Stopford Augustus Brooke

English Literature

Stopford Augustus Brooke

English Literature

ISBN/EAN: 9783337737856

Printed in Europe, USA, Canada, Australia, Japan

Cover: Foto ©Andreas Hilbeck / pixelio.de

More available books at **www.hansebooks.com**

BY

STOPFORD A. BROOKE, M.A.

New York

THE MACMILLAN COMPANY

LONDON: MACMILLAN & CO., Ltd.

1897

CONTENTS

CHAPTER I

CHAPTER VII

CHAPTER VIII

ENGLISH LITERATURE

CHAPTER I

WRITERS BEFORE THE NORMAN CONQUEST, 670–1066

1. **The History of English Literature** is the story of what great English men and women thought and felt, and then wrote down in good prose and beautiful poetry in the English language. The story is a long one. It begins in England about the year 670; it had its unwritten beginnings still earlier on the Continent, in the old Angle-Land; it was still going on in the year which closes this book, 1832; nor has our literature lost any of its creative force in the years which have followed 1832. Into this little book then is to be briefly put the story of nearly 1200 years of the thoughts, feelings, and imagination of a great people. Every English man and woman has good reason to be proud of the work done by their forefathers in prose and poetry. Every one who can write a good book or a good song may say to himself, " I belong to a noble company, which has been teaching

and delighting the world for more than 1000 years." And that is a fact in which those who write and those who read English literature ought to feel a noble pride.

2. **The English and the Welsh.** — This literature is written in English, the tongue of our fathers. They lived, while this island of ours was still called Britain, in North and South Denmark, in Hanover and Friesland — Jutes, Angles, and Saxons. Their common tongue and name were *English;* but, either because they were pressed from the inland, perhaps by Attila, or for pure love of adventure, they took to the sea, and, landing at various parts of Britain at various times, drove back, after 150 years of hard fighting, the Britons, whom they called Welsh, to the land now called Wales, to Strath-clyde, and to Cornwall. It is well for those who study English literature to remember that in these places the Britons remained as a distinct race with a distinct literature of their own, because the stories and the poetry of the Britons crept afterwards into English literature and had a great influence upon it. Moreover, in the later days of the Conquest, a great number of the Welsh were amalgamated with the English. The whole tale of King Arthur, of which English poetry and even English prose is so full, was a British tale. Some then of the imaginative work of the conquered afterwards took captive their fierce conquerors.

3. **The English Tongue.** — The earliest form of our English tongue is very different from modern English in form, pronunciation, and appearance; but still the lan-

guage written in the year 700 is the same as that in which the prose of the Bible is written, just as much as the tree planted a hundred years ago is the same tree to-day. It is this sameness of language, as well as the sameness of national spirit, which makes our literature one literature for 1200 years.

4. **Of English Literature written in this tongue** we have no extant prose until the time of King Ælfred. Men like Bæda and Ealdhelm wrote their prose in Latin. But we have, in a few manuscripts, a great deal of poetry written in English, chiefly before the days of Ælfred. There is (1) the MS. under the name of *Cædmon's Paraphrase*, a collection of religious poems by various writers, now in the Bodleian. There is (2) the MS. of *Beowulf* and of the last three books of *Judith*. There is (3) the *Exeter Book*, a miscellaneous collection of poems, left by Leofric, Bishop of Exeter, to his cathedral church in the year 1071. There is (4) the *Vercelli Book*, discovered at Vercelli in the year 1822, in which, along with homilies, there is a collection of six poems. A few leaflets complete the list of the MSS. containing poems earlier than Ælfred. All together they constitute a vernacular poetry which consists of more than twenty thousand lines.

5. **The metre of the poems** is essentially the same, un-like any modern metre, without rhyme, and without any fixed number of syllables. Its essential elements were accent and alliteration. Every verse is divided into two half-verses by a pause, and has four accented syllables,

while the number of unaccented syllables is indifferent.
These half-verses are linked together by alliteration. The
two accented syllables of the first half, and one of the
accented syllables in the second half, begin with the same
consonant, or with vowels which were generally different
one from another. This is the formal rule. But to give
a greater freedom there is often only one alliterative
letter in the first half-verse. Here is an example of the
usual form : —

> And *deáw-dr*ías : on *d*ege weorðeð
> Winde geondsâwen.

> And the *dew-d*ownfall : at the *d*ay-break is
> Winnowed by the wind.

This metre was continually varied, and was capable,
chiefly by the addition of unaccented syllables, of many
harmonious changes. The length of the lines depended
on the nature of the things described, or on the rise and
fall of the singer's emotion ; the emphatic words in which
the chief thought lay were accented and alliterated, and
probably received an additional force by the beat of the
hand upon the harp. All the poetry was sung, and the
poet could alter, as he sang, the movement of the verse.
But, however the metre was varied, it was not varied
arbitrarily. It followed clear rules, and all its develop-
ments were built on the simple original type of four
accents and three alliterated syllables. This was the
vehicle, interspersed with some rare instances in which
rhymes were employed, in which all English poetry was

sung and written till the French system of rhymes, metres, and accents was transferred to the English tongue ; and it continued, alongside of the French system, to be used, sometimes much and sometimes little, until the sixteenth century. Nor, though its use was finished then, was its influence lost. Its habits, especially alliteration, have entered into all English poetry.

6. **The Characters of this Poetry.** — (1) It is marked by parallelism. It frequently repeats the same statement or thought in different ways. But this is not so common as it is, for example, in Hebrew poetry. (2) It uses the ordinary metaphorical phrases of Teutonic poetry, such as the *whale's-road* for the sea, but uses them with greater moderation or with less inventiveness than the Icelandic poets. Elaborate similes are not found in the earlier poetry, but later poets, Cynewulf especially, invent them, not frequently, but well. (3) A great variety of compound words, chiefly adjectives, also characterise it, by the use of which the poet strove to express with brevity a number of qualities belonging to his subject. When Tennyson used such adjectives as *hollow-vaulted*, *dainty woeful*, he was returning to the custom of his ancient predecessors. (4) At times the poetry is concise and direct, but this is chiefly found in those parts of the poems which have some relation to heathen times. For the most part, save when the subject is war or sea-voyaging, the poetry is diffuse, and wearies by a constant repetition. But we owe a great deal of this repetition to the introduction of extempore matter

by the bards as they sung. There is not much of it in
poems which have been carefully edited, as many were
in the time of Ælfred. Nor do I think that the original
lays which the bards expanded were more diffuse than
the early Icelandic lays. (5) It is the earliest extant
body of poetry in any modern language. It began to
be written in England towards the close of the seventh
century, and all its best work was done before the close
of the eighth. (6) Its width of range is very remarkable.
The epic is represented in it by *Beowulf*. *Judith* is an
heroic saga. The earlier *Genesis* is a paraphrase with
original episodes. The later *Genesis* is an epic fragment
with dramatic conversations, and in other poems there
are traces of what might have formed a basis for a
dramatic literature. The *Exodus* is an heroic narrative,
freely invented on the Biblical story. The *Christ* of
Cynewulf is a threefold poem, conceived like a trilogy,
in the honour of Christ, the Hero. Narrative poetry is
represented by Cynewulf's poems of the life of Saint
Guðlac, of the martyrdom of Saint Juliana, by the *Elene*
and the *Andreas*. There is one pure lyric, and there
are sacred hymns of joy among Cynewulf's poems which
have all the quality of lyrics. There are five elegiac
poems. There are a number of Riddles, some of
which are poems of pure natural description. There
are didactic, gnomic, and allegorical poems. Almost
every form of poetry is represented. (7) It is the
only early poetry which has poems wholly dedicated to
descriptions of nature. Of such descriptions there is no

trace in the Icelandic poetry. For anything resembling them we must look forward to the nineteenth century. (8) Many of the poems are extraordinarily modern in feeling. The hymns of Cynewulf might have been written by Crashaw. The sentiment of the *Wanderer* and the *Ruin* might belong to this century. The *Seafarer* has the same note of feeling for the sea which prevails in the sea-poetry of Swinburne and Tennyson. (9) There is no trace of any Norse influence or religion on early English poetry. Old Saxon poetry influenced the later English verse, but may itself have been derived from England. The poetry of natural description owes much to the Celtic influence which was largely present in Northumbria, but otherwise there is no Celtic note in early English poetry. There is a classic note. Virgil and other Latin poets were read by those whom Bæda taught, and the ancient models had their wonted power. The unexpected strain of culture, so remarkable in this poetry, must, I think, be due to this influence. (10) The greater part of this poetry was written in Northumbria, and before the coming of the Danes. This has been questioned, but it seems not wisely. The only examples of any importance outside of this statement are the war-lyrics in the *Chronicle* and that portion of the Cædmonic poems which it is now believed was translated from an Old Saxon original, probably in the time of Ælfred.

7. **The First English Poems.** — Our forefathers, while as yet they were heathen and lived on the Continent,

made poems, and of this poetry we *may* possess a few remains. The earliest is The Song of the Traveller — *Widsith*, the far-goer — but it has been filled up by later insertions. It is not much more than a catalogue of the folk and the places whither the minstrel said he went with the Goths, but when he expands concerning himself, he shows so pleasant a pride in his art that he wins our sympathy. *Deor's Complaint* is another of these poems. Its form is that of a true lyric. The writer is a bard at the court of the Heodenings, from whom his rival takes his place and goods. He writes this complaint to comfort his heart. Weland, Beado-hild, Theodric knew care and sorrow. " *That* they overwent, *this* also may I." This is the refrain of all the verses of our first, and, I may say, our only early English lyric. The *Fight at Finsburg* is an epic fragment. It tells, and with all the fire of war, of the attack on Fin's palace in Friesland, and another part of the same story is to be found in *Beowulf*. It is plain there was a full Fin-saga, portions of which were sung at feasts. This completes, with those parts of *Beowulf* which we may refer to heathen traditionary songs, the list of the English poetry which we may possibly say belonged to the older England over seas. There are two fragments of a romance of *Waldhere* of the date or place of which we know nothing. In the so-called *Rune Song* — which, as we have it, is not old — there is one verse at least which alludes to the times of the heroic sagas. But the poems where we find most traces of early English paganism are the so-called *Charms.*

8. **Beowulf** is our old English epic, and it recounts the great deeds and death of Beowulf. It may have arisen before the English conquest of Britain in the shape of short songs about the hero, and we can trace, perhaps, three different centres for the story. The scenery is laid among the Danes in Seeland and among the Geats in South Sweden, on the coast of the North Sea and the Kattegat. There is not a word about our England in the poem. Coming to England in the form of short poems, it was wrought together into a complete tale of two parts, the first of which we may again divide into two ; and was afterwards edited, with a few Christian applications, and probably by a Northumbrian poet, in the eighth century. In this form we possess it.

The story is of Hrothgar, one of the kingly race of Jutland, who builds his hall, Heorot, near the sea, on the edge of the moorland. A monster called Grendel, half-human, half-fiend, dwells in a sea-cave, near the moor over which he wanders by night, and hating the festive noise, carries off thirty of the thegns of Hrothgar and devours them. He then haunts the hall at night, and after twelve years of this distress, Beowulf, thegn of Hygelac, sails from Sweden to bring help to Hrothgar, and at night, when Grendel breaks into the hall, wrestles with him, tears away his arm, and the fiend flies away to die. The second division of the first part of the poem begins with the vengeance taken by Grendel's

mother. She slays Æschere, a trusty thegn of Hrothgar. Then Beowulf descends into her sea-cave and
slays her also; feasts in triumph with Hrothgar, and
returns to his own land. The second part of the poem
opens fifty years later. Beowulf is now king; his land
is happy under his rule. But his fate is at hand. A
fire-drake, who guards a treasure, is robbed and comes
from his den to harry and burn the country. The gray-
haired king goes forth to fight his last fight, slays the
dragon, but dies of its fiery breath, and the poem closes
with the tale of his burial, burned on a lofty pyre on
the top of Hronesnæs.

Its social interest lies in what it tells us of the manners and customs of our forefathers before they came
to England. Their mode of life in peace and war is
described; their ships, their towns, the scenery in which
they lived, their feasts, amusements — we have the account of a whole day from morning to night — the close
union between the chieftain and his war-brothers; their
women and the reverence given them; the way in which
they faced death, in which they sang, in which they gave
gifts and rewards. The story is told with Homeric directness and simplicity, but not with Homeric rapidity. A
deep fatalism broods over it. "Wyrd (the fate-goddess)
goes ever as it must," Beowulf says, when he thinks he
may be torn to pieces by Grendel. "It shall be," he
cries when he goes to fight the dragon, "for us in the
fight as Wyrd shall foresee." But a daring spirit fills
the fatalism. "Let him who can," he says, "gain honour

ere he die." "Let us have fame or death." Out of the
fatalism naturally grew the dignity and much of the
pathos of the poem. It is most poetical in the vivid
character-drawing of men and women, and especially
in the character of the hero, both in his youth and in
his age; in the fateful pathos of the old man's last
fight for his country against certain death, in the noble
scene of the burial, in the versing of the grave and
courteous interchange of human feeling between the
personages. Moreover, the descriptions of the sea and
the voyage, and of the savage places of the cliffs and
the moor, are instinct with the spirit which is still alive
among our poetry, and which makes dreadful and lonely
wildernesses seem dwelt in — as if the places needed a
king — by monstrous beings. In the creation of Grendel and his mother, the savage stalkers of the moor,
that half-natural, half-supernatural world began, which,
when men grew gentler and the country more cultivated,
became so beautiful as fairyland. Here is the description of the dwelling-place of Grendel : —

> There the land is hid in gloom,
> Where they ward; wolf-haunted slopes, windy headlands
>   o'er the sea.
> Fearful is the marish-path, where the mountain torrent
> 'Neath the Nesses' mist, nither makes its way.
> Under earth the flood is, not afar from here it lies;
> But the measure of a mile, where the mere is set.
> Over it, outreaching, hang the ice-nipt trees :
> Held by roots the holt is fast, and o'er-helms the water.

There an evil wonder, every night, a man may see —
In the flood a fire!
                Not unhaunted is the place!
Thence the welter of the waves is upwhirled on high,
Wan towards the clouds, when the wind is stirring
Wicked weather up; till the lift is waxing dark,
And the welkin weeping!

The whole poem, Pagan as it is, is English to its very root.
It is sacred to us, our Genesis, the book of our origins.

9. **Christianity and English Poetry.** — When we came
to Britain we were great warriors and great sea pirates
— "sea wolves," as a Roman poet calls us; and all our
poetry down to the present day is full of war, and still
more of the sea. No nation has ever written so much
sea-poetry. But we were more than mere warriors. We
were a home-loving people when we got settled either in
Sleswick or in England, and all our literature from the
first writings to the last is full of domestic love, the dear-
ness of home, and the ties of kinsfolk. We were a religious people, even as heathen, still more so when we
became Christian, and our poetry is as much of religion
as of war. But with Christianity a new spirit entered
into English poetry. The war spirit did not decay, but
into the song steals a softer element. The fatalism is
modified by the faith that the fate is the will of a good
God. The sorrow is not less, but it is relieved by an on-
look of joy. The triumph over enemies is not less, but
even more exulting, for it is the triumph of God over His
foes that is sung by Cædmon and Cynewulf. Nor is the

imaginative delight in legends and in the supernatural less. But it is now found in the legends of the saints, in the miracles and visions of angels that Bæda tells of the Christian heroes, in fantastic allegories of spiritual things, like the poems of the *Phœnix* and the *Whale*. The love of nature lasted, but it dwells now rather on gentle than on savage scenery. The human sorrow for the hardness of life is more tender, and when the poems speak of the love of home, it is with an added grace. One little bit still lives for us out of the older world.

> Dear the welcomed one
> To his Frisian wife, when his Floater's drawn on shore,
> When his keel comes back, and her man returns to home ;
> Hers, her own food-giver. And she prays him in,
> Washes then his weedy coat, and new weeds puts on him !
> O lythe it is on land to him whom his love constrains.

If that was the soft note of home in a Pagan time, it was softer still when Christianity had mellowed manners. Yet, with all this, the ancient faith still influences the Christian song. Christ is not only the Saviour, but the Hero who goes forth against the dragon. His overthrow of the fiends is described in much the same terms as that of Beowulf's wrestling with Grendel. " Bitterly grim, gripped them in his wrath." The death of Christ, at which the universe trembles and weeps, was mixed up afterwards with the story of the death of Balder. The old poetry penetrated the new, but the spirit of the new transformed that of the old.

10. **Cædmon.** — The poem of *Beowulf* has the grave
Teutonic power, but it is not, as a whole, native to our
soil. It is not the first true English poem. That is the
work of CÆDMON, and it was done in Northumbria. The
story of it, as told by Bæda, proves that the making of
songs was common at the time. Cædmon was a servant
to the monastery of Hild, an abbess of royal blood, at
Whitby in Yorkshire. He was somewhat aged when the
gift of song came to him, and he knew nothing of the
art of verse, so that at the feasts when for the sake of
mirth all sang in turn he left the table. One evening,
having done so and gone to the stables, for he had the care
of the cattle that night, he fell asleep, and One came to
him in vision and said, "Cædmon, sing me some song."
And he answered, "I cannot sing; for this cause I left
the feast and came hither." Then said the other, "However, you shall sing." "What shall I sing?" he replied.
"Sing the beginning of created things," answered the
other. Whereupon he began to sing verses to the praise
of God, and, awaking, remembered what he had sung,
and added more in verse worthy of God. In the morning he came to the town-reeve, and told him of the gift
he had received, and, being brought to Hild, was ordered
to tell his dream before learned men, that they might
give judgment whence his verses came. And when they
had heard, they all said that heavenly grace had been
conferred on him by our Lord. This story ought to be
loved by us, for it tells of the beginning in England of
the wonderful life of English Poetry. Nor should we

fail to reverence the place where it began. Above the small and land-locked harbour of Whitby rises and juts out towards the sea the dark cliff where Hild's monastery stood, looking out over the German Ocean. It is a wild, wind-swept upland, above the furious sea; and standing there we feel that it is a fitting birthplace for the poetry of the sea-ruling nation. Nor is the verse of the first poet without the stormy note of the sea-scenery among which it was written, nor without the love of the stars and the high moorlands that Cædmon saw from Whitby Head. Cædmon's poems were done before 680, in which year he died. Bæda tells us that he sang the story of Genesis and Exodus, many other tales in the Sacred Scriptures, and the story of Christ and the Apostles and of Heaven and Hell to come. "Others after him tried to make religious poems, but none could compare with him for he learnt the art of song not from men, but, divinely aided, received that gift." It is plain then that he was the founder of a school. It is equally plain, it seems, from this passage, that at Bæda's death the later school of religious poets, of whom Cynewulf was the chief, had not begun to write. Cædmon's poems, then, were widely known. Bæda quotes their first verses. They were copied from monastery to monastery. Ælfred got them from the north, and no doubt gave them to the great schools at Winchester. They were however lost. Only their fame survived.

11. **The Junian Cædmon.** — Archbishop Ussher, hunting for books for Trinity College, Dublin, found an Old

English MS. which Francis Dujon (Junius) printed in
Amsterdam about 1650, and published as the work of
Cædmon, because its contents agreed with Bæda's description of Cædmon's poems and of his first hymn.
Junius was a friend of Milton, and Milton was one of the
first to hear what the earliest English poet was supposed
to have written on the Fall of the Angels and the Fall of
Man. Since then critics have wrought their will upon
this MS. Some say that Cædmon did not write a line of
it ; others allow him some share in it. It pleases us to
think, and the judgment is possible, that the more
archaic portion of the first poem in the MS. — the *Genesis*
— which describes the Fall of the Angels and the Creation, the Flood, and perhaps the battle of Abraham with
the kings of the East is by Cædmon himself. In the
midst of the *Genesis* there is however a second description of the Fall of the Angels and an elaborate account of
the council in Hell, and of the temptation in the Garden.
This is held to be an after-insertion, made perhaps in the
time of Ælfred. It differs in feeling, in subtlety, and in
manner of verse from the rest. A conjecture was made
that it was a translation of a part of an Old Saxon poem,
and this seems to be borne out by the discovery in 1894
of a fragment of Old Saxon poetry in which there are
lines similar to those of this separated portion of the
Genesis. The next poem in the MS. is the *Exodus*. It
is certainly not by Cædmon. It is not a paraphrase ; it
is a triumphal poem of war, boldly invented, on the passage of the Red Sea. The *Daniel*, the third poem of the

MS., is so dull that it is no matter who wrote it or when
it was written. The second part of the MS. is in a different handwriting from the first, and is a series of Psalm-
like poems on the Fall of the Angels, the Harrowing of
Hell, the Resurrection, Ascension, Pentecost, the Judgment Day, and the Temptation. They are a kind of
Paradise Regained.

12. **The interest of these poems** is not found in any
paraphrase of the Scriptures, but in those parts of them
which are the invention of the poets, in the drawing of
the characters, in the passages instinct with the genius of
our race, and with the individuality of the writers. The
account of the creation in the *older Genesis* has the
grandeur of a nature-myth. The description of the flood
is full of the experience of one who had known the sea in
storm. The battle of Abraham is a fine clash of war, and
might be the description of the repulse by some Northumbrian king of the northern tribes. The ruin of the
angels and the peace of Heaven, set in contrast, have the
same kind of proud pathos as Milton's work on the same
subject. The *later Genesis* is even more Teutonic than
the first. Satan's fierce cry of wrath and freedom against
God from his bed of chains in Hell is out of the heart of
heathendom. The northern rage of war and the northern
tie of war-brotherhood speak in all he says, in all that his
thegns reply. The pleasure of the northern imagination
in swiftness and joy is just as marked as its pleasure in
dark pride and in revenge. The burst of exulting vengeance when the thegn of Satan succeeds in the tempta-

c

tion is magnificent. His master, he cries, will lie softly
and be blithe of heart in the dusky fire, now that his
revenge is gained. There is true dramatic power in the
dialogue between Eve and the fiend, and so much subtlety
of thought that it cannot belong to Cædmon's time.   It is
characteristic of Teutonic manners that the motives of
the woman for eating the fruit are all good, and the passionate and tender conscientiousness of the love and
repentance of Adam and Eve is equally characteristic of
the gentler and more religious side of the Teutonic
nature. "Dark and true and tender is the North."

The *Exodus* is remarkable for its descriptions of war
and a marching host, and especially for the elaborate
painting of the breaking up of the sea, which was probably done by one who had himself battled with a whirling
gale on the German Ocean.   On the whole, we have in
the two parts of the *Genesis*, and in the *Exodus*, in the
midst of spaces of dulness, original and imaginative
pieces of poetry well worthy of the beginnings of English
song.

13. **English in the South.** — While Cædmon was still
alive, Theodore, Archbishop of Canterbury, and his sub-
deacon Hadrian set up a celebrated school of learning at
Canterbury, which flourished for a short time and then
decayed.   One of Theodore's scholars was EALDHELM.
A young man when Cædmon died in 680, his name is
connected with English poetry. As Abbot of Malmesbury and Bishop of Sherborne he spread the learning of
Canterbury over the south of England, and sent his in-

fluence into Northumbria, where his *Riddles* were imitated by Cynewulf. But our chief interest in him is that he was himself an English poet. It is said that he had not his equal in the making and singing of English verse. One of his songs was popular in the twelfth century. Ælfred had some in his possession, and a pretty story tells that when the traders came into the towns, Ealdhelm used, like a gleeman, to stand on the bridge or the public way and sing songs to them in the English tongue, that he might lure them by the sweetness of his speech to hear the word of God.

14. **English Poetry in the North after Cædmon — "Judith."** — We have seen that English poetry began with religion in the poems of Cædmon, and the greater part of the written poetry which followed him is also religious. One of the best of these pieces is the *Judith*. Originally composed in twelve books, we only possess the three last which tell of the banquet of Holofernes, his slaughter, and the attack of the Jews on the Assyrian camp. It is a poem made after Bæda's death, full of the flame and joy of war. Nor is the drawing of the person and character of Judith unworthy of a race which has always honoured women. She stands forth clear, a Jewish Velleda. To call the poem, however, as some have done, the finest of the Old English poems, is to say a great deal too much. We may date, about the same time, in the eighth century, a fine fragment on the *Harrowing of Hell*, some poems on Christian legends, perhaps the allegorical poems of the *Whale* and the

Panther, and some lyrical translations of the Psalms in the Kentish and West Saxon dialects.

15. **There are five Elegies** in the *Exeter Book*, which from their excellence deserve to be isolated from the rest of the minor poems. The first of these has been called the *Ruin*. It is the mourning of a traveller over a desolated city, and certain phrases in it seem to show that the city was Bath, utterly overthrown by Ceawlin in 577. If so, the date of the poem may be between 676 when Osric founded a monastery among the ruins, and 781 when Offa rebuilt the town. The second, the *Wanderer*, expands the mourning "motive" of the *Ruin* over the desolation of the whole world of man. It may have been originally a heathen poem, edited afterwards with a Christian Prologue and Epilogue. Of all the Old English poems it is the most of an artistic whole, and a noble piece of work it is. In its grave and fateful verse an exile bewails his own lost happiness and the sorrowful fates of men. The third, the *Seafarer*, apparently a dialogue between an old and a young sailor about the dangers and the fascination of the sea, breathes the spirit which filled the heart of our forefathers while they sang and sailed, and is extraordinarily modern in note. The blank-verse manner of Tennyson is in it, and the spirit of it is strangely re-echoed in the *Sailor Boy*. The same may be said of the two other elegies — the *Wife's Complaint* and the *Husband's Message*. They are not of so fine a quality as the *Wanderer* or the *Seafarer*, but they both have love-passion, otherwise

unrepresented in Old English poetry. To these must be added the dramatic monologue, formerly regarded as the *First Riddle*. As recently interpreted, it should be known as *Wulf and Eadwacer*.

16. **Cynewulf** was the greatest of the northern singers, and wrote, most people think, during the latter half of the eighth century. His name is known to us, and he is the only one of these poets of whose personality and life we have some clear image, and whose work is so wide in range and so varying in quality that it may be divided into periods. He has signed his name in its runic letters to four of his poems. The riddling commentary he linked on to the runes gives some account of his life, and the poems are throughout as personal as Milton's. He was often a wandering singer, but seems to have had, in his youth, a fixed place at the court of some northern noble — a wild and gay young man, a rider, a singer at the feasts, fond of sports and war, indifferent to religion, sensitive to love and beauty, and at home with all classes of men. It must have been during this time that he wrote the greater number of the *Riddles*. They prove that he had a poet's sympathy with the life of man and nature. They are written by one who knew the sea and its dangers, the iron coasts and storms of Northumbria, who knew and had taken part in war, who knew the forest-land, the scattered villages and their daily life ; who loved the wild animals and the birds, and who, strange to say at this early time, wrote about nature with an observant and loving eye

and in a way we do not meet again in English poetry
for many centuries. The poem on the Hurricane is
an artistic whole, and may not be unjustly compared
with Shelley's *Ode to the West Wind*. There is scarcely
a trace of Christianity in these early poems. Trouble
then fell on Cynewulf, and with it repentance for his
"sinful life," and he tells in the *Dream of the Rood*
of how comfort was brought to him at last. He then
turned to write religious poems, and to this part of his
life we may allot the *Juliana*, and perhaps the first part
of the *Guðlac*. He then wrote, and with a far higher
art, the *Crist*, a long, almost an epical, poem of the
Incarnation, the Descent into Hell, the Ascension, and
the Last Judgment, a noble and continuous effort, full
of triumphant verse. He had now reached full peace
of mind, and as much mastery over his art as was possible at that early time. He may then have composed,
from a poem now given to Lactantius, the allegorical
poem of the *Phœnix*, in which there is a famous passage
describing the sinless land; the second part of the
Guðlac, as fine as the first is poor; and still later on
in life, and with a free recurrence to the war-poetry
of heathendom, the *Elene* and the *Andreas*, the first,
the finding of the True Cross by the Empress Helena,
and remarkable for its battle-fervour; the second equally
remarkable for its imaginative treatment of the voyage
of St. Andrew for the conversion of the Marmedonians.
Then, before he died, and to leave his last message
to his folk, he wrote, using perhaps part of an older

poem, the *Dream of the Holy Rood*, and showed that even in his old age his imagination and his versing were as vivid as in his youth.

17. **Poetry during and after Ælfred's Reign.** — When Ælfred set up learning afresh in the south, it had perished in Northumbria. But no great poetry arose in the south. There was alliterative versing, but it had neither imagination, originality, nor music. The English alliterative version of the *Metra* of Boethius may be Ælfred's own ; if so, he was plainly not a poet. The second part of the *Genesis* may belong to this time, but it is asserted now to be a translation. I do not believe that the last poems in the Cædmonic MS. are of this time, but of the Northumbrian School. It was a time, however, of collections of the poetry of the past. Nearly all the Old English poetry, as we have it, is in the West-Saxon Dialect. Ælfred had a *Handbook*, into which, tradition says, he copied some English songs. It is extremely likely that the poems in the *Exeter Book* were brought together in Ælfred's time. In that book itself there are gnomic and didactic poems, as, for example, the *Fates of Men* and the *Gifts of Men*, which are collections of short verses belonging to various times, and some of them are very old. At a later period than Ælfred's reign, these gnomic verses took the form of dialogues, partly in prose and partly in verse, and we have two incomplete specimens of this in the *Solomon and Saturnus*, in which a Judaic legend is curiously mingled with Teutonic forms of thought. To the same period may be allotted the

Menologium, a poetical calendar, the best portions of which seem borrowed from the past. The rest of the verse up to the Conquest is chiefly made up of alliterative sermons and the war songs.

18. **The War-poetry** was probably always as plentiful as the religious, but was not likely to be written down by the monks. When, however, Ælfred developed the *Chronicle* into a national history, the writers seized on popular songs, and inserted them in the *Chronicle*. In that way we have at least one fine war-poem handed down to us — *The Song of Brunanburh*, 937. It describes the fight of King Æthelstan with Anlaf the Dane and the Scots under Constantine. Another war-poem is the *Fight at Maldon*, the story of the death of Byrhtnoth, an East Saxon Ealdorman, in battle with a band of Vikings. They are the fitting source, in their simplicity and patriotism, of such war-songs as the *Battle of the Baltic* and the *Siege of Lucknow*. Of the two the *Fight at Maldon* is the finer, the most human and varied, but the *Song of Brunanburh* is lyrical as the latter is not. They are two different types of poetry. Both of them have some Norse feeling, and we may link with them from this point of view the *Rhyme Song*, which recalls the motive and spirit of the earlier *Ruin*, but which, having rhymes along with alliteration, resembles the Scandinavian form called *Runhenda*, and has induced critics to attribute it to the influence of the warrior and scald, Egil Skalagrimsson, who twice visited King Æthelstan. Two fragmentary odes, among some other short poems, inserted

in the *Chronicle*, one on the deliverance of the five cities
from the Danes by King Eadmund, 942 ; and another
on the coronation of King Eadgar, are the last records
of a war-poetry which naturally decayed when the English were trodden down by the Normans. When Taille-
fer rode into battle at Hastings, singing songs of Roland
and Charlemagne, he sang more than the triumph of the
Norman over the English ; he sang the victory for a time
of French Romance over Old English poetry.

19. **Old English Prose.** — It is pleasant to think that
we may not unfairly make English prose begin with
BÆDA.   He was born about 673, and was like Cædmon,
a Northumbrian.   After 683, he spent his life at Jarrow,
"in the same monastery," he says, "and while attentive
to the rule of mine order, and the service of the Church,
my constant pleasure lay in learning, or teaching, or
writing."   He enjoyed that pleasure for many years, for
his quiet life was long, and his toil unceasing.   Forty-
five works prove his industry ; and their fame over the
whole of learned Europe proves their value.   His learning was as various as it was great.   All that the world
then knew of theology, science, music, rhetoric, medicine, arithmetic, astronomy, and physics was brought
together by him ; his *Ecclesiastical History* is our best
authority for Early England ; accuracy and delightful-
ness are at one in it.   It reveals his charming character ;
and indeed, his life was as gentle, and himself as loved,
as his work was great.   His books were written in Latin,
and with these we have nothing to do, but he strove to

make English prose a literary language, for his last work was a *Translation of the Gospel of St. John*, as almost his last words were in English verse. In the story of his death told by his disciple Cuthbert is the first record of English prose writing. When the last day came, the dying man called his scholars to him that he might dictate more of his translation. "There is still a chapter wanting," said the scribe, "and it is hard for thee to question thyself longer." "It is easily done," said Bæda, "take thy pen and write swiftly." Through the day they wrote, and when evening fell, "There is yet one sentence unwritten, dear master," said the youth. "Write it quickly," said the master. "It is finished now." "Thou sayest true," was the reply, "all is finished now." He sang the "Glory to God" and died. It is to that scene that English prose looks back as its sacred source, as it is in the greatness and variety of Bæda's Latin work that English scholarship strikes its key-note.

When Bæda died, Northumbria was the centre of European literature. Wilfrid of York had founded libraries and monasteries, but the true beginner of all the Northumbrian learning was Benedict Biscop, who collected two brother libraries at Wearmouth and Jarrow, and whose scholars were Ceolfrid and Bæda. Six hundred scholars gathered round Bæda, and he handed on all his learning to his pupil Ecgberht, who as Archbishop of York established the famous library, and founded the great school, or, as it may be called, the University of York. To this place, for more than sixty years, all

Europe sent pupils to win the honey of learning. Alcuin, Ecgberht's pupil, finally took with him to the court
of Charles the Great, in 792, all the knowledge which
Bæda had won and the School of York had expanded.
Through Alcuin then, whom we may call Charles's Min-
ister of Education, England was the source of the new
education which slowly spread over the vast sphere of
the Frankish Empire. This was done just at the right
moment, for Alcuin had scarce left the English shores
for the last time when the Danes descended on Northumbria, and blotted out the whole of its literature and
learning.

20. **Ælfred.** — Though the long battle with the in-
vaders was lost in the north, it was gained for a time by
Ælfred the Great in Wessex; and with Ælfred's literary
work, learning changed its seat from the north to the
south. Ælfred's writings and translations, being in English and not in Latin, make him, since Bæda's work is
lost, the true father of English prose. As Whitby is the
cradle of English poetry, so is Winchester of English
prose. At Winchester the king took the English tongue
and made it the tongue in which history, philosophy,
law, and religion spoke to the English people. No work
was ever done more eagerly or more practically. He
brought scholars from different parts of the world. He
set up schools in his monasteries "where every free-born
youth, who has the means, shall attend to his book till
he can read English writing perfectly." He presided
over a school in his own court. He made himself a

master of a literary English style, and he did this that
he might teach his people. He translated the popular
manuals of the time into English, but he edited them
with large additions of his own, needful as he thought,
for English use. He gave his nation moral philosophy
in Boethius's *Consolation of Philosophy;* a universal history, with geographical chapters of his own, "of the
highest literary and philological value as specimens of his
natural prose," in his translation of *Orosius;* an ecclesiastical history of England in Bæda's History, giving to
some details a West-Saxon form ; and a religious handbook, with a preface of his own, in the *Pastoral Rule* of
Pope Gregory. He induced Bishop Werferth to translate
into English the *Dialogues* of Gregory, a book which had
a far-reaching influence on mediæval literature and theology. We do not quite know whether he worked himself at the *English* or *Anglo-Saxon Chronicle*, but at
least it was in his reign that this chronicle rose out of
meagre lists into a full narrative of events. To him,
then, we English look back as the fountain of English
prose literature.

21. **The Later Old English Prose.** — The impulse he
gave soon died away, but it was revived under King Ead-
gar the Peaceful, whose seventeen years of government
(958-75) were the most prosperous and glorious of the
West-Saxon Empire. Under him and his predecessors,
Æthelwold, Bishop of Winchester, founded and kept up
English schools, and, working together with Archbishop
Dunstan and Oswald of Worcester, recreated monastic

life, classic learning, and the education of the clergy.
Their labours were the origin of the famous Blickling
Homilies, 971. About twenty years after, Ælfric, called
"Grammaticus" from his Englished Latin Grammar,
began to write. He turned into English the Pentateuch,
Joshua, and part of Job. The rest of his numerous
works are some of the best models we possess of the
literary English of the beginning of the eleventh century.
The two collections of *Homilies* we owe to him, and
his *Lives of the Saints*, are written in a classic prose,
and his *Glossary and Colloquy*, afterwards edited by
Ælfric Bata, served for a kind of English-Latin text-
book. His prose in his later life was somewhat spoiled
by his over-mastering fancy for alliteration, but he is
always a clear and forcible writer of English. But this
revival had no sooner begun to take root than the North-
men came again in force upon the land and conquered it.
We have in Wulfstan's (Archbishop of York, 1002–23)
Address to the English, a terrible picture, written in impassioned prose, of the demoralisation caused by the in-
roads of the Danes. During the fresh interweaving of
Danes and English together under Danish kings from
1013 to 1042, no English literature arose, but Latin prose
intruded more and more on English writing. It was
towards the reign of Edward the Confessor that English
writing again began to live. But no sooner was it born
than the Norman invasion repressed, but did not quench
its life.

22. **The English Chronicle.** One great monument,

however, of Old English prose lasts beyond the Conquest. It is the *English Chronicle*, and in it our literature is continuous from Ælfred to Stephen. At first it was nothing but a record of the births and deaths of bishops and kings, and was probably a West-Saxon Chronicle. Among these short notices there is, however, one tragic story, of Cynewulf and Cyneheard, under the date 755 — but the true date is 784 — so rude in style, and so circumstantial, that it is probably contemporary with the events themselves. If so, it is the oldest piece of historical prose in any Teutonic tongue. More than a hundred years later Ælfred took up the Chronicle, caused it to be edited from various sources, added largely to it from Bæda, and raised it to the dignity of a national history. The narrative of Ælfred's wars with the Danes, written, it is likely, by himself at the end of his reign, enables us to estimate the great weight Ælfred himself had in literature. "Compared with this passage," says Professor Earle, "every other piece of prose, not in these Chronicles merely, but throughout the whole range of extant Saxon literature, must assume a secondary rank." After Ælfred's reign, and that of his son Eadward, 901–25, the Chronicle becomes scanty, but songs and odes are inserted in it. In the reign of Æthelred and during the Danish kings its fulness returns, and growing by additions from various quarters, it continues to be our great contemporary authority in English history till 1154, when it abruptly closes with the death of Stephen. "It is the first history of any Teutonic people in their own language ; it is the earliest and most venerable monument of English prose." In it Old English poetry sang its last extant song, in its death Old English prose dies. It is not till the reign of John that English poetry, in any form but that of short poems, appears again in the *Brut* of Laya-mon. It is not till the reign of Henry III. that original English prose begins again in the *Ancren Riwle* (the Rule of Anchoresses), in the *Wooing of our Lord*, and in the charming homily entitled the *Sawles Warde*.

CHAPTER II

FROM THE CONQUEST TO CHAUCER'S DEATH, 1066–1400

23. **General Outline.** — The invasion of Britain by the English made the island, its speech, and its literature, English. The invasion of England by the Danes left our speech and literature still English. The Danes were of our stock and tongue, and we absorbed them. The invasion of England by the Normans seemed likely to crush the English people, to root out their literature, and even to threaten their speech. But that which happened to the Danes happened to the Normans also, and for the same reason. They were originally of like blood to the English, and of like speech; and though during their settlement in Normandy they had become French in manner and language, and their literature French, yet the old blood prevailed in the end. The Norman felt his kindred with the English tongue and spirit, became an Englishman, and left the French tongue that he might speak and write in English. We absorbed the Normans, and we took into our literature and speech the French elements they had brought with them. It was a process slower in literature than it was in the political history,

but it began from the political struggle. Up to the time
of Henry II. the Norman troubled himself but little about
the English tongue. But when French foreigners came
pouring into the land in the train of Henry and his sons
the Norman allied himself with the Englishman against
these foreigners, and the English tongue began to rise into
importance. Its literature grew slowly, but as quickly
as most of the literatures of Europe. Moreover it never
quite ceased. We are carried on to the year 1154 by the
prose of the English Chronicle. There are traces in the
Norman Chroniclers of the use they made of lost English war-songs. There are Old English homilies which
we may date from 1120. The so-called *Moral Ode*, an
English rhyming poem, was compiled about the year 1170.
It made almost a school ; it gave rise to some impassioned
poems to the Virgin, and it is found in a volume of homilies of the same date. In the reign of Henry II., the
old Southern-English Gospels of King Æthelred's time
were modernised after 200 years or less of use. The
Sayings of Ælfred, written in English for the English,
were composed about the year 1200. About the same
date the Old English Charters of Bury St. Edmunds were
translated into the dialect of the shire, and now, early in
the thirteenth century, at the central time of the strife
between English and foreign elements, after the death of
Richard I., the *Brut* of Layamon and the *Orrmulum*
come forth within ten years of each other to prove the
continuity, the survival, and the victory of the English
tongue. When the patriotic struggle closed in the reign

of Edward I., English literature had again risen, through
the song, the religious poems, the alliterative romance
and homily, the lives of saints and the translations of
French romances, into importance, and was written by a
people made up of Norman and Englishman welded into
one by the fight against the French foreigner. But
though the foreigner was driven out, his literature influenced, and continued to influence, the new English
poetry, for in this revival our literature was chiefly poetical. Prose, with but few exceptions, was still written
in Latin.

24. **Religious and Story-telling Poetry** are the two
main streams into which this poetical literature divides
itself. The religious poetry is for the most part English
in spirit, and a poetry of the people, from the *Orrmulum*, about 1215, to *Piers Plowman*, in which poem the
distinctly English poetry reached its truest expression in
1362. The story-telling poetry may be called English at
its beginning in the *Brut* of Layamon, but becomes more
and more influenced by the romantic poetry of France,
and in the end grows in Chaucer's hands into a poetry
of the court and of fine allegory, a literary in contrast
with a popular poetry. But Chaucer, at first thus influenced by French and then by Italian subjects, becomes
at last entirely English in feeling and in subjects, and the
Canterbury Tales are the best example of English story-
telling we possess. The struggle then of England against
the foreigner to become and remain England finds its
parallel in the struggle of English poetry against the

influence of foreign poetry to become and remain English. Both struggles were long and varied, but in both England was triumphant. She became a nation, and she won a national literature. It is the course of this struggle we have now to trace along the two lines already laid down — the poetry of religion and the poetry of story-telling; but to do so we must begin in both instances with the Norman Conquest.

25. **The Religious Poetry.** — The religious revival of the eleventh century was strongly felt in Normandy, and both the knights and Churchmen who came to England with William the Conqueror and during his son's reign, were founders of abbeys, from which, as centres of learning and charity, the country was civilised. Where Lanfranc and Anselm lived, religion or scholastic learning was not likely to go to sleep. A frequent communication was kept up with French scholarship through the University of Paris. Schools and libraries multiplied. The Latin learning of England steadily developed. Its scholars in the twelfth and thirteenth centuries wrote not only on theology, but on many various subjects; and some of their books influenced the whole of European thought. In Henry I.'s reign the religion of England was further quickened by missionary monks sent by Bernard of Clairvaux. London was stirred to rebuild St. Paul's, and abbeys rose in all the well-watered valleys of the north. Thus the English citizens of London and the English peasants in the country received a new religious life from the foreign noble and

the foreign monk, and both were drawn together through
a common worship. When this took place a desire arose
for religious handbooks in the English tongue. Orrmin's
Orrmulum may be taken as a type of these. We may
date it, though not precisely, at 1215, the date of the
Great Charter. It is English; its sources are Ælfric
and Bæda; its Danish writer loves his native dialect;
not five French words are to be found in it. It is a
metrical version of the Gospel of each day with the
addition of a sermon in verse. "This book is named
Orrmulum for that Orrm it wrought." It marks the
rise of English religious literature, and its religion is
simple and rustic. Orrm's ideal monk is " a very pure
man, and altogether without property, except that he
shall be found in simple meat and clothes." He will
have "a hard and stiff and rough and heavy life to
lead. All his heart and desire ought to be aye toward
heaven, and to serve his Master well." This was English religion in the country at this date. It was continued in English prose writing by the *Ancren Riwle* —
the Rule of the Anchoresses — written about 1220. The
original MS. was probably in the Dorsetshire dialect.
The *Genesis* and then the *Exodus*, biblical poems of
about 1250, were made by the pious writers to make
Christian men as glad as birds at the dawning for the
story of salvation. A Northumbrian Psalter of 1250
is only one example out of many devotional pieces,
homilies, metrical creeds, hymns to the Virgin (mostly
imitated from the French), which, with the metrical

Lives of the Saints (a large volume, the lives translated
from Latin or French prose into English verse), carry
the religious poetry up to 1300. Among these the
most important are the lives of three saints, *Marherete*,
Juliane, and *Katerine*, and the homily on *Hali Meiden-
had* (Holy Maidenhood) all in alliterative verse, written
in southern England, and beginning a new and vital
class of poetry, the poetry of impassioned love to
Christ and the Virgin.

26. **Literature and the Friars.** — There was little
religion in the towns, but this was soon changed. In
1221 the Mendicant Friars came to England, and they
chose the towns for their work. The first Friars who
learnt English that they might preach to the people
were foreigners, and spoke French. Many English
Friars studied in Paris, and came back to England,
able to talk to Norman noble and English peasant.
Their influence, exercised both on Norman and English, was thus a mediatory and uniting one, and Normans
as well as English now began to write religious works in
English. The people, of course, had to be served with
stories, and in the early years of the fourteenth century
a number of Christian legends of the childhood of Jesus,
of the Virgin, the Apostles and Saints, and of miracles,
chiefly drawn from the French, were put into varying
poetic forms; and, recited everywhere, added a large
number of materials to the imagination of England. A
legend-cycle was thus formed, and this cycle was chiefly
made by writers in the *south of England*. In 1303

Robert Mannyng of Brunne, in Lincolnshire, freely translated, to please plain people, a French work, the Manual of Sins (written thirty years earlier by William of Waddington), under the title of *Handlyng Synne*. William of Shoreham translated the whole of the Psalter into English prose about 1327, and wrote poems which might be called treatises in rhyme. The *Cursor Mundi*, written about 1320, in Northumbria, and thought " the best book of all " by men of that time, was a metrical recast of the history of the Old and New Testament, interspersed, as was the *Handlyng Synne*, with legends of saints. This book started a whole series of verse-homilies tagged with tales, which created in *northern England* a legend-cycle similar to that created in the south. Some scattered Sermons, and in 1340 the *Ayenbite of Inwyt* (the Sting of Conscience), translated from the French, mark how *English prose* was rising through religion. About the same year Richard Rolle, the Hermit of Hampole, wrote in Latin and in Nor-thumbrian English for the "unlearned," a poem called the *Pricke of Conscience*. This poem is the last dis-tinctly religious poem of any importance before the *Vision of Piers Plowman*, unless we are led to except those written by the author of *The Grene Knight*. At its date, 1340, the religious influence of the Friars was swiftly decaying. In *Piers Plowman* their influence for good is gone. In that poem, which brings religious poetry, in the death of its author, up to 1400, the re-ligious literature of England strikes the last note of

the old religious impulse and the boldest music of the
new. The Friar is slain, the Puritan survives.

27. **History and the Story-telling Poetry.** — The
Normans brought an historical taste with them to
England, and created a valuable historical literature.
It was written in Latin, and we have nothing to do
with it till English story-telling grew out of it about
the time of the Great Charter. But it was in itself
of such importance that a few things must be said
concerning it.

(1) The men who wrote it were called CHRONICLERS.
At first they were only annalists — that is, they jotted
down the events of year after year without any attempt
to bind them together into a connected whole. Of these,
the most important, and indeed they were something
more than mere annalists, were Ordericus Vitalis, and
his predecessors, Florence of Worcester and Simeon of
Durham. But afterwards, from the time of Henry I.,
another class of men arose, who wrote, not in scattered
monasteries, but at the Court. Living at the centre of
political life, their histories were written in a philosophic
spirit, and wove into a whole the growth of law and
national life and the story of affairs abroad. They are
our great authorities for the history of these times. They
begin with William of Malmesbury, whose book ends in
1142, and die out after Matthew Paris, 1235–73. Historical prose in England is only represented after the
death of Henry III. by a few dry Latin annalists till it
rose again in modern English prose in 1513, when Sir

Thomas More's *Life of Edward V. and Usurpation of Richard III.* is said to have been written.

(2) *A distinct English feeling* soon sprang up among these Norman historians. English patriotism was far from having died among the English themselves. The *Sayings of Ælfred* were written in English by the English. These and some ballads, as well as the early English war-songs, interested the Norman historians and were collected by them. William of Malmesbury, who was born of English and Norman parents, has sympathies with both peoples, and his history marks how both were becoming one nation. The same welding together of the conquered and the conquerors is seen in Henry of Huntingdon and others, till we come to Matthew Paris, whose view of history is entirely that of an Englishman. When he wrote, Norman noble and English yeoman, Norman abbot and English priest, were, and are in his pages, one in blood and one in interests.

28. **English Story-telling** grew out of this historical literature. There was a Welsh priest at the court of Henry I., called GEOFFREY OF MONMOUTH, who, inspired by the Genius of romance, composed in Latin twelve short books (1132–35), which he playfully called History. He had been given, he said, an ancient Welsh book to translate which told in verse the history of Britain from the days when Brut, the great-grandson of Æneas, landed on its shores, through the whole history of King Arthur down to Cadwallo, a Welsh king who died in 689. The real historians were angry at the fiction, and declared

that throughout the whole of it " he had lied saucily and shamelessly." It was indeed only a clever putting together and invention of a number of Welsh and other legends, but it was *the beginning of story-telling* after the Conquest. Every one who read it was delighted with it ; it made, as we should say, a sensation, and as much on the Continent as in England. Geoffrey may be said to have created the heroic figure of Arthur, which had been only sketched in the compilation which passes under the name of Nennius. In it the Welsh invaded English literature, and their tales have never since ceased to live in it. They charm us as much in Tennyson's *Idylls of the King* as they charmed us in the days of Henry I. But the stories Geoffrey of Monmouth told were in Latin prose. They were put first into French verse by Geoffrey Gaimar for the wife of his patron, Ralph FitzGilbert, a northern baron. They got afterwards to France and, added to from Breton legends, were made into a poem and decked out with the ornaments of French romance. In that form they came back to England as the work of Wace, a Norman of Caen, the writer also of the *Roman de Rou*, who called his poem the *Geste des Bretons* (afterwards the *Brut*), and completed it in 1155, shortly after the accession of Henry II. Spread far and wide in France, it led to an immense development there and elsewhere of the Legend of Arthur and his Knights.

29. **Layamon's "Brut."** — In this French form the story drifted through England. and at last falling into the hands of an English priest in Worcestershire, he resolved

to tell it in alliterative English verse to his countrymen, and so doing became the writer of our first important English poem after the Conquest. We may roughly say that its date is 1205, ten years or so before the *Orrmu-lum* was written, ten years before the Great Charter. It is plain that its composition, though it told a Welsh story, was looked on as a patriotic work by the writer. "There was a priest in the land," he writes of himself, "whose name was Layamon; he was son of Leovenath: May the Lord be gracious unto him! He dwelt at Earnley, a noble church on the bank of Severn, near Radstone, where he read books. It came in mind to him and in his chiefest thought that he would tell the noble needs of England, what the men were named, and whence they came, who first had English land." And it was truly of great importance. The poem opened to the imagination of the English people an immense, though a fabled, past for the history of the island they dwelt in, and made a common bond of interest between Norman and Englishman. It linked also the Welsh to the English and the Norman. Written on the borders of Wales, it introduces a number of Briton legends of which Wace knew nothing, and of English stories also down to the days of Æthelstan. It enlarged Arthur before the eyes of men, and even Teutonic sagas enter into the story. In the realm of poetry all nations meet and are reconciled. Though a great deal of it is rendered from the French, there are not fifty French words in its 30,000 lines. The old English alliterative metre is kept up with a few rare rhymes.

In battle, in pathetic story, in romantic adventure, in invention, in the sympathy of sea and storm with heroic
deeds, he is a greater and more original poet than those
who followed him, till we come to Chaucer. He touches
with one hand the ancient England before the Conquest,
he touches with another the romantic poetry after it. Indeed, what Cædmon was to early English poetry, Layamon
is to English poetry after the Conquest. He is the first
of the new singers.

30. **Story-telling becomes entirely French in Form.** —
After an interval the desire for story-telling increased in
England, and France satisfied the desire. The French
tales were carried over our land by the travelling merchant and friar, by the gleemen and singers who translated them, or sung translations of them, not only to the
castle and the farm, but to the village and the town.
Floriz and Blancheflur and the *Romance of Sir Tristrem*
were versified before 1300, and many other romantic
tales. The lay of *Havelok the Dane* was perhaps adapted
from the French towards the close of the thirteenth century, and so was the song of *King Horn*. Their English
origin is also maintained, and at least both rest on Teutonic
tradition. The first took form in northern England, and
shares in the rough vigour of the north. The second is a
southern tale, and has been entirely transformed by the
romantic spirit. English in rhythm, it is thoroughly
French in feeling. The romances of *King Alexander* and
of *Richard Cœur de Lion*, and of *Arthour and Merlin*,
while romantic in form, preserve an English sentiment

and originality which make us remember that, when they
were written, Edward I. was making Norman and English
into one people. About 1300 the story-telling verged
into historical poems, and Robert of Gloucester wrote
his *Rhyming Chronicle*, from Brutus to Edward I. As the
dates grow nearer to 1300, the amount of French words
increases, and the French romantic manner of story-telling.
In the Romance of *Alexander*, to take one example as a
type of all, the natural landscape, the conventional intro-
ductions to the parts, the gorgeous descriptions of pomps,
and armour, and cities, the magic wonders, the manners,
and feasts, and battles of chivalry, especially the love
affairs and feelings, are all steeped in the colours of
French romantic poetry. Now this romance was originally adapted by a Frenchman about the year 1200. It
took therefore nearly a century before the French
romantic manner of poetry could be naturalised in
English ; and it was naturalised, curious to say, at the
very time when England as a nation had lost its French
attachments and become entirely English.

31. **Cycles of Romance.** — At this time, then, the
French romance of a hundred years earlier was made
English in England. There were four great romantic
stories. The first was that of *King Arthur*, and Geoffrey
of Monmouth began it in England about 1132. Before
1150 it was taken up in Normandy, sent therefrom into
France, and independent invention soon began to play
upon it. Of these inventors the first was Crestien of
Troyes, but we owe to Robert de Boron, a knight of the

Vosges country, the first poem on the Graal, the Holy Dish with which Christ celebrated the Last Supper, and which in the hands of Joseph of Arimathea received his blood. The origin of the legend may be traced to Celtic stories, and this may partly account for its swift development in the west of England. Two more romances on the subject, *Le Grand St. Graal* and *La Queste del St. Graal*, in which Galahad appears, are attributed to Walter Map, a friend of Henry II., and they were certainly written in England in that king's reign. It is due to the Anglo-Normans and the Normans that this Graal-story, in which the Arthur legends were bound up with the highest doctrine of the Church, took its great development, not only in France but in Germany. Alongside of the Arthurian Saga arose the Tristan story, and, at first independent, it was afterwards linked on to the tale of Arthur. These two together, along with stories invented concerning all the Knights of the Round Table, and chiefly Launcelot and Gawaine, were worked over in a multitude of romantic tales, most of which became popular in England, and were sung and made into English verse from the thirteenth to the sixteenth century.

The second romantic story was that of *Charlemagne and his twelve peers*. Begun in France with the *Song of Roland*, a huge tale of Charlemagne was forged about 1110 in the name of Archbishop Turpin. In this, Charlemagne's wars were bound up with oriental legend, with the Holy Sepulchre, with every kind of story. A great number of Carlovingian romances followed. This cycle, however, owing perhaps to the alienation of the Anglo-Normans in England from the French, was not much developed in England at the beginning of our romance-writing. The most popular of the Carlovingian poems was the poem of *Otinel* in the reign of Edward II.; but the most beautiful was *Amis et Amiloun*, the English version of which so wholly leaves out its connexion with Charlemagne that it has been supposed to be an original Anglo-Norman-English poem. The *Roland*, the *Charlemagne and Roland*, a *Siege of Milan*, *Sir Ferumbras* and the humorous *Rauf Coilyear* almost exhaust the English poems of this cycle.

The third Romantic story is that of the *Life of Alexander*, derived from a Latin version (fourth century) of the Greek story made in Alexandria under the name of *Callisthenes*. Its romantic wonders, fictions, and magic, largely added to from the Arabian books about Eskander, were doubled by the imagination and coloured with all the romance of chivalry in the eleventh or twelfth century; and the story became so common in England that "every wight that hath discrecioune," says Chaucer, had heard of Alexander's fortune. No doubt it was sung all over England, but we have only a few poems concerning it in English, the last of which, a free translation of a French original, *The Buik of the most noble and vailzeand Conquerour*, belongs to the fourth decade of the fifteenth century.

The fourth romantic story, first in date, but last in im-

portance in England, was that of the *Siege of Troy*. Two
Latin pieces, bearing the names of *Dares Phrygius* and
of *Dictys Cretensis*, composed about the story of Troy
in the decline of Latin literature, were worked over by
Benoit de Sainte More, with fabulous and romantic inventions of his own, in the *Roman de Troie*, about 1160.
Guido della Colonne, of Messina, took them up about
1270, and with additions woven into them from the
Theban and Argonautic stories, made a great Latin story
out of them which Lydgate used. Virgil supplied materials for a romance of *Æneas;* Statius for a *Roman de
Thebes*. During the crusades Byzantine and oriental
stories entered into French romance, and especially into
this Cycle of Troy. The *Gest Historiale* (XIV. Cent.)
of the Destruction of Troy, first introduced the story of
Troilus (invented by Benoit) to readers of English verse.
This cycle does not seem to have much entered into our
literature till Chaucer's time, but it attracted both Chaucer and Lydgate.

These were the four great Romantic cycles which were
used by English poets. But the desire for romances
was not satisfied with these. A few collected round Old
English traditions or history. There was a poem about
Wade, the father of Weland, to which Chaucer alludes.
It has long been lost, but a small fragment of it has lately
been discovered. I have already mentioned the stories
of Horn and Havelok. The romances of *Guy of War-
wick* and of *Bevis of Hampton*, though both translated
from the French, take us back to the time of Æthelstan

and Eadgar, but are as unhistorical as the tales of Troy
and Alexander. A number of other romances from various sources belong to the time of the Edwards, and were
all derived from the French. Short tales also sprang up,
taken from the *fabliaux*, from the *Roman de Renart*,
from the French *lais*, some satirical, some of love, some
in the form of "debates." Compilations of tales were
made. The *Sevyn Sages* was worked from the oriental
stock of the *Book of the Seven Wise Men*; and the *Gesta
Romanorum*, a book of stories which began to be used
in England in the reign of Edward I., supplied the material for tales in England as well as all over Europe. The
country was therefore swarming with tales, chiefly French,
and its poetic imagination with the fancies, the fables,
the love, and the ornaments of French romance, translated and imitated in English, and written in the metres
of France and in rhyme.

32. **Alliterative English Poems, 1350.** — In the midst
of all this French imitation, something national begins
to gleam, and it comes from the west, from the lands on
the edge of Wales and Cumbria. This is the recovery
of the Old English metre, that fine, elastic, marching,
epic, alliterative metre which Layamon used, and which
takes us back to Cynewulf. The things written now in
this national metre are still romantic and French in subject, feeling, and manners; but their Teutonic metre
slides a fresh, even a vigorous originality, into the conventional phrasing of the romantic poetry. This reaction
from a French to an English type began in the middle

of the fourteenth century, and runs parallel with the general victory of the English language over the French in the time of Edward III. At least twelve important poems are written in this alliterative metre, the last of which in this century was Langland's *Vision*. Among these, but not altogether alliterative, are the poems of a northern, perhaps a Lancashire poet. These are *Sir Gawayne and the Grene Knight; Pearl;* and *Cleanness and Patience* (Clannesse and Pacience). This poet, who probably had finished his poems just as Chaucer and Langland began to write, stands quite apart from his fellows in excellence, and, indeed, along with Langland and only below Chaucer. Though *Sir Gawayne* is romantic, it escapes at many points from the French spirit. It is more original, it is more imaginative, it is far more intense in feeling, than the ordinary romances. It describes natural scenery at first hand, and the scenery is that of the poet's own country. It is moral in aim, it is composed into an organic whole. It is full of new inventions. In the *Pearl*, our earliest *In Memoriam*, there is an extraordinary personal passion of grief and of religious exultation pervading a lovely symbolism, which is quite unique. The same strong personality, mixed with a more distinctly moral purpose, fills the writer's two other poems, and brings him as a religious poet into range with Langland on the one hand, and with Cynewulf on the other. No one can crudely mix him up with France. He is as English, at the last, as Langland or Chaucer.

E

33. English Lyrics. — In the midst of all this story-
telling, like prophecies of what should afterwards be so
lovely in our poetry, rose, no one can tell how, some
lyric poems, country idylls, love songs, and, later on,
some war-songs. The English ballad, sung from town
to town by wandering gleemen, had never altogether
died. A number of rude ballads collected round the
legendary *Robin Hood*, and the kind of poetic literature which sang of the outlaw and the forest, and afterwards so fully of the wild border life, gradually took
form. About 1280 a beautiful little idyll called the
Owl and the Nightingale was written, probably in Dorsetshire, in which the rival birds submit their quarrel for
precedence to the possible writer of the poem, Nicholas
of Guildford. About 1300 we meet with a few lyric
poems, full of charm. They sing of spring-time with its
blossoms, of the woods ringing with the thrush and nightingale, of the flowers and the seemly sun, of country
work, of the woes and joys of love, and many other
delightful things. They are tinged with the colour of
French romance, but they have an English background.
This lyrical movement began with hymns to the Virgin
and Christ, touched with the sentiments of Latin and
Norman-French amorous poetry. These changed into
frank love-poems in the hands of the wandering stu-
dents. Many arose on the Welsh marches, and were
tinged with Celtic feeling. Some are no doubt literary
renderings of English folk-songs, such as "Sumer is
ycumen in," "Blow, northerne wind," and are full of

love of women and love of nature. After these, a new
type of religious lyrics blossomed, in which, as in all
future English poetry, the love of nature was mingled
with the love of God and the longing of the soul for
perfect beauty. Satirical lyrics also arose, and the pro-
verbial poetry of France gave an impulse to collections
like the *Proverbs of Hendyng.* Most of these were of
the time of Henry III. and Edward I. Political ballads
now began, in Edward I.'s reign, to be frequently written
in English, but the only dateable ballads of importance
are that on the battle of Lewes, 1264, and the ten war
lyrics of Laurence Minot, who, in 1352, sang the great
deeds and battles of Edward III.

34. **The King's English.** — After the Conquest, French
or Latin was the language of the literary class. The English tongue, spoken only by the people, fell back from the
standard West-Saxon English of the *Chronicle* into that
broken state of anarchy in which each part of the country
has its own dialect, and each writer uses the dialect of
his own dwelling-place. All the poems then of which we
have spoken were written in dialects of English, not in a
fixed English common to all writers. During the prev-
alence of French, and the continued translation of
French poems, English had been invaded by French
words, and though it had become, in Edward III.'s
reign, the national tongue, it had been transformed as a
language. The old inflections had mostly disappeared.
French endings and prefixes were used, till even so early
as the end of Edward I.'s reign, in Robert of Brunne's

work, a third of his nouns, adverbs, and verbs, are French. His work was still however in a dialect — the East-Midland dialect. This dialect grew into the language of literature, *the standard English*. In Robert of Brunne, it was most literary and most French, but we must remember that the same dialect belonged to the two centres of learning, Oxford and Cambridge, and that London, on this side the Thames was contained in the same Anglian boundaries. This conquering dialect, when it became the standard English, did not prevent the *Vision concerning Piers Plowman* and Wyclif's translation of the Bible from being written in a dialect, but it became the English in which all future English literature was to be written. It was fixed into clear form by Chaucer. It was the language talked at the court and in the court society to which that poet belonged. It was the *King's English*, and the fact that it was the tongue of the best and most cultivated society, as well as the great excellence of the works written in it by Chaucer, made it at once the tongue of literature.

35. **Religious Literature in Langland and Wyclif.** — We have traced the work of " transition English," as it has been called, along the lines of popular religion and story-telling. The first of these, in the realm of poetry, reaches its goal in the work of William Langland ; in the realm of prose it reaches its goal in Wyclif. In both these writers, the work differs from any that went before it, by its popular power, and by the depth of its religious feeling. It is plain that it represented a society

much more strongly moved by religion than that of
the beginning of the fourteenth century.   In Wyclif, the
voice comes from the university and it went all over the
land in the body of preachers whom, like Wesley, he sent
forth.   In Langland's *Vision* we have a voice from the
centre of the people themselves; his poem is written
in old alliterative English verse, and in the Old English
manner.   The very ploughboy could understand it.   It
became the book of those who desired social and Church
reform.   It was as eagerly listened to by the free labourers
and fugitive serfs who collected round John Ball and Wat
Tyler.   It embodied a puritan reaction against the Friars
who had fallen away from the religious revival they had
so nobly instituted.   The strongest cry of this regenerated
religion was for truth as against hypocrisy, for purity in
State and Church and private life, for honest labour, and
against ill-gotten wealth and its tyrannical persecution.
There was also a great movement at this time against the
class system of the Middle Ages.   This was made a religious movement when the equality of all men before
God was maintained, and a social movement when it pro-
tested against the oppression of the poor and on behalf
of their misery.   The French wars had increased this
misery.   Heavy taxation and severe laws ground down the
peasantry.   The " Black Death " deepened the wretchedness into panic.   In 1349, 1362, and 1369 it swept over
England.   Grass grew in the towns ; whole villages were
left uninhabited ; a wild terror fell upon the people,
which was added to by a fierce tempest in 1362 that to

men's minds told of the wrath of God. In their panic
then, as well as in their pain, they fled to religion.

36. **Piers Plowman.** — All these elements are to be
found fully represented in the *Vision of William concerning Piers Plowman*, followed by that concerning *Dowel,
Dobet, and Dobest.* Its author, WILLIAM LANGLAND,
though we are not certain of his surname, was born, about
1332, at Cleobury Mortimer, in Shropshire. His *Vision*
begins with a description of his sleeping on the Malvern
Hills, and the first text of it was probably written in the
country in 1362. At the accession of Richard II., 1377,
he was in London. The great popularity of his poem
made him in that year, and again about the year 1398,
send forth two more texts of his poem. In these texts
he made so many additions to the first text that he nearly
doubled the length of the original poem. In 1399, he
wrote his last poem, *Richard the Redeless*, and then died,
probably in 1400, and we may hope in the quiet of the
West country.

37. **His Vision.** — He paints his portrait as he was
when he lived in Cornhill, a tall, gaunt figure, whom men
called Long Will ; clothed in the black robes in which he
sang for a few pence at the funerals of the rich ; hating
to take his cap off his shaven head to bow to the lords
and ladies that rode by in silver and furs as he stalked
in observant moodiness along the Strand. It is this
figure which in indignant sorrow walks through the
whole poem. The dream of the " field full of folk,"
with which it begins, brings together nearly as many

typical characters as the Tales of Chaucer do. In the
first part, the truth sought for is righteous dealing in
Church, and Law, and State. After the Prologue of the
" field full of folk " and in it the Tower of Truth and the
Dungeon where the Father of Falsehood lives, the *Vision*
treats of Holy Church who tells the dreamer of Truth.
Where is Falsehood? he asks. She bids him turn, and
he sees Falsehood and Lady Meed, and learns that
they are to be married. Theology interferes and all the
parties go to London before the King. Lady Meed,
arraigned on Falsehood's flight, is advised by the King
to marry Conscience, but Conscience indignantly pro-
claims her faults, and prophesies that one day Reason
will judge the world. On this the King sends for Reason,
who, deciding a question against Wrong and in spite of
Meed (or bribery), is begged by the King to remain
with him. This fills four divisions or " Passus." The
fifth Passus contains the confession of the Seven Deadly
Sins, and is full of vivid pictures of friars, robbers, nuns,
of village life, of London alehouses, of all the vices of the
time. It ends with the search for Truth being taken up
by all the penitents, and then for the first time Piers
Plowman appears and describes the way. He sets all
who come to him to hard work, and it is here that the
passages occur in which the labouring poor and their evils
are dwelt upon. The seventh Passus introduces the bull
of pardon sent by Truth (God the Father) to Piers. A
Priest declares it is not valid, and the discussion between
him and Piers is so hot that the Dreamer awakes and

ends with a fine outburst on the wretchedness of a trust
in indulgences and the nobleness of a righteous life.
This is the first part of the poem.

In the second part the truth sought for is that of
righteous life, to *Do Well*, to *Do Better*, to *Do Best*, the
three titles of a new vision and a new pilgrimage. In a
series of dreams and a highly-wrought allegory, *Do Well*,
Do Bet, and *Do Best* are finally identified with Jesus
Christ, who now appears as Love in the dress of Piers
Plowman. *Do Well* is full of curious and important
passages. *Do Bet* points out Christ as the Saviour of the
World, describes His death, resurrection, and victory over
Death and Sin. And the dreamer awakes in a transport
of joy, with the Easter chimes pealing in his ears. But
as Langland looked round on the world, the victory did
not seem real, and the stern dreamer passed out of
triumph into the dark sorrow in which he lived. He
dreams again in *Do Best*, and sees, as Christ leaves the
earth, the reign of Antichrist. Evils attack the Church
and mankind. Envy, Pride, and Sloth, helped by the
Friars, besiege Conscience. Conscience cries on Contrition to help him, but Contrition is asleep, and Conscience,
all but despairing, grasps his pilgrim staff and sets out to
wander over the world, praying for luck and health, " till
he have Piers the Plowman," till he find the Saviour.
And then the dreamer wakes for the last time, weeping
bitterly. This is the poem which displays to us that side
of English society which Chaucer had not touched, and
which wrought so strongly in men's minds that its moral

influence was almost as widely spread as Wyclif's in the revolt which had now begun against Latin Christianity. Its fame was so great, that it produced imitators. About 1394, another alliterative poem was set forth by an unknown author, with the title of *Pierce the Ploughman's Crede;* and the *Plowman's Tale,* wrongly attributed to Chaucer, is another witness to the popularity of Langland.

38. Wyclif. — At the same time as the *Vision* was being read all over England, JOHN WYCLIF, about 1378, determined to give a full translation of the Bible to the English people in their own tongue. He himself translated the New Testament. His assistant, Nicholas of Hereford, finished the Old Testament as far as Baruch, and Wyclif completed it. Some time after, John Purvey, under Wyclif, revised the whole, corrected its errors, did away with its Latinisms, and made it a book of sterling English — a book which had naturally a great power to fix and preserve words in our language. But Wyclif did much more than this for our tongue. He made it the popular language of religious thought and feeling. In 1381 he was in full battle with the Church on the doctrine of transubstantiation, and was condemned to silence. He replied by appealing to the whole of England in the speech of the people. He sent forth tract after tract, sermon after sermon, couched not in the dry, philosophic style of the schoolmen, but in short, sharp, stinging sentences, full of the homely words used in his own Bible, denying one by one almost all the doctrines, and denouncing the practices, of the Church of

Rome. He was our first Protestant. It was a new
literary vein to open, the vein of the pamphleteer. With
his work then, and with Langland's, we bring up to the
year 1400 the English prose and poetry pertaining to
religion, the course of which we have been tracing since
the Conquest.

39. **Story-telling** is the other line on which we have
placed our literature, and it is now represented by JOHN
GOWER. He belongs to a school older than Chaucer,
inasmuch as he is scarcely touched by the Italian, but
chiefly by the French influence. However, he had read
Petrarca. Fifty *Balades* prove with what clumsy ease he
could write in the French tongue about the affairs of love.
As he grew older he grew graver, and partly as the
religious and social reformer, and partly as the story-
teller, he fills up the literary space between the spirit
of Langland and Chaucer. In the church of St. Saviour, at Southwark, his head is still seen resting on his
three great works, the *Speculum Meditantis*, the *Vox
Clamantis*, the *Confessio Amantis*, 1393. It marks the
unsettled state of our literary language, that each of
these was written in a different tongue, the first in
French, the second in Latin, the third in English. The
first of these has been lost, but has lately been discovered at Cambridge. The second is a dream which
passes into a sermon, cataloguing all the vices of the
time, and is suggested by the peasant rising of 1381.

The third, his English work, is a dialogue between a
lover and his confessor a priest of Venus, and in its

course, and with an imitation of Jean de Meung's part of the *Roman de la Rose*, all the passions and studies which may hinder love are dwelt upon, partly in allegory, and their operation illustrated by apposite stories, borrowed from the *Gesta Romanorum* and from the Romances. But the book is in reality a better and larger collection of tales than was ever made before in English. The telling of the tales is wearisome, and the smoothness of the verse makes them more wearisome. But Gower was a careful writer of English; and in his satire of evils, and in his grave reproof of the follies of Richard II., he rises into his best strain. The king himself, even though reproved, was a patron of the poet. It was as Gower was rowing on the Thames that the royal barge drew near, and he was called to the king's side. "Book some new thing," said the king, " in the way you are used, into which book I myself may often look ; " and the request was the origin of the *Confession of a Lover*. He ended by writing *The Tripartite Chronicle*. It is with pleasure that we turn from the learned man of talent to Geoffrey Chaucer — to the genius who called Gower, with perhaps some of the irony of an artist, " the moral Gower."

40. **Chaucer's French Period.** — GEOFFREY CHAUCER was the son of John Chaucer, a vintner, of Thames Street, London, and was born in 1340 or a year or two earlier. He lived almost all his life in London, in the centre of its work and society. When he was sixteen he became page to the wife of Lionel, Duke of Clarence,

and continued at the court till he joined the army in
France in 1359. He was taken prisoner, but ransomed
before the treaty of Bretigny, in 1360. We then know
nothing of his life for seven years ; but from items in the
Exchequer Rolls, we find that he was again connected
with the court, from 1366 to 1372. He was made a
valet of the king's chamber, and in 1368 an "esquire
of less degree." It was during this time that he began
to write. We seem to have evidence that he composed
in his wild youthful days a number of love poems, none
of which have survived, but which gave him some fame
as a poet. It is said that the *A, B, C,* a prayer to the
Virgin, is the first of his extant poems, but some are in-
clined to put it later. The translation of the *Roman de
la Rose* which we possess is, with the exception of the
first 1705 lines, denied to be his, but it is certain that he
did make a translation of the French poem ; and there
are a few who think that Chaucer's translation was made
about 1380, and that it is completely lost. It is commonly said that he wrote the *Compleynt unto Pite,* a
tender and lovely little poem, before 1369. This was
followed by the *Boke of the Duchesse,* in 1369, a pathetic
allegory of the death of Blanche of Castile, whose husband, John of Gaunt, was Chaucer's patron. These,
being written under the influence of French poetry, are
classed under the name of Chaucer's first period. There
are lines in them which seem to speak of a luckless love
affair, and in this broken love it has been supposed we
find some key to Chaucer's early life. However that

may be, he was married to Philippa Chaucer at some period between 1366 and 1374. Of the children of this marriage we only know certainly of one, Lewis, for whom he made his treatise on the Astrolabe.

41. Chaucer's Italian Period. — Chaucer's second poetic period may be called the period of Italian influence, from 1372 to 1384. During these years he went for the king on four, perhaps five, diplomatic missions. Two of these were to Italy — the first to Genoa, Pisa, and Florence, 1372–3; the second to Lombardy, 1378–9. At that time the great Italian literature which inspired then, and still inspires, European literature, had reached an astonishing excellence, and it opened to Chaucer a new world of art. His many quotations from Dante show that he had read the *Divina Commedia*, and we may well think that he then first learnt the full power and range of poetry. He read the Sonnets of Petrarca, and he learnt what is meant by "form" in poetry; but Petrarca never had the same power over him which Dante possessed. He read the tales and poems of Boccaccio, who made Italian prose, and in them he first saw how to tell a story exquisitely. Petrarca and Boccaccio he may even have met, for they died in 1374 and 1375, and Petrarca was in 1373 at Arquà, close to Padua, an l employed on the Latin version of the story of Grisilde, the version which Chaucer translated in the Clerk's tale. But Dante he could not see, for he had died at Ravenna in 1321. When he came back from these journeys he was a new man. He threw aside the roman-

tic poetry much in vogue, and perhaps laughed at it then
in his gay and kindly manner in the *Rime of Sir Thopas*,
one of the *Canterbury Tales*. His chief work of this
time bears witness to the influence of Italy. It was
Troilus and Criseyde, 1380–3, a translation, with many
changes and additions, of the *Filostrato* of Boccaccio.
The additions (and he nearly doubled the poem) are
stamped with his own peculiar tenderness, vividness, and
simplicity. His changes from the original are all towards the side of purity, good taste, and piety. We
meet the further influence of Boccaccio in the birth of
some of the *Canterbury Tales*, and of Petrarca in the
Tales themselves. To this time is now referred the *Lyf
of Seint Cecyle*, afterwards made the Second Nun's tale ;
and the passionate religious fervour and repentance of
this poem has seemed to point to a period of penitence
in his life for his early sensuousness. It did not last
long, and he now wrote the *Story of Grisilde*, the Clerk's
tale ; the *Story of Constance*, the Man of Law's tale ;
the Monk's tale ; the *Compleynt of Mars;* the *Compleynt to his Lady; Anelida and Arcyte; Troilus and
Criseyde;* the *Lines to Adam Scrivener; To Rose-
mounde; The Parlement of Foules; Boece*, a prose version of the *De Consolatione;* the *Hous of Fame*, and
the *Legende of Good Women*. In these two last poems
we may trace, not only an Italian, but a classical period
in the work of Chaucer. This is the record of the work
of the years between 1373 and 1384 : and almost all
these poems are either influenced by Dante or adapted

from Petrarca and Boccaccio.   In the passion with which
Chaucer describes the ruined love of Troilus or Anelida,
some have traced the lingering sorrow of his early love
affair.   But if this be true, it was now passing away, for
in the creation of Pandarus in the *Troilus*, and in the
delightful fun of that enchanting poem the *Parlement
of Foules*, a new Chaucer appears, the humorous poet
of some of the *Canterbury Tales*.   The noble art of the
Parlement, as well as that of the *Troilus*, lifts Chaucer
already on to that eminence apart where sit the great
poets of the world.   Nothing like this had appeared
before in England.   Nothing like it appeared again till
Spenser.   In the active business life he led during the
period his poetry was likely to win a closer grasp on
human life, for he was not only employed on service
abroad, but also at home.   In 1374 he was Comptroller
of the Wool Customs, in 1382 of the Petty Customs,
and in 1386 Knight of the Shire for Kent.

42. **Chaucer's English Period.** — It is in the next
period, from 1384 to 1390, that he left behind (except
in the borrowing of his subjects) Italian influence as he
had left French, and became entirely himself, entirely
English.   The comparative poverty in which he now
lived, and the loss of his offices in 1386, for in John of
Gaunt's absence court favour was withdrawn from him,
and the death of his wife in 1387, may have given him
more time for study and the retired life of a poet.   His
appointment as Clerk of the Works in 1389 brought him
again into contact with men.   He superintended the

repairs and building at the Palace of Westminster, the Tower, and St. George's Chapel, Windsor, till July, 1391, when he was superseded, and lived on pensions allotted to him by Richard II. and by Henry IV., after he had sent Henry in 1399 his *Compleint to his Purse*. Before 1390, however, he had added to his great work its most English tales; those of the Miller, the Reeve, the Cook, the Wife of Bath, the Merchant, the Friar, the Nun's Priest, the Pardoner, and perhaps the Sompnour. The Prologue was probably written in 1388. In these, in their humour, in their vividness of portraiture, in their ease of narration, and in the variety of their characters, Chaucer shines supreme. A few smaller poems belong to this time, such as the *Former Age ; Fortune ; Truth ; Gentilesse ;* and the *Lak of Steadfastnesse*.

During the last ten years of his life, which may be called the period of his decay, he wrote some small poems, and along with the *Compleynt of Venus*, and a prose treatise on the Astrolabe, three more Canterbury tales, the Canon's-yeoman's, Manciple's, and Parson's. The last was written the year of his death, 1400. Having done this work he died in a house under the shadow of the Abbey of Westminster. Within the walls of the Abbey Church, the first of the poets who lies there, that "sacred and happy spirit" sleeps.

43. **Chaucer's Character.** — Born of the tradesman class, Chaucer was in every sense of the word one of our finest gentlemen : tender, graceful in thought, glad of heart, humorous, and satirical without unkindness ; sensitive to

every change of feeling in himself and others, and therefore full of sympathy; brave in misfortune, even to mirth,
and doing well and with careful honesty all he undertook.
His first and great delight was in human nature, and he
makes us love the noble characters in his poems, and feel
with kindliness towards the baser and ruder sort. He
never sneers, for he had a wide charity, and we can
always smile in his pages at the follies and forgive the
sins of men. He had a quiet and true religion, much
like that we conceive Shakespeare to have had; nor was
he without a high philosophic strain. Both were kept in
order by his imagination and his humour. He had a
true and chivalrous regard for women of his own class,
and his wife and he ought to have been very happy if
they had fulfilled the ideal he had of marriage. He lived
in aristocratic society, and yet he thought him the greatest gentleman who was the most courteous and the most
virtuous. He lived frankly among men, and as we have
seen, saw many different types of men, and in his own
time filled many parts as a man of the world and of business. Yet, with all this active and observant life, he was
commonly very quiet and kept much to himself. "Flee
from the press and dwell with steadfastness" is the first
line of his last ballad, and it embodies, with the rest of
that personal poem, the serious part of his life. The
Host in the Tales japes at him for his lonely, abstracted
air. "Thou lookest as thou wouldest find a hare, And
ever on the ground I see thee stare." Being a good
scholar, he read morning and night alone, and he says

F

that after his (office) work he would go home and sit at
another book as dumb as a stone, till his look was dazed.
While at study and when he was making of songs and
ditties, "nothing else that God had made" had any interest for him. There was but one thing that roused him
then, and that too he liked to enjoy alone. It was the
beauty of the morning and the fields, the woods, and
streams, and flowers, and the singing of the little birds.
This made his heart full of revel and solace, and when
spring came after winter, he rose with the lark and cried
"Farewell, my book and my devotion." He was a keen
observer of the nature he cared for, especially of colour.
He loved the streams and the birds and soft grassy
places and green trees, and all sweet, ordered gardens,
and flowers. He could spend the whole day, he says, in
gazing alone on the daisy, and though what he says is
symbolic, yet we may trace through the phrase that
lonely delight in natural scenery which is so special a
mark of our later poets. He lived thus a double life, in
and out of the world, but never a gloomy one. For he
was fond of mirth and good-living, and when he grew
towards age, was portly of waist, no poppet to embrace.
But he kept to the end his elfish countenance, the shy,
delicate, half-mischievous face which looked on men
from its gray hair and forked beard, and was set off by
his dark-coloured dress and hood. A knife and ink-horn
hung on his dress; we see a rosary in his hand; and
when he was alone he walked swiftly.

44. The Canterbury Tales. — Of his work it is not

easy to speak briefly, because of its great variety.   Enough
has been said of it, with the exception of his most complete creation, the *Canterbury Tales*.   It will be seen
from the dates given above that they were not written at
one time.   They are not, and cannot be looked on as a
whole.   Many were written independently, and then fitted
into the framework of the Prologue.   Many, which he
intended to write in order to complete his scheme, were
never written.   But we may say that the full idea of his
work took shape about 1385, after he had finished *The
Legende of Good Women*, and that the whole existing
body of the Tales was completed, with the exception of
the last three already mentioned, before the close of
1390.   At intervals, from time to time, he added a tale ;
in fact, the whole was done much in the same way as
Tennyson has written his *Idylls of the King*.   The manner
in which he knitted them together was very simple, and
likely to please the English people.   The holiday ex-
cursions of the time were the pilgrimages, and the most
famous and the pleasantest pilgrimage to go, especially
for Londoners, was the three or four days' journey to see
the shrine of St. Thomas at Canterbury.   Persons of all
ranks in life met and travelled together, starting from a
London inn.   Chaucer had probably made the pilgrimage
to Canterbury in the spring of 1385 or 1387, and was led
by this experience to the framework in which he set his
pictures of life.   He grouped around the jovial host of
the Tabard Inn men and women of every class of society
in England, set them on horseback to ride to Canterbury

and home again, intending to make each of them tell
tales. No one could hit off a character better, and in
his Prologue, and in the prologues to the several Tales,
a great part of the new, vigorous English society which
had grown up since Edward I. is painted with astonishing
vividness. " I see all the pilgrims in the *Canterbury
Tales*," says Dryden, "their humours, their features, and
the very dress, as distinctly as if I had supped with them
at the Tabard in Southwark." The Tales themselves
take in the whole range of the poetry and the life of the
Middle Ages ; the legend of the saint, the romance of the
knight, the wonderful fables of the traveller, the coarse
tale of common life, the love story, the allegory, the
animal-fable, and the satirical lay. And they are pure
tales. He is not in any sense a dramatic writer ; he is
our greatest story-teller in verse. All the best tales are
told easily, sincerely, with great grace, and yet with so
much homeliness, that a child would understand them.
Sometimes his humour is broad, sometimes sly, sometimes gay, but it is also exquisite and affectionate. His
pathos does not go into the far depths of sorrow and pain,
but it is always natural. He can bring tears into our eyes,
and he can make us smile or be sad as he pleases.

His eye for colour was superb and distinctive. He
had a very fine ear for the music of verse, and the tale
and the verse go together like voice and music. Indeed,
so softly flowing and bright are they, that to read them
is like listening in a meadow full of sunshine to a clear
stream rippling over its bed of pebbles. The English in

which they are written is almost the English of our
time; and it is literary English. Chaucer made our
tongue into a true means of poetry. He did more, he
welded together the French and English elements in
our language and made them into one English tool for
the use of literature, and all our prose writers and poets
derive their tongue from the language of the *Canterbury
Tales.* They give him honour for this, but still more for
that he was so fine an artist. Poetry is an art, and the
artist in poetry is one who writes for pure and noble
pleasure the thing he writes, and who desires to give to
others the same or a similar pleasure by his poems
which he had in writing them. The things he most
cares about are that the form in which he puts his
thoughts or feelings may be perfectly fitting to the subjects : and that subject, matter, and form should be as
beautiful as possible — but for these he cares very
greatly; and in this Chaucer stands apart from the other
poets of his time. Gower wrote with a set object, and
nothing can be less beautiful than the form in which he
puts his tales. The author of *Piers Plowman* wrote with
the object of reform in social and ecclesiastical affairs,
and his form is uncouth and harsh. Chaucer wrote because he was full of emotion and joy in his own thoughts,
and thought that others would weep and be glad with
him, and the only time he ever moralises is in the tales of
the Canon's Yeoman and the Manciple, written in his decay. He has, then, the best right to the poet's name. He
is, within his own range, the clearest of English artists.

Finally, his position in the history of English poetry and towards his own time resembles that of Dante, whom he loved so well, in the history and poetry of Italy. Dante embodied all the past elements of the Middle Ages in his work, and he began the literature, the thoughts, and the power of a new age. He was the Evening Star of the Mediæval day and the Morning Star of the Renaissance. Chaucer also represented medievalism though in a much more incomplete way than Dante, but he had, so far as poetry in England is concerned, more of the Renaissance spirit than Dante. He is more humanistic than even Spenser. England needed to live more than a century to get up to the level of Chaucer. Lastly, both Dante and he made their own country's tongue the tongue of noble literature.

45. **The Travels of Sir John Maundevile** belong to this place which treats of story-telling. Whatever other English prose arose in the fourteenth century was theological or scientific. John of Trevisa had, among other English translations, turned into English prose, 1387, the *Polychronicon* of Ranulf Higden. Various other prose treatises, beginning with those of Richard Rolle, had appeared. Chaucer himself translated two of his tales, that of the Parson, and that of Melibœus, from the French into an involved prose; and wrote in the same rude vehicle, his *Boece*, and his book on the Astrolabe. We have already noticed the prose of Wyclif. But *Maundevile's Travels* is a story-book. Maundevile himself, the quaint and pleasant knight, is as

much an invention as Robinson Crusoe, and the travels
as much an imposture as Geoffrey's *History of the Kings
of Britain*. But they had a similar charm, and when
made up originally by Jean de Bourgogne, a physician
who died at Liège in 1372, were received with delight
and belief by the world, and nowhere with greater
pleasure than in England, where they were translated
into English prose by an anonymous writer of the late
fourteenth or more probably fifteenth century. The
prose is garrulous and facile, gliding with a pleasure
in itself from legend to travellers' tales, from dreams
to facts, from St. Albans to Jerusalem, from Cairo to
Cathay. The book became a model of prose, and may
even be called an early classic.

CHAPTER III

FROM CHAUCER'S DEATH 1400, TO ELIZABETH, 1558

46. **The Fifteenth Century Poetry.** — The last poems
of Chaucer and Langland bring our story up to 1400.
The hundred years that followed are the most barren
in our literature. The influence of Chaucer lasted, and
of the poems attributed to him, but now rejected by
scholars, some certainly belong to the first half of this
century. There are fifty poems, making up 17,000 lines,
which have been wrongly attributed to Chaucer, and
though some of them were contemporary with him, a
number are by imitators of his in the fifteenth century.
Some of these have a great charm. *The Cuckoo and
the Nightingale* is a pleasant thing. *The Complaint of
the Black Knight* is by Lydgate. *The Court of Love*
and *Chaucer's Dream* are good but late imitations of
the master. *The Flower and the Leaf* is by a woman
whose name we should like to know, for the poem is
lovely. "*Moder of God and Virgin undefouled*" is by
Hoccleve, and was long attributed to Chaucer. The
triple Roundel, *Merciles Beaute*, is given by Professor
Skeat to Chaucer, and at least is worthy of the poet;

and the *Amorous Compleint* and a *Ballade of Com-pleynt,* may possibly be also his. There was then a considerable school of imitators, who followed the style, who had some of the imaginative spirit, but who failed in the music and the art of Chaucer.

47. **Thomas Hoccleve and John Lygate.** — Two of these imitators stand out from the rest by the extent of their work. Hoccleve, a London man, was a monotonous versifier of the reigns of the three Henries, but he loved Chaucer well. In the MS. of his longest poem, the *Governail of Princes,* written before 1413, he caused to be drawn, with fond idolatry, the portrait of his "master dear and father reverent," who had enlumined all the land with his books. He had a style of his own. Sometimes, in his playful imitations of Chaucer's *Balades,* and in his devotional poetry, such as his *Moder of God,* he reached excellence ; but his didactic and controversial aims finally overwhelmed his poetry.

48. **John Lydgate** was a more worthy follower of Chaucer. A monk of Bury, and thirty years of age when Chaucer died, he yet wrote nothing of much importance till the reign of Henry V. He was a gay and pleasant person, though a long-winded poet, and he seems to have lived even in his old age, when he recalls himself as a boy "weeping for naught, anon after glad," the fresh and natural life of one who enjoyed everything ; but, like many gay persons, he had a vein of melancholy, and some of his best work, at

least in the poet Gray's opinion, belongs to the realms
of pathetic and moral poetry. But there was scarcely
any literary work he could not do. He rhymed history,
ballads, and legends, till the monastery was delighted.
He made pageants for Henry VI., masques and May-
games for aldermen, mummeries for the Lord Mayor,
and satirical ballads on the follies of the day. It is
impossible here to mention the tenth part of his multifarious works, many of which are as yet unpublished.
They are a strange mixture of the poet striving to be
religious, and of the monk carried away by his passions
and his gaiety. He may have been educated at Oxford,
and perhaps travelled in France and Italy; he knew
the literature of his time, and he even dabbled in the
sciences. He was as much a lover of nature as Chaucer, but cannot make us feel the beauty of nature in
the same way. It is his story-telling which links him
closest to his master. His three chief poems are, first,
The Troye Book, which is adapted from Guido's *Historia Trojana;* secondly, the *Storie of Thebes*, which
is introduced as an additional Canterbury Tale, and is
worked up from French romances on this subject.
The third is the *Falles of Princes*, 1424–5, at which
he worked till he was sixty years of age. It is a free
translation of a French version of Boccaccio's *De Cas-
ibus Virorum et Feminarum Illustrium*. It tells the
tragic fates of great men and women from the time
of Adam to the capture of King John of France at
Poitiers. The plan is picturesque; the sorrowful dead

appear before Boccaccio, pensive in his library, and
each tells of his downfall. This is Lydgate's most important, but by no means his best, poem ; and it had
its influence on the future, for in the *Mirror for Magistrates*, at least eight Elizabethan poets united at different times to supplement his *Falles of Princes*.

A few minor poets do no more now than keep poetry
alive. Another version of the Troy Story in Henry VI.'s
time ; Hugh de Campeden's *Sidrac*, Thomas Chestre's
Lay of Sir Launfal, and the translation of the *Earl of
Toulouse*, prove that romances were still taken from the
French. William Lichfield's *Complaint between God and
Man*, and William Nassington's *Mirrour of Life*, carry
on the religious, and the *Tournament of Tottenham* the
satirical, poetry. John Capgrave's translation of the *Life
of St. Catherine* is less known than his *Chronicle of
England* dedicated to Edward IV. He, with John Hard-
ing, a soldier of Agincourt, whose rhyming Chronicle
belongs to Edward IV.'s reign, continue the historical
poetry. A number of obscure versifiers, Thomas Norton,
and George Ripley who wrote on alchemy, and Dame
Juliana Berners' book on Hunting, bring us to the reign
of Henry VII., when Skelton first began to write. Mean-
while poetry, which had decayed in England, was
flourishing in Scotland.

49. **Ballads,** lays, fragments of romances, had been
sung in England from the earliest times, and popular
tales and jokes took form in short lyric pieces, to be accompanied with music and dancing. In fact, the ballad

went over the whole land among the people. The trader, the apprentices, and poor of the cities, the peasantry, had their own songs. They tended to collect themselves round some legendary name like Robin Hood, or some historical character made legendary, like Randolf, Earl of Chester. In the fourteenth century, Sloth, in *Piers Plowman*, does not know his paternoster, but he does know the rhymes of these heroes. Robin Hood was then well known in 1370. A crowd of minstrels sang them through city and village. The very friar sang them, "and made his English swete upon his tonge." The *Tale of Gamelyn* is a piece of minstrel poetry, of the forest type, and drew to it, as we know, the attention of Chaucer. Chaucer and Langland mention the French ballads which were sung in London, and these were freely translated. The popular song, "When Adam dalf and Eve span," was a type of a class of socialistic ballads. *The Battle of Otterbourne* and *The Hunting of the Cheviot* were no doubt composed in the fourteenth century, but were not published till now. Two collections of Robin Hood ballads and *The Nut Brown Maid*, printed about the beginning of the sixteenth century, show that a fresh interest had then awakened in this outlaw literature to which we owe so much. It was not, however, till much later that any large collection of ballads was made ; and few, in the form we possess them, can be dated farther back than the reign of Elizabeth.

50. **Prose Literature.** — Four men continued English prose into the fifteenth century. The religious war be-

tween the Lollards and the Church raged during the reigns
of Henry V. and Henry VI., and in the time of the
latter REGINALD PECOCK took it out of Latin into homely
English.   He fought the Lollards with their own weapons,
with public sermons in English, and with tracts in English ; and after 1449, when Bishop of Chichester, published
his works, *The Repressor of overmuch Blaming of the
Clergy* and *The Book of Faith*. They pleased neither
party. The Lollards disliked them because they defended
the customs and doctrines of the Church. Churchmen
burnt them because they agreed with the "Bible-men,"
that the Bible was the only rule of faith. Both abjured
them because they said that doctrines were to be proved
from the Bible by reason. Pecock is the first of all the
Church theologians who wrote in English, and his books
are good examples of our early prose.

SIR JOHN FORTESCUE'S book on the *Difference between
Absolute and Limited Monarchy*, in Edward IV.'s reign,
is less fine an example of the prose of English politics
than SIR THOMAS MALORY'S *Morte Darthur* is of the
prose of chivalry. This book, arranged and modelled
into a labyrinthine story from French and contemporary
English materials, is the work of a man of genius, and
was ended in the ninth year of Edward IV., fifteen years
before Caxton had finished printing it. Its prose, in its
joyous simplicity, may well have charmed CAXTON, who
printed it with all the care of one who "loved the noble
acts of chivalry." Caxton's own work added to the
prose of England. Born of Kentish parents, he went to

the Low Countries in 1440, and learned his trade. The first book said to have been printed in this country was *The Game and Playe of the Chesse*, 1474. The first book that bears the inscription, " Imprynted by me, William Caxton, at Westmynstre," is *The Dictes and Sayings of Philosophers*. But the first English book Caxton made, and finished at Cologne in 1471, was his translation of the *Recuyell of the Historyes of Troy*, and in this book, and in his translation of *Reynard the Fox* from the Dutch, in his translation of the *Golden Legend*, and his re-editing of Trevisa's *Chronicle*, in which he " changed the rude and old English," he kept, by the fixing power of the press, the Midland English, which Chaucer had established as the tongue of literature, from further degradation. Forty years later Tyndale's New Testament fixed it more firmly, and the Elizabethan writers kept it in its purity.

51. The Foundations of the Elizabethan Literature. — The first of these may be found in Caxton's work. John Shirley, a gentleman of good family, and Chaucer's contemporary, who died, a very old man, in 1449, deserves mention as a transcriber and preserver of the works of Chaucer and Lydgate, but Caxton fulfilled the task Shirley had begun. He printed Chaucer and Lydgate and Gower with zealous care. He printed the *Chronicle of the Brut ;* he secured for us the *Morte Darthur.* He had a tradesman's interest in publishing the romances, for they were the reading of the day ; but he could scarcely have done better for the interests of the coming literature. These books nourished the imagination of England, and supplied poet after poet with fine subjects for work, or fine frames for their subjects. He had not a tradesman's, but a loving literary, interest in printing the old English poets; and in sending them out from his press Caxton kept up the continuity of English poetry. The poets after him at once began on the models of Chaucer and Gower and Lydgate; and the books themselves being more widely read, not only made poets but a public that loved poetry. The imprinting of old English poetry was one of the sources in this century of the Elizabethan literature.

The second source was the growth of an interest in classic literature. All through the last two-thirds of this century, though so little creative work was done, the interest in that literature grew among men of the upper classes. The Wars of the Roses did not stop the reading of books. *The Paston Letters*, 1422–1509, the correspondence of a country family from Henry VI. to Henry VII., are pleasantly, even correctly written, and contain passages which refer to translations of the classics and to manuscripts sent to and fro for reading. A great number of French translations of the Latin classics were read in England. Henry V. and VI., Edward IV., and some of the great nobles were lovers of books. Men like Duke Humphrey of Gloucester made libraries and brought over Italian scholars to England to translate Greek works. There were even scholars in England, like John, Lord Tiptoft, Earl of Worcester, who had won fame in the schools of Italy, and whose translations of Cicero's *De Amicitiâ* and of Cæsar's *De Bello Gallico* prove, with his Latin letters, how worthy he was of the praise of Padua and the gratitude of Oxford. He added many MSS. to the library of Duke Humphrey. The two great universities were also now reformed; new colleges were founded, new libraries were established, Greek, Latin, and Italian MSS. were collected in them. The New Learning had begun to move in these great centres. A number of university men went to study in Italy, to Padua, Bologna, and Ferrara. Among these were Robert Flemmyng, Dean of Lincoln; John Gunthorpe, Dean of Wells; William Grey, Bishop of Ely; John Phreas, Provost of Balliol; William Sellynge, Fellow of All Souls, all of whom collected MSS. in Italy of the classics, with which they enriched the libraries of England. It is in this growing influence of the great classic models of literature that we find the gathering together of another of the sources of that Elizabethan literature which seems to flower so suddenly, but which had been long preparing.

52. **The Italian Revival of Learning.** — The impulse, as we see, came from Italy, and was due to that great humanistic movement which we call the Renaissance, and which had properly begun in Italy with Dante and his circle, with Petrarca and Boccaccio, with Giotto and Nicolo Pisano. It carried with it, as it went on reviving the thought, literature and law of Greece and Rome, the overthrow of Feudalism and the romantic poetry of the Middle Ages. It made classic literature and art the basis

of a new literature and a new art, which was not at first imitative, save of excellence of form. It began a new worship of beauty, a new worship of knowledge, and a new statesmanship. It initiated those new views of man and of human life, of its aims, rights, and duties, of its pleasures and pains, of religion, of knowledge, and of the whole course of the history of the world, which produced, as they fell on various types of humanity, the Reformation, a semi-pagan freedom of thought and life, the theories and ideas which took such furious form in the French Revolution, the boundless effort which attempted all things, and the boundless curiosity which penetrated into every realm of thought and feeling, and considered nothing too sacred or too remote for investigation by knowledge or for representation in art. At every one of those points it has affected literature up to the present day.

No sooner had Petrarca and Boccaccio started it than Italy began to send eager searchers over Europe and chiefly to Constantinople. For more than seventy years before that city was taken by the Turk, shoals of MSS. had been carried from it into Italy together with a host of objects of ancient art. Before 1440 the best Latin classics and many of the Greek, were known, and were soon studied, lectured on, imitated, and translated. By 1460 Italy, in all matters of thought, life, art, literature, and knowledge, was like a hive of bees in a warm summer. We have seen with what slowness this vast impulse was felt in England in the fifteenth century. But it had begun, and in Elizabeth's time, pouring into England, it

G

went forth conquering and to conquer. As France dominated the literature of England after the Conquest, till Chaucer, touched by Italy, made it English, so Italy dominated it till Shakespeare and his fellows, touched also by Italy, made it again English.

53. **There was now a Transition Period both in Prose and Poetry.** — The reigns of Richard III. and Henry VII. brought forth no prose of any worth, but the country awakened into its first Renaissance with the accession of Henry VIII., 1509. John Colet, Dean of St. Paul's, with William Lilly, the grammarian, set on foot a school where the classics were taught in a new and practical way, and between the year 1500 and the Reformation twenty grammar-schools were established. Erasmus, who had all the enthusiasm which sets others on fire, had come to England in 1497, and found Grocyn and Linacre at Oxford, teaching the Greek they had learnt from Chalcondylas at Florence. He learnt Greek from them, and found eager admiration of his own scholarship in Bishop Fisher, Sir Thomas More, Colet, and Archbishop Warham. From these men a liberal and moderate theology spread, which soon, however, perished in the heats of the Reformation. But the New Learning they had started grew rapidly, assisted by the munificence of Wolsey; and Cambridge, under Cheke and Smith, excelled even Oxford in Greek learning. The study of the great classics set free the minds of men, stirred and gave life to letters, woke up English prose from its sleep, and kindled the young English intelligence in the universities. Its earliest

prose was its best. It was in 1513 (not printed till 1557) that THOMAS MORE wrote the history in English, of Edward V.'s life and Richard III.'s usurpation. The simplicity of his genius showed itself in the style, and his wit in the picturesque method and the dramatic dialogue that graced the book. This stately historical manner was laid aside by More in the tracts of nervous English with which he replied to Tyndale, but both his styles are remarkable for their purity. Of all the " strong words " he uses, three out of four are Teutonic. More's most famous work, the *Utopia*, 1516, was written in Latin, but was translated afterwards, in 1551, by Ralph Robinson. It tells us more of the curiosity the New Learning had awakened in Englishmen concerning all the problems of life, society, government, and religion, than any other book of the time. It is the representative book of that short but well-defined period which we may call *English Renaissance before the Reformation.* We see in all this movement another of the sources of the Elizabethan outburst. Much of the progress of prose was due to the patronage of the young king. It was the king who asked Lord Berners to translate *Froissart,* a translation which in 1523 made a landmark in our tongue. It was the king who supported Sir Thomas Elyot in his effort to improve education, and encouraged him to write books (1531–46) in the vulgar tongue that he might please his countrymen. It was the king who made Leland, our first English writer on antiquarian subjects, the " King's Antiquary," 1533. It was the king to whom

Roger Ascham dedicated his first work, and who sent
him abroad to pursue his studies. This book, the
Toxophilus, or the *School of Shooting*, 1545, was written for the pleasure of the yeomen and gentlemen of
England in their own tongue. Ascham apologises for
this, and the apology marks the state of English prose.
" Everything has been done excellently well in Greek
and Latin, but in the English tongue so meanly that no
man can do worse." But " I have written this English
matter, in the English tongue for English men." Ascham's
quaint English has its charm, and he did not know that
the very rudeness of language of which he complained
was in reality laying the foundations of an English more
Teutonic and less Latin than the English of Chaucer.

54. **Prose and the Reformation.** —The bigotry, the
avarice, and the violent controversy of the Reformation
killed for a time the New Learning, but the Reformation
did a vast work for English literature, and prepared the
language for the Elizabethan writers, by its version of
the Bible. WILLIAM TYNDALE's *Translation of the New
Testament*, 1525, fixed our standard English once for all,
and brought it finally into every English home. Tyndale
held fast to pure English. In his two volumes of political tracts " there are only twelve Teutonic words which
are now obsolete, a strong proof of the influence his
translation of the Bible has had in preserving the old
speech of England." Of the 6000 words of the *Authorised Version*, still in a great part his translation, only 250
are not now in common use. " Three out of four of his

nouns, adverbs, and verbs are Teutonic." And he spoke
sharply enough to those who said our tongue was so rude
that the Bible could not be translated into it. "It is not
so rude as they are false liars. For the Greek tongue
agreeth more with the English than the Latin; a thousand parts better may it be translated into the English
than into the Latin."

Tyndale was helped in his English Bible by William
Roy, a runaway friar; and his friend Rogers, the first
martyr in Queen Mary's reign, added the translation of
the *Apocrypha*, and made up what was wanting in Tyndale's translation from Chronicles to Malachi out of
Coverdale's translation. It was this Bible which, revised by Coverdale and edited and re-edited as *Cromwell's Bible*, 1539, and again as *Cranmer's Bible*, 1540,
was set up in every parish church in England. It got
north into Scotland and made the Lowland English more
like the London English. It passed over to the Protestant settlements in Ireland. After its revisal in 1611
it went with the Puritan Fathers to New England and
fixed the standard of English in America. Many mill-
ions of people now speak the English of Tyndale's Bible,
and there is no book which has had, through the Authorised Version, so great an influence on the style of
English literature and the standard of English prose. In
Edward VI.'s reign also Cranmer edited the *English
Prayer Book*, 1549-52. Its English is a good deal
mixed with Latin words, and its style is sometimes weak
or heavy, but on the whole it is a fine example of stately

prose. It also steadied our speech. LATIMER, on the
contrary, whose *Sermon on the Ploughers* and others were
delivered in 1549 and in 1552, wrote in a plain, shrewd
style, which by its humour and rude directness made him
the first preacher of his day. On the whole the Reformation fixed and confirmed our English tongue, but at the
same time it brought in through theology a large number
of Latin words. The pairing of English and Latin words
(*acknowledge* and *confess*, etc.) in the Prayer Book is
a good example of both these results.

**55. Poetry in the Sixteenth Century under the In-
fluence of Chaucer.**—One source, we have said, of the
Elizabethan literature, before Elizabeth, was the recovery,
through Caxton's press, of Chaucer and his men. It is
probable that the influence of Italian literature on English
poets was now kept from becoming overwhelming by the
strong English element in Chaucer. At least this was
one of the reasons for the clear poetic individuality of
England ; and we can easily trace its balancing effect
in Spenser. It was of importance, then, that before
Surrey and Wyatt again brought Italian elements into
English verse, there should be a revival of Chaucer,
both in England and Scotland. This transition period,
short as it was, is of interest. STEPHEN HAWES, in the
reign of Henry VII., represented the transition by an
imitation of the old work. Amid many poems, some
more imitative of Lydgate than of Chaucer, his long allegorical poem, entitled the *Pastime of Pleasure*, is the
best. In fact, it is the first, since the middle of the

fifteenth century, in which Imagination again began to
plume her wings and soar.   Within the realm of art, it
corresponded to that effort to resuscitate the dead body
of the Old Chivalry which Henry VIII. and Francis I.
attempted.   It goes back for its inspiration to the *Romance of the Rose*, and is an allegory of the right education of a knight, showing how Grand Amour won at last
La Bel Pucell.   But, like all soulless resurrections, it
died quickly.

On the other hand, JOHN SKELTON represents the
transition by at first following the old poetry, and then,
pressed upon by the storm of human life in the present,
by taking an original path.   His imitative poetry belongs
mostly to Henry VII.'s time, but when the religious and
political disturbances began in Henry VIII.'s time,
Skelton became excited by the cry of the people for
Church reformation.   His poem, *Why come ye not to
Court?* was a fierce satire on the great Cardinal.   That
of *Colin Clout* was the cry of the country Colin, and of
the Clout or mechanic of the town against the corruption
of the Church ; and it represents the whole popular feeling of the time just before the movement of the Reformation took a new turn from the opposition of the Pope to
Henry's divorce.   Both are written in short " rude rayling
rimes, pleasing only the popular ear," and Skelton chose
them for that purpose.   He had a rough, impetuous
power, but Skelton could use any language he pleased.
He was an admirable scholar.   Erasmus calls him the
" glory and light of English letters," and Caxton says

that he improved our language.   His poem, the *Bowge of Court* (rewards of court), is full of powerful satire against the corruption of the times, and of vivid impersonations of the virtues and vices.   But he was not only the satirist. The pretty and new love lyrics that we owe to him fore-shadow the Elizabethan imagination and life ; and the *Boke of Phyllyp Sparowe*, which tells, in imitation of Catullus, the grief of a nun called Jane Scrope for the death of her sparrow, i. a gay and inventive poem. Skelton stands — a landmark in English literature — be-tween the mere imitation of Chaucer and the rise of a new Italian influence in England in the poems of Surrey and Wyatt.   In his own special work he was entirely original. The *Ship of Fooles*, 1508, by Barclay, is of this time, but it has no value.   It is a paraphrase of a famous German work by Sebastian Brandt, published at Basel. It was popular because it attacked the follies and ques-tions of the time.   Its sole interest to us is in its pictures of familiar manners and popular customs.   But Barclay did other work, and he established the eclogue in Eng-land.   With him the transition time is over, and the curtain is ready to rise on the Elizabethan age of poetry. While we wait, we will make an interlude out of the work of the poets of Scotland.

SCOTTISH POETRY

56 **Scottish Poetry** is poetry written in the English tongue by men living in Scotland.   These men, though calling themselves Scotsmen, are of good English blood.

But the blood, as I think, was mixed with a larger infusion of Celtic blood than elsewhere.

Old Northumbria extended from the Humber to the Firth of Forth, leaving however on its western border a strip of unconquered land, which took in Lancashire, Cumberland, and Westmoreland in our England, and, over the border, most of the western country between the Clyde and Solway Firth. This unconquered country was the Welsh kingdom of Strathclyde, and was dwelt in by the Celtic race. The present English part of it was conquered and the Celts absorbed. But in the part to the north of the Solway Firth the Celts were not conquered and not absorbed. They remained, lived with the Englishmen who were settled over the old Northumbria, intermarried with them, and became under Scot kings a people with the Celtic elements more dominant in them than in the rest of our nation. English literature in the Lowlands of Scotland would then retain more of these Celtic elements than elsewhere ; and there are certain peculiarities infused through the whole of English poetry in Scotland which are especially Celtic.

57. **Celtic Elements of Scottish Poetry.** — The first of these is *the love of wild nature for its own sake.* There is a passionate, close, and poetical observation and description of natural scenery in Scotland from the earliest times of its poetry, such as we do not possess in English poetry till the time of Thomson. The second is *the love of colour.* All early Scottish poetry differs from English in the extraordinary way in which colour is in-

sisted on, and at times in the lavish exaggeration of it.
The third is *the wittier and coarser humour* in the Scottish poetry, which is distinctly Celtic in contrast with
that humour which has its root in sadness and which belongs to the Teutonic races. Few things are really more
different than the humour of Chaucer and the humour of
Dunbar, than the humour of Cowper and the humour of
Burns. These are the special Celtic elements in the
Lowland poetry.

58. But there are also **national elements** in it which,
exaggerated and isolated as they were, are also Celtic.
The wild individuality of the Gaelic clans was not unrepresented in the Lowland kingdom, and became there
as assertive a nationality as Ireland has ever proclaimed.
The English were as national as the Scots, but they were
not oppressed. But for nearly forty years the Scots re-
sisted for their very life the efforts of England to conquer
them. And the war of freedom left its traces on their
poetry from Barbour to Burns and Walter Scott in the
almost obtrusive way in which Scotland, and Scottish
liberty, and Scottish heroes are thrust forward in their
verse. Their passionate nationality appears in another
form in their descriptive poetry. The natural description of Chaucer, Shakespeare, or even Milton, is not
distinctively English. But in Scotland it is always the
scenery of their own land that the poets describe. Even
when they are imitating Chaucer they do not imitate his
conventional landscape. They put in a Scottish landscape ; and in the work of such men as Gawin Douglas

the love of Scotland and the love of nature mingle their influences together to make him sit down, as it were, to paint, with his eye on everything he paints, a series of Scottish landscapes.

59. The first of the Scottish poets, omitting Thomas of Erceldoune, is JOHN BARBOUR, Archdeacon of Aberdeen. His long poem of *The Bruce*, 1375-7, represents the whole of the eager struggle for Scottish freedom against the English which closed at Bannockburn ; and the national spirit, which I have mentioned, springs in it, full grown, into life. But it is temperate, it does not pass into the fury against England, which is so plain in writers like BLIND HARRY, who, about 1461, composed a long poem in the heroic couplet of Chaucer on the deeds of *William Wallace*. In Henry V.'s reign, ANDREW OF WYNTOUN wrote his *Oryginale Cronykil of Scotland*, one of the rhyming chronicles of the time. It is only in the next poet that we find the full influence of Chaucer, and it is thereafter continuous till the Elizabethan time. JAMES THE FIRST of Scotland was prisoner in England for nineteen years, till 1422. There he read Chaucer, and fell in love with Lady Jane Beaufort, niece of Henry IV. The poem which he wrote — *The King's Quair* (the quire or book) — is done in imitation of Chaucer, and in Chaucer's seven-lined stanza, which from James's use of it is called " Rime Royal." In six cantos, sweeter, tenderer, and purer than any verse till we come to Spenser, he describes the beginning of his love and its happy end. " I must write," he says, " so

much because I have come so from Hell to Heaven." Though imitative of Chaucer, his work has an original element in it. The natural description is more varied, the colour is more vivid, and there is a modern self-reflective quality, a touch of mystic feeling which does not belong to Chaucer.

ROBERT HENRYSON, who died about 1500, a school-master in Dunfermline, was also an imitator of Chaucer, and his *Testament of Cresseid* continues Chaucer's *Troilus*. But he did not do only imitative work. He treated the fables of Æsop in a new fashion. In his hands they are long stories, full of pleasant dialogue, political allusions, and with elaborate morals attached to them. They have a peculiar Scottish tang, and are full of descriptions of Scottish scenery. He also reanimated the short pastoral in his *Robin and Makyne*. It is a natural, prettily-turned dialogue; and a flashing Celtic wit, such as charms us in *Duncan Gray*, runs through it. The individuality which reformed two modes of poetic work in these poems appears again in his sketch of the graces of womanhood in the *Garment of Good Ladies;* a poem of the same type as those thoughtful lyrics which describe what is best in certain phases of professions, or of life, such as Sir H. Wotton's *Character of a Happy Life*, or Wordsworth's *Happy Warrior*.

But among many poets whom we need not mention, the greatest is WILLIAM DUNBAR. He carries the in-fluence of Chaucer on to the end of the fifteenth century and into the sixteenth. His genius, though masculine,

loved beauty, and his work was as varied in its range as
it was original. He followed the form and plan of Chaucer in his two poems of *The Thistle and the Rose*, 1503,
and the *Golden Terge*, 1508, the first on the marriage of
James IV. to Margaret Tudor, the second an allegory of
Love, Beauty, Reason, and the poet. In both, though
they begin with Chaucer's conventional May morning,
the natural description becomes Scottish, and in both the
national enthusiasm of the poet is strongly marked. But
he soon ceased to imitate. The vigorous fun of the
satires and of the satirical ballads that he wrote is only
matched by their coarseness, a coarseness and a fun that
descended to Burns. Perhaps Dunbar's genius is still
higher in a wild poem in which he personifies the seven
deadly sins, and describes their dance, with a mixture of
horror and humour which makes the little thing unique.

A man as remarkable as Dunbar is GAWIN DOUGLAS,
Bishop of Dunkeld, who died in 1522, at the Court of
Henry VIII., and was buried in the Savoy. He translated into verse Ovid's *Art of Love*, now lost, and afterwards, with truth and spirit, the *Æneids* of Virgil, 1513.
To each book of the Æneid he wrote a prologue of his
own. Three of them are descriptions of the country in
May, in Autumn, and in Winter. The scenery is altogether Scottish, and the few Chaucerisms that appear
seem absurdly out of place in a picture of nature which
is painted with excessive care and directly from the truth.
The colour is superb, but the landscape is not composed
by any art into a whole. There is nothing like it in

England till Thomson's *Seasons*, and Thomson was a Scotsman. Only the Celtic love of nature can account for the vast distance between work like this and contemporary work in England such as Skelton's. Of Douglas's other original work, one poem, the *Palace of Honour*, 1501, continues the influence of Chaucer.

There were a number of other Scottish poets who are all remembered by Dunbar in his *Lament for the Makars*, and praised by SIR DAVID LYNDSAY, whom it is best to mention in this place, because he still connects Scottish poetry with Chaucer. He was born about 1490, and was the last of the old Scottish school, and the most popular. He is the most popular because he is not only the poet, but also the reformer. His poem the *Dreme*, 1528, links him back to Chaucer. It is in the manner of the old poet. But its scenery is Scottish, and instead of the May morning of Chaucer, it opens on a winter's day of wind and sleet. The place is a cave over the sea, whence Lyndsay sees the weltering of the ocean. Chaucer goes to sleep over Ovid or Cicero, Lyndsay falls into a dream as he thinks of the "false world's instability," wavering like the sea waves. The difference marks not only the difference of the two countries, but the different natures of the men. Chaucer did not care much for the popular storms, and loved the Court more than the Commonweal. Lyndsay in the *Dreme* and in two other poems — the *Complaint to the King*, and the *Testament of the King's Papyngo* — is absorbed in the evils and sorrows of the people, in the desire to reform the abuses of the Church.

of the Court, of party, of the nobility. In 1539 his *Satire of the Three Estates*, a Morality interspersed with interludes, was represented before James V. at Linlithgow. It was a daring attack on the ignorance, profli- • gacy, and exactions of the priesthood, on the vices and flattery of the favourites — " a mocking of abuses used in the country by diverse sorts of estates." A still bolder poem, and one thought so even by himself, is the *Monarchie*, 1553, his last work. He is as much the reformer, as he is the poet, of a transition time. Still his verse hath charms, but it was neither sweet nor imaginative. He had genuine satire, great moral breadth, much preaching power in verse, coarse, broad humour in plenty, and more dramatic power and invention than the rest of his fellows.

60. **The Elizabethan Dawn: Wyatt and Surrey.** — While poetry under Skelton and Lyndsay became an instrument of reform, it revived as an art at the close of Henry VIII.'s reign in SIR THOMAS WYATT and LORD HENRY HOWARD, Earl of Surrey. They were both Italian travellers, and in bringing back to England the inspiration they had gained from Italian and classic models they re-made English poetry. They are our first really modern poets ; the first who have anything of the modern manner. Though Italian in sentiment, their language is more English than Chaucer's, that is, they use fewer romance words. They handed down this purity of English to the Elizabethan poets, to Sackville, Spenser,

and Shakespeare. They introduced a new kind of poetry, the amourist poetry — a poetry extremely personal, and personal as English poetry had scarcely ever been before. The amourists, as they are called, were poets who composed a series of poems on the subject of the joys and sorrows of their loves — sonnets mingled with lyrical pieces after the manner of Petrarca, and sometimes in accord with the love philosophy he built on Plato. They began with Wyatt and Surrey. They did not die out till the end of James I.'s reign. The subjects of Wyatt and Surrey were chiefly lyrical, and the fact that they imitated the same model has made some likeness between them. Like their personal characters, however, the poetry of Wyatt is the more thoughtful and the more strongly felt, but Surrey's has a sweeter movement and a livelier fancy. Both did this great thing for English verse — they chose an exquisite model, and in imitating it "corrected the ruggedness of English poetry." A new standard was made below which the future poets should not fall. They also added new stanza measures to English verse, and enlarged in this way the "lyrical range." Surrey was the first, in his translation of the Second and Fourth Books of *Virgil's Æneid*, to use the ten-syllabled, unrhymed verse, which we now call blank verse. In his hands it is not worthy of praise. Sackville, Lord Buckhurst, introduced it into drama ; Marlowe made it the proper verse of the drama. In plays it has a special manner of its own ; in poetry proper it was, we may say, not only created but perfected by Milton.

The new impulse thus given to poetry was all but arrested by the bigotry that prevailed during the reigns of Edward VI. and Mary, and all the work of the New Learning seemed to be useless. But Thomas Wilson's book in English on *Rhetoric and Logic* in 1553, and the publication of Thomas Tusser's *Pointes of Husbandrie* and of Tottel's *Miscellany of Uncertain Authors*, 1557, in the last year of Mary's reign, proved that something was stirring beneath the gloom. The *Miscellany* contained 40 poems by Surrey, 96 by Wyatt, 40 by Grimoald, and 134 by uncertain authors. The date should be remembered, for it is the first printed book of modern English poetry. It proves that men cared now more for the new than the old poets, that the time of mere imitation of Chaucer was over, and that of original creation begun. It ushers in the Elizabethan literature.

H

CHAPTER IV

THE ELIZABETHAN LITERATURE

61. **Elizabethan Literature,** as a literature, may be said to begin with Surrey and Wyatt. But as their poems were published shortly before Elizabeth came to the throne, we date the beginning of the *early period* of Elizabethan literature from the year of her accession, 1558. That period lasted till 1579, and was followed by the great literary outburst of the days of Spenser and Shakespeare. The apparent suddenness of this outburst has been an object of wonder. I have already noticed its earliest sources in the last hundred years. And now we shall best seek its nearest causes in the work done during the early years of Elizabeth. The flood-tide which began in 1579 was preceded by a very various, plentiful, but inferior literature, in which new forms of poetry and prose-writing were tried, and new veins of thought opened. These twenty years from the *Mirror for Magistrates*, 1559, to the *Shepheard's Calendar*, 1579, sowed seeds which when the time came broke into flower. We wonder at the flower, but it grew naturally through seed and stem, leaves and blossom. They made the flower, since the

circumstances were favourable. And never in England,
save in our own century, were they so favourable.

62. First Elizabethan Period, 1558–1570. — (1.) The
literary prose of the beginning of this time is represented
by the *Scholemaster* of ASCHAM, published in 1570. This
book, which is on education, is the work of the scholar of
the New Learning of the reign of Henry VIII. who has
lived on into another period. It is not, properly speaking, Elizabethan; it is like a stranger in a new land and
among new manners.

(2.) Poetry is first represented by SACKVILLE, Lord
Buckhurst. The *Mirror for Magistrates*, for which he
wrote, 1563, the *Induction* and one tale, is a series of
tragic poems on the model of Boccaccio's *Falls of Princes*,
already imitated by Lydgate. Seven poets at least, with
Sackville, contributed tales to it, but his poem is poetry
of so fine a quality that it stands absolutely alone during
these twenty years. The *Induction* paints the poet's
descent into Avernus, and his meeting with Henry
Stafford, Duke of Buckingham, whose fate he tells with
a grave and inventive imagination, and with the first true
music which we hear since Chaucer. Being written in
the manner and stanza of the elder poets, this poem has
been called the transition between Lydgate and Spenser.
But it does not truly belong to the old time; it is as
modern as Spenser, and its allegorical representations
are in the same manner as those of Spenser. GEORGE
GASCOIGNE, whose satire, the *Steele Glas*, 1576, is our
first long satirical poem, deserves mention among a

crowd of poets who came after Sackville. They wrote legends, pieces on the wars and discoveries of the Englishmen of their day, epitaphs, epigrams, songs, sonnets, elegies, fables, and sets of love poems ; and the best things they did were collected in such miscellaneous collections as the *Paradise of Dainty Devices*, in 1576. This book, with Tottel's, set on foot both now and in the later years of Elizabeth a crowd of other miscellanies of poetry which represent the vast number of experiments made in Elizabeth's time, in the subjects, the metres, and the various kinds of lyrical poetry. At present, all we can say is that lyrical poetry, and that which we may call " occasional poetry," were now in full motion. The popular *Ballads* also took a wide range. The registers of the Stationers' Company prove that there was scarcely any event of the day, nor almost any controversy in literature, politics, religion, which was not the subject of verse, and of verse into which imagination strove to enter. The ballad may be said to have done the work of the modern weekly review. It stimulated and informed the popular intellectual life of England.

(3.) *Frequent translations* were now made from the classical writers. We know the names of more than twelve men who did this work, and there must have been many more. Already in Henry VIII.'s and Edward VI.'s time, ancient authors had been made English ; and now before 1579, Virgil, Ovid, Cicero, Demosthenes, Plutarch, and many Greek and Latin plays, were translated. Among the rest, Phaer's *Virgil*, 1562, Arthur Golding's

Ovid's Metamorphoses, 1567, and George Turbervile's *Historical Epistles of Ovid*, 1567, are, and especially the first, remarkable. The English people in this way were brought into contact, more than before, with the classical spirit, and again it had its awakening power. We cannot say that either the fineness or compactness of classic work appeared in these heterogeneous translations, though one curious result of them was the craze which followed, and which Gabriel Harvey strove, fortunately in vain, to impose on Spenser, for reproducing classical metres in English poetry. Nor were the old English poets neglected. Though Chaucer and Lydgate, Langland, and the rest, were no longer imitated in this time when fresh creation had begun, they were studied, and they added their impulse of life to original poets like Spenser.

(4.) *Theological Reform* stirred men to another kind of literary work. A great number of polemical ballads, pamphlets, and plays issued every year from obscure presses and filled the land. Poets like George Gascoigne and still more Barnaby Googe, represent in their work the hatred the young men had of the old religious system. It was a spirit which did not do much for literature, but it quickened the habit of composition, and made it easier. The Bible also became common property, and its language glided into all theological writing and gave it a literary tone ; while the publication of John Foxe's *Acts and Monuments* or *Book of Martyrs*, 1563, gave to the people all over England a

book which, by its simple style, the ease of its story-
telling, and its popular charm made the very peasants
who heard it read feel what is meant by literature.

(5.) The *history* of the country and its manners was
not neglected. A whole class of antiquarians wrote
steadily, if with some dulness, on this subject. Grafton,
Stow, Holinshed, and others, at least supplied materials
for the study and use of historical dramatists.

(6.) The *love of stories* grew quickly. The old English tales and ballads were eagerly read and collected.
Italian tales by various authors were translated and
sown so broadcast over London by William Painter in
his collection. *The Palace of Pleasure*, 1566, by George
Turbervile, in his *Tragical Tales* in verse, and by
others, that it is said they were to be bought at every
bookstall. The Romances of Spain and Italy poured
in, and *Amadis de Gaul*, and the companion romances
the *Arcadia* of Sannazaro and the *Ethiopian History*,
were sources of books like Sidney's *Arcadia*, and, with
the classics, supplied materials for the pageants. A
great number of subjects for prose and poetry were
thus made ready for literary men, and prose fiction
became possible in English literature.

(7.) All over Europe, and especially in Italy, now
closely linked to England, the Renaissance had produced a wild spirit of exhausting all the possibilities
of human life. Every form, every game of life, was
tried, every fancy of goodness or wickedness followed
for the fancy's sake. Men said to themselves " Attempt,

Attempt." The act accompanied the thought. England at last shared in this passion, but in English life
it was directed. There was a great liberty given to
men to live and do as they pleased, provided the
queen was worshipped and there was no conspiracy
against the State. That much direction did not apply
to purely literary production. Its attemptings were
unlimited. Anything, everything was tried, especially
in the drama.

(8.) The *masques, pageants, interludes*, and *plays* that
were written at this time are scarcely to be counted.
At every great ceremonial, whenever the queen made
a progress or visited one of the great lords or a university, at the houses of the nobility, and at the Court
on all important days, some obscure versifier, or a
young scholar at the Inns of Court, at Oxford or at
Cambridge, produced a masque or a pageant, or wrote
or translated a play. The habit of play-writing became
common ; a kind of school, one might almost say a
manufacture of plays, arose, which partly accounts for
the rapid production, the excellence, and the multitude
of plays that we find after 1576. Represented all over
England, these masques, pageants, and dramas were
seen by the people, who were thus accustomed to take
an interest, though of an uneducated kind, in the larger
drama that was to follow. The literary men on the
other hand ransacked, in order to find subjects and
scenes for their pageants, ancient and mediæval, magi-
cal, and modern literature, and many of them in doing

so became not fine but multifarious scholars. The imagination of England was quickened and educated in this way, and as Biblical stories were well known and largely used, the images of oriental life were kept among the materials of dramatic imagination.

(9.) Another influence bore on literature. It was that given by the *stories of the voyagers*, who, in the new commercial activity of the country, penetrated into remote lands, and saw the strange monsters and savages which the poets now added to the fairies, dwarfs, and giants of the Romances. Before 1579, books had been published on the north-west passage. Frobisher had made his voyages, and Drake had started, to return in 1580, to amaze all England with the story of his sail round the world and of the riches of the Spanish Main. We may trace everywhere in Elizabethan literature the impression made by the wonders told by the sailors and captains who explored and fought from the North Pole to the Southern Seas.

(10.) Then there was the freest possible play of literary criticism. Every wine-shop in London, every room at the university, was filled with the talk of young men on any work which was published and on the manuscripts which were read. Out of this host emerged the men of genius. Moreover, far apart from these, there were in England now, among all the noise and stir, quiet scholars, such as Contarini and Pole had been in Italy, followers of Erasmus and Colet, precursors of Bacon, who kept the lamp of scholarship burning, and who,

when literature became beautiful, nurtured and praised
it. Nor were the young nobles, who like Surrey had
been in Italy and had known what was good, less useful
now.   There were many men who, when Shakespeare
and Spenser came, were able to say — "'This is good,"
and who drew the new genius into light.

(11.) Lastly, we have proof that there was a large
number of persons writing who did not publish their
works. It was considered at this time, that to write for
the public injured a man, and unless he were driven by
poverty he kept his manuscript by him. But things
were changed when a great genius like Spenser took the
world by storm ; when Lyly's *Euphues* enchanted court
society; when a fine gentleman like Sir Philip Sidney
was known to be a writer. Literature was made the
fashion, and the disgrace being taken from it, the production became enormous. Manuscripts written and
laid by were at once sent forth ; and when the rush
began it grew by its own force. Those who had previously been kept from writing by its unpopularity now
took it up eagerly, and those who had written before
wrote twice as much now. The great improvement also
in literary quality is also accounted for by this — that
men strove to equal such work as Sidney's or Spenser's,
and that a wider and more exacting criticism arose.
Nor must one omit to say, that owing to this employment of life on so vast a number of subjects, and to the
voyages, and to the new literatures searched into, and to
the heat of theological strife, a multitude of new words

streamed into the language, and enriched the vocabulary of imagination. Shakespeare uses 15,000 words.

63. **The Later Literature of Elizabeth's Reign, 1579-1602**, begins with the publication of Lyly's *Euphues*, 1579, and Spenser's *Shepheards Calendar*, also in 1579, and with the writing of Sir Philip Sidney's *Arcadia* and his *Apology for Poetrie*, 1580-1.   It will be best to leave the poem of Spenser aside till we come to write of the poets.

The *Euphues* was the work of JOHN LYLY, poet and dramatist.   It is in two parts, *Euphues the Anatomie of Wit*, and *Euphues and his England*.   In six years it ran through five editions, so great was its popularity.   Its prose style is odd to an excess, "precious" and sweetened, but it has care and charm, and its very faults were of use in softening the solemnity and rudeness of previous prose.   The story is long, and is more a loose framework into which Lyly could fit his thoughts on love, friendship, education, and religion, than a true story.   It made its mark because it fell in with all the fantastic and changeable life of the time.   Its far-fetched conceits, its extravagance of gallantry, its endless metaphors from the classics and especially from natural history, its curious and gorgeous descriptions of dress, and its pale imitation of chivalry, were all reflected in the life and talk and dress of the court of Elizabeth.   It became the fashion to talk "Euphuism," and, like the *Utopia* of More, Lyly's book has created an English word.

The *Arcadia* was the work of SIR PHILIP SIDNEY, and

though written about 1580, did not appear till after his
death.   It is more poetic and more careless in style than
the *Euphues*, but it endeavours to get rid of the mere
quaintness for quaintness' sake, and of the far-fetched
fancies, of Euphuism.   It is less the image of the time
than of the man.   We know that bright and noble figure,
the friend of Spenser, the lover of Stella, the last of the
old knights, the poet, the critic, and the Christian, who,
wounded to the death, gave up the cup of water to a
dying soldier.   We find his whole spirit in the story of
the *Arcadia*, in the first two books and part of the third,
which alone were written by him.   It is a pastoral romance, after the fashion of the Spanish romances, coloured by his love of his sister, Lady Pembroke, and by
the scenery of Wilton under the woods of which he wrote
it.   The characters are real, but the story is confused
by endless digressions.   The sentiment is too fine and
delicate for the world of action.   The descriptions are
picturesque ; a quaint or poetic thought or an epigram
appear in every line.   There is no real art in it, nor is it
true prose.   But it is so full of poetical thought that it
became a mine into which poets dug for subjects.

64. **Poetic Criticism** began before the publication of
the *Faerie Queene*, and its rise shows the interest now
awakened in poetry.   The *Discourse of English Poetrie*,
1586, written by William Webbe "to stirre up some other
of meet abilitie to bestow travell on the matter," was
followed three years after by the *Art of English Poesie*,
attributed to George Puttenham, an elaborate book,

"written," he says, "to help the courtiers and the gen-
tlewomen of the court to write good poetry, that the art
may become vulgar for all Englishmen's use," and the
phrase marks the interest now taken in poetry by the
highest society in England. Sidney himself joined in
this critical movement. His *Apology for Poetrie*, the
style of which is much more like prose than that of his
Arcadia, defended against Stephen Gosson's *School of
Abuse* in which poetry and plays were attacked from the
Puritan point of view, the nobler uses of poetry. But
he, with his contemporary, Gabriel Harvey, was so en-
thralled by the classical traditions that he also defended
the "unities" and attacked all mixture of tragedy and
comedy, that is, he supported all that Shakespeare was
destined to violate. *The Defence of Rhyme*, written
much later by Samuel Daniel, and which finally destroyed
the attempt to bring classical metres into our poetry;
and also Campion's effort, in his *Observations*, in favour
of rhymeless verse, must be mentioned here. Their
matter belongs to this time.

65. **Later Prose Literature.** — (1.) *Theological Literature* remained for some years after 1580 only a literature
of pamphlets. Puritanism, in its attack on the stage,
and in the Martin Marprelate controversy upon episcopal
government in the Church, flooded England with small
books. Lord Bacon even joined in the latter controversy, and Nash the dramatist made himself famous in
the war by the vigour and fierceness of his wit. Periodical writing was, as it were, started on its course. Over

this troubled and multitudinous sea rose at last the
stately work of RICHARD HOOKER.   It was in 1594 that
the first four books of *The Laws of Ecclesiastical Polity*,
a defence of the Church against the Puritans, were given
to the world.   Before his death he finished the other
four.   The book has remained ever since a standard
work.   It is as much moral and political as theological.
Its style is grave, clear, and often musical.   He adorned
it with the figures of poetry, but he used them with
temperance, and the grand and rolling rhetoric with
which he often concludes an argument is kept for its
right place.   On the whole, it is the first monument of
splendid literary prose that we possess.

(2.) We may place beside it, as other great prose of
Elizabeth's later time, the development of *The Essay* in
LORD BACON'S *Essays*, 1597, and Ben Jonson's *Discoveries*, published after his death.   The highest literary
merit of Bacon's Essays is their combination of charm
and of poetic prose with conciseness of expression and
fulness of thought.   But the oratorical and ideal manner
in which, with his variety, he sometimes wrote, is best
seen in his *New Atlantis*, that imaginary land in the
unreachable seas.

(3.) *The Literature of Travel* was carried on by the
publication in 1589 of HAKLUYT'S *Navigation, Voyages,
and Discoveries of the English Nation*.   The influence of
a compilation of this kind, containing the great deeds of
the English on the seas, has been felt ever since in the
literature of fiction and poetry.

(4.) *In the Tales*, which poured out like a flood from the " university wits," from such men as Peele, and Lodge, and Greene, we find the origin of English fiction, and the subjects of many of our plays ; while the fantastic desire to revive the practices of chivalry which was expressed in the *Arcadia*, found food in the continuous translation of romances, chiefly of the Charlemagne cycle, but now more from Spain than from France ; and in the reading of the Italian poets, Boiardo, Tasso, and Ariosto, who supplied a crowd of our books with the machinery of magic, and with conventional descriptions of nature and of women's beauty.

66. **Edmund Spenser.** — The later Elizabethan poetry begins with the *Shepheards Calendar* of Spenser. Spenser was born in London in 1552, and educated at the Merchant Taylors' Grammar School, which he left for Cambridge in April, 1569. There seems to be evidence that in this year the *Sonnets of Petrarca* and the *Visions of Bellay* afterwards published in 1591, were written by him for a miscellany of verse and prose issued by Van der Noodt, a refugee Flemish physician. At sixteen or seventeen, then, he began literary work. At college Gabriel Harvey, a scholar and critic, and the *Hobbinoll* of Spenser's works, and Edward Kirke, the E. K. of the *Shepheards Calendar*, were his friends. In 1576 he took his degree of M.A., and before he returned to London spent some time in the wilds of Lancashire, where he fell in love with the " Rosalind " of his poetry, a " fair widowe's daughter of the glen." His love was

not returned, a rival interfered, but he clung fast until
his marriage to this early passion. His disappointment
drove him to the South, and there, 1579, he was made
known through Leicester to Leicester's nephew, Philip
Sidney. With him, and perhaps at Penshurst, the *Shepheards Calendar* was finished for the press, and the
Faerie Queene conceived. The publication of the former work, 1579, made Spenser the first poet of the day,
and so fresh and musical, and so abundant in new life
were its twelve eclogues, that men felt that at last England had given birth to a poet as original, and with as
much metrical art as Chaucer. Each month of the year
had its own eclogue ; some were concerned with his
shattered love, two of them were fables, three of them
satires on the lazy clergy ; one was devoted to fair Eliza's
praise : one, the Oak and the Briar, prophesies his
mastery over allegory. The others belong to rustic
shepherd life. The English of Chaucer is imitated, but
the work is full of a new spirit, and as Spenser had begun
with translating Petrarca, so here, in two of the eclogues,
he imitates Clément Marot. The " Puritanism " of the
poem is the same as that of the *Faerie Queene* which he
now began to compose. Save in abhorrence of Rome,
Spenser does not share in the politics of Puritanism.
Nor does he separate himself from the world. He is as
much at home in society and with the arts as any literary
courtier of the day. He was Puritan in his attack on the
sloth and pomp of the clergy ; but his moral ideal, built
up, as it was, out of Christianity and Platonism, rose far
above the narrower ideal of Puritanism.

In the next year, 1580, he went to Ireland with Lord Grey of Wilton as secretary, and afterwards saw and learnt that condition of things which he described in his *View of the Present State of Ireland.* He was made Clerk of Degrees in the Court of Chancery in 1581, and Clerk of the Council of Munster in 1586, and it was then that the manor and castle of Kilcolman were granted to him. Here, at the foot of the Galtees, and bordered to the north by the wild country, the scenery of which is frequently painted in the *Faerie Queene,* and in whose woods and savage places such adventures constantly took place in the service of Elizabeth as are recorded in the *Faerie Queene,* the first three books of that great poem were finished.

67. **The Faerie Queene.** — The plan of the poem is described in Spenser's prefatory letter to Raleigh. The twelve books were to tell the warfare of twelve Knights, in whom twelve virtues were represented. They are sent forth from the court of Gloriana, Queen of Fairyland, and their warfare is against the vices and errors, impersonated, which opposed those virtues. In Arthur, the Prince, the Magnificence of the whole of virtue is represented, and he was at last to unite himself in marriage to the Faerie Queene, that divine glory of God to which all human act and thought aspired. Six books of this plan were finished ; the legends of Holiness, Temperance, and Chastity, of Friendship, Justice, and Courtesy. The two posthumous cantos on Mutability seem to have been part of a seventh legend, on Constancy, and their splendid

work makes us the more regret that the story of the poem being finished is not true. Alongside of the spiritual allegory is the historical one, in which Elizabeth is Gloriana, and Mary of Scotland Duessa ; and Leicester, and at times Sidney, Prince Arthur, and Lord Grey is Arthegall, and Raleigh Timias, and Philip II. the Soldan, or Grantorto. In the midst, other allegories slip in, referring to events of the day, and Elizabeth becomes Belphœbe and Britomart, and Mary is Radegund, and Sidney is Calidore, and Alençon is Braggadochio. At least, these are considered probable attributions. The dreadful " justice " done in Ireland, by the " iron man," and the wars in Belgium, and Norfolk's conspiracy, and the Armada, and the trial of Mary are also shadowed forth.

The allegory is clear in the first two books. Afterwards it is troubled with digressions, sub-allegories, genealogies, with anything that Spenser's fancy led him to introduce. Stories are dropt and never taken up again, and the whole tale is so tangled that it loses the interest of narrative. But it retains the interest of exquisite allegory. It is the poem of the noble powers of the human soul struggling towards union with God, and warring against all the forms of evil ; and these powers become real personages, whose lives and battles Spenser tells in verse so musical and so gliding, so delicately wrought, so rich in imaginative ornament, and so inspired with the finer life of beauty, that he has been called the poets' Poet. But he is the poet of all men who love poetry.

I

Descriptions like those of the House of Pride and the
Mask of Cupid, and of the Months, are so vivid in form
and colour, that they have always made subjects for
artists; while the allegorical personages are, to the very
last detail, wrought out by an imagination which describes not only the general character, but the special
characteristics of the Virtues or the Vices, of the Months
of the year, or of the Rivers of England.   In its ideal
whole, the poem represents the new love of chivalry,
of classical learning; the delight in mystic theories of
love and religion, in allegorical schemes, in splendid
spectacles and pageants, in wild adventure; the love of
England, the hatred of Spain, the strange worship of the
queen, even Spenser's own new love.   It takes up and
uses the popular legends of fairies, dwarfs, and giants, all
the recovered romance and machinery of the Italian
epics, and mingles them up with the wild scenery of
Ireland, with the savages and wonders of the New World.
Almost the whole spirit of the Renaissance under Elizabeth, except its coarser and baser elements, is in its
pages.   Of anything impure, or ugly, or violent, there
is no trace.   And Spenser adds to all his own sacred
love of love, his own pre-eminent sense of the loveliness
of loveliness, walking through the whole of this woven
world of faerie —

" With the moon's beauty and the moon's soft pace."

The first three books were finished in Ireland, and
Raleigh listened to them in 1589 at Kilcolman Castle,

among the alder shades of the river Mulla that fed the lake below the castle. Delighted with the poem, he brought Spenser to England, and the queen, the court, and the whole of England soon shared in Raleigh's delight. It was the first great ideal poem that England had produced; it places him side by side with Milton, but on a throne built of wholly different material. It has never ceased to make poets, and it will live, as he said in his dedication to the queen, " with the eternitie of her fame."

68. **Spenser's Minor Poems.** — The next year, 1591, Spenser, being still in England, collected his smaller poems, most of which seem to be early work, and published them. Among them *Mother Hubberd's Tale* is a remarkable satire, somewhat in the manner of Chaucer, on society, on the evils of a beggar soldiery, of the Church, of the court, and of misgovernment. The *Ruins of Time*, and still more the *Tears of the Muses*, support the statement that literature was looked on coldly previous to 1580. Sidney had died in 1586, and three of these poems bemoan his death. The others are of slight importance, and the whole collection was entitled *Complaints*. His *Daphnaida* seems to have also appeared in 1591. Returning to Ireland, he gave an account of his visit and of the court of Elizabeth in *Colin Clout's come Home again*, and at last, after more than a year's pursuit, won, in 1594, his second love for his wife, and found with her perfect happiness. A long series of lovely " Sonnets " — the *Amoretti*, records the progress of his wooing ; and

the *Epithalamion*, his exultant marriage hymn, is the most glorious love-song in the English tongue. These three were published in 1595. At the close of 1595 he brought to England in a second visit the last three books of the *Faerie Queene*. The next year he spent in London, and published these books, as well as the *Prothalamion* on the marriage of Lord Worcester's daughters, the *Hymns on Love and Beauty* and *on Heavenly Love and Beauty*. The two first hymns were rapturously written in his youth; the two others, now written, and with even greater rapture, enshrine that love philosophy of Petrarca which makes earthly love a ladder to the love of God. The close of his life was sorrowful. In 1598, Tyrone's rebellion drove him out of Ireland. Kilcolman was sacked and burnt, one of his children perished in the flames, and Spenser and his family fled for their lives to England. Broken-hearted, poor, but not forgotten, the poet died in a London tavern. All his fellows went with his body to the grave, where, close by Chaucer, he lies in Westminster Abbey. London, "his most kindly nurse," takes care also of his dust, and England keeps him in her love.

69. **Later Elizabethan Poetry : Translations.** — There are three translators that take literary rank among the crowd that carried on the work of the earlier time. Two mark the influence of Italy, one the more powerful influence of the Greek spirit. Sir John Harington in 1591 translated Ariosto's *Orlando Furioso*, Fairfax in 1600 translated Tasso's *Jerusalem*, and his book is "one of the

glories of Elizabeth's reign." But the noblest translation
is that of Homer's whole work by GEORGE CHAPMAN, the
dramatist, the first part of which appeared in 1598. The
vivid life and energy of the time, its creative power and
its force, are expressed in this poem, which is " more an
Elizabethan tale written about Achilles and Ulysses "
than a translation. The rushing gallop of the long fourteen-syllable stanza in which it is written has the fire and
swiftness of Homer, but it has not his directness or dignity. Its "inconquerable quaintness" and diffuseness
are wholly unlike the pure form and light and measure of
Greek work. But it is a distinct poem of such power
that it will excite and delight all lovers of poetry, as it
excited and delighted Keats. John Florio's *Translation
of the Essays of Montaigne*, 1603, and North's *Plutarch*,
are also, though in prose, to be mentioned here, because
Shakespeare used the books, and because we must mark
Montaigne's influence on English literature even before
his retranslation by Charles Cotton.

70. **The Four Phases of Poetry after 1579.** — Spenser
reflected in his poems the romantic spirit of the English
Renaissance. The other poetry of Elizabeth's reign
reflected the whole of English Life. The best way to
arrange it — omitting as yet the Drama — is in an order
parallel to the growth of the national life, and the proof
that it is the best way is, that on the whole such an historical order is a true chronological order. *First*, then,
if we compare England after 1580, as writers have often
done, to an ardent youth, we shall find in the poetry of

the first years that followed that date all the elements of
youth. It is a poetry of love, and romance, and imagination, — of Romeo and Juliet. *Secondly*, and later on,
when Englishmen grew older in feeling, their enthusiasm,
which had flitted here and there in action and literature
over all kinds of subjects, settled down into a steady
enthusiasm for England itself. The country entered on
its early manhood, and parallel with this there is the
great outbreak of historical plays, and a set of poets whom
I will call the Patriotic Poets. *Thirdly*, and later still,
the fire and strength of the people, becoming inward,
resulted in a graver and more thoughtful national life,
and parallel with this are the tragedies of Shakespeare
and the poets who have been called philosophical.
These three classes of poets overlapped one another,
and grew up gradually, but on the whole their succession is the image of a real succession of national thought
and emotion.

A *fourth* and separate phase does not represent, as these
do, a new national life, a new religion, and new politics,
but the despairing struggle of the old faith against the
new. There were numbers of men, such as Wordsworth
has finely sketched in old Norton in the *Doe of Rylstone*,
who vainly and sorrowfully strove against all the new
national elements. ROBERT SOUTHWELL, of Norfolk, a
Jesuit priest, was the poet of Roman Catholic England.
Imprisoned for three years, racked ten times, and finally
executed, he wrote, while confessor to Lady Arundel, a
number of poems published at various intervals, and

finally collected under the title, *St. Peter's Complaint,
Mary Magdalen's Tears, with other works of the Author,
R.S.* The *Mæoniæ*, and a short prose work *Marie Magdalen's Funerall Tears*, became also very popular. It
marks not only the large Roman Catholic element in the
country, but also the strange contrasts of the time that
eleven editions of books with these titles were published
between 1595 and 1609, at a time when, the *Venus and
Adonis* of Shakespeare led the way for a multitude of
poems — following on Marlowe's *Hero and Leander* and
Lodge's *Glaucus and Scylla* — which sang devotedly of
love and amorous joy.

71. **The Love Poetry.** — I have called it by this name
because all its best work is almost limited to that subject
— the subject of youth. The Love sonnets, written in
a series, are a feature of the time. The best are Sidney's
Astrophel and Stella, Daniel's *Delia*, Constable's *Diana*,
Drayton's *Idea*, Spenser's *Amoretti*, and Shakespeare's
Sonnets. More than twelve collections of these love
sonnets, each dedicated to one lady, and often a hundred in number, were published between 1593 and 1596,
and these had been preceded by many others.

The Miscellanies, to which I have already alluded,
and the best of which were *The Passionate Pilgrim,
England's Helicon*, and *Davison's Rhapsody*, were
scarcely less numerous than the Song-books published
with music, full of delightful lyrics. The wonder is that
the lyrical level in such a multitude of short poems is
so high throughout. Some songs reach a first-rate ex-

cellence, but even the least good have the surprising
spirit of poetry in them. The best of them are " old
and plain, and dallying with the innocence of love,"
childlike in their natural sweetness and freshness, but
full also of a southern ardour of passion. Shakespeare's
excel the others in their gay rejoicing, their firm reality,
their exquisite ease, and when in the plays, gain a
new beauty from their fitness to their dramatic place.
Others possess a quaint pastoralism like shepherd life
in porcelain, such as Marlowe's well-known song, " Come
live with me, and be my love ; " others a splendour of
love and beauty as in Lodge's *Song of Rosaline*, and
Spenser's on his marriage. To specialise the various
kinds would be too long, for there never was in our
land a richer outburst of lyrical ravishment and fancy.
England was like a grove in spring, full of birds in
revel and solace. Love poems of a longer kind were
also made, such as Marlowe's *Hero and Leander*, the
Venus and Adonis and, if we may date them here, the
Elegies of John Donne. I mention only a few of these
poems, the mark of which is a luscious sensuousness.
There were also religious poems, the reflection of the
Puritan and Church elements in English society. They
were collected under such titles as the *Handful of
Honeysuckles*, the *Poor Widow's Mite*, *Psalms and
Sonnets*, and there are some good things among them
written by William Hunnis.

72. **The Patriotic Poets.** — Among all this poetry of
Romance, Religion, and Love, rose a poetry which

devoted itself to the glory of England. It was chiefly historical, and as it may be said to have had its germ in the *Mirror for Magistrates*, so it had its perfect flower in the historical dramas of Shakespeare. Men had now begun to have a great pride in England. She had stepped into the foremost rank, had outwitted France, subdued internal foes, beaten and humbled Spain on every sea. Hence the history of the land became precious, and the very rivers, hills, and plains honourable, and to be sung and praised in verse. This poetic impulse is best represented in the works of three men — WILLIAM WARNER, SAMUEL DANIEL, and MICHAEL DRAYTON. Born within a few years of each other, about 1560, they all lived beyond the century, and the national poetry they set on foot lasted when the romantic poetry lost its wealth and splendour.

William Warner's great book was *Albion's England*, 1586, a history of England in fourteen-syllable verse from the Deluge to Queen Elizabeth. It is clever, humorous, now grave, now gay, crowded with stories, and runs to 10,000 lines. Its popularity was great, and the English in which it was written deserved it. Such stories in it as *Argentile and Curan*, and the *Patient Countess*, prove Warner to have had a true, pathetic vein of poetry. His English is not however so good as that of "well-languaged Daniel," who, among tragedies and pastoral comedies, the noble series of sonnets to Delia and poems of pure fancy, wrote *The Complaint of Rosamond*, far more poetical than his

steadier, even prosaic *Civil Wars of York and Lancaster.* Spenser saw in him a new "shepherd of poetry
who did far surpass the rest," and Coleridge says that
the style of his *Hymen's Triumph* may be declared
"imperishable English." Of the three the easiest poet
was Drayton. *The Barons' Wars, England's Heroical
Epistles,* 1597, *The Miseries of Queen Margaret,* and
Four Legends, together with the brilliant *Ballad of
Agincourt* prove his patriotic fervour. Not content with
these, he set himself to glorify the whole of his land in
the *Polyolbion,* thirty books, and nearly 100,000 lines.
It is a description in Alexandrines of the "tracts,
mountains, forests, and other parts of this renowned
isle of Britain, with intermixture of the most remarkable stories, antiquities, wonders, pleasures, and com-
modities of the same, digested into a poem." It was
not a success, though it deserved success. Its great
length was against it, but the real reason was that this
kind of poetry had had its day. It appeared in 1613,
in James I.'s reign. He, as well as Daniel, did other
work. Indeed Drayton is a striking instance of the way
in which these divisions, which I have made for the sake
of a general order, overlapped one another. He is as
much the love poet as the patriotic poet in his eclogues
of 1593 and in his later *Idea;* he is also a religious, a
satirical, a lyrical, and a fairy poet. He plays on every
kind of harp.

73. **Philosophical Poets.** — Before the date of the
Polyolbion a change had come. As the patriotic poets

on the whole came after the romantic, so the patriotic,
on the whole, were followed by the philosophical poets.
The land was settled; enterprise ceased to be the first
thing; men sat down to think, and in poetry questions
of religious and political philosophy were treated with
" sententious reasoning, grave, subtle, and condensed."
Shakespeare, in his passage from comedy to tragedy, in
1601, illustrates this change. The two poets who best
represent it are SIR JNO. DAVIES and FULKE GREVILLE,
Lord Brooke. In Davies himself we find an instance of
it. His earlier poem of the *Orchestra*, 1596, in which
the whole world is explained as a dance, is as exultant
as Spenser. His later poem, 1599, is compact and vigorous reasoning, for the most part without fancy. Its
very title, *Nosce te ipsum* — Know Thyself — and its
divisions, 1. "On humane learning," 2. "The immortality of the soul " — mark the alteration. Two little
poems, one of Bacon's, on the *Life of Man*, as a bubble,
and one of Sir Henry Wotton's, on the *Character of a
Happy Life*, are instances of the same change. It is still
more marked in Lord Brooke's long. obscure poems *On
Human Learning, on Wars, on Monarchy, and on Religion*. They are political and historical treatises, not
poems, and all in them, said Lamb, " is made frozen
and rigid by intellect." Apart from poetry, " they are
worth notice as an indication of that thinking spirit
on political science which was to produce the riper
speculations of Hobbes, Harrington, and Locke."
Brooke too, in a happier mood, was a lyrist; and his

collection, *Cælica*, has some of the graces of love and
its imagination.

74. **Satirical Poetry,** which lives best when imaginative
creation begins to decay, arose also towards the end of
Elizabeth's reign.   It had been touched in the beginning before Spenser by Gascoigne's *Steele Glas,* but had
no further growth save in prose until 1593, when John
Donne is supposed to have written some of his *Satires.*
Thomas Lodge. Joseph Hall, John Marston, wrote satirical poems in the last part of the sixteenth century.
These satires are all written in a rugged, broken style,
supposed to be the proper style for satire.   Donne's are
the best, and are so because he was a true poet.   Though
his work was mostly done in the reign of James I., and
though his poetical reputation, and his influence (which
was very great) did not reach their height till after the
publication in 1633 of all his poems, he really belongs,
by dint of his youthful sensuousness, of his imaginative
flame, and of his sad and powerful thought, to the Elizabethans.   So also does William Drummond, of Haw-
thornden, whose work was done in the reign of James I.,
and whose name is linke 1 by poetry and friendship to
Sir William Alexander, Earl of Stirling.   Both are the
result of the Elizabethan influence extending to Scotland.
Drummond's sonnets and madrigals have some of the
grace of Sidney. and he rose at intervals into grave and
noble verse, as in his sonnet on John the Baptist.   We
turn now to the drama, which in this age grew into
magnificence.

THE DRAMA

75. Early Dramatic Representation in England. —
The English Drama grew up through the Mystery and
the Miracle play, the Morality and the Interlude, the
rude farce of the strolling players and the pageant.
The *Mystery* was the representation (at first in or near
the Church, and by the clergy; and then in the towns,
and by the laity) of the events of the Old and New
Testaments which bore on the Fall and the Redemption
of Man. The *Miracle play*, though distinct elsewhere
from the Mystery, was the common name of both in
England, and was the representation of some legendary
story of a saint or martyr. These stories gave more
freedom of speech, a more worldly note, and a greater
range of characters to the mystery plays. They also
supplied a larger opportunity for the comic element. The
Miracle plays of England fell before long into two classes,
represented at the feasts of Christmas Day and Easter
Day; and about 1262 the town-guilds took them into
their hands. At Christmas the Birth of Christ was represented, and the events which made it necessary, back
to the Fall of Man. At Easter the Passion was represented in every detail up to the Ascension, and the play
often began with the raising of Lazarus. Sometimes even
the Baptism was brought in, and finally, the Last Judgment was added to the double series, which thus em-
braced the whole history of man from the creation to the
close. About the beginning of the fourteenth century

these two series were brought together into one, and acted on Corpus Christi Day on a great moveable stage in the open spaces of the towns. The whole series consisted of a number of short plays written frequently by different authors, and each guild took the play which suited it best. In a short time, there was scarcely a town of any importance in England from Newcastle to Exeter which had not its Corpus Christi play, and the representations lasted from one day to eight days. Of these sets of plays we possess the Towneley plays, 32 in all, those of York, 48 in all, those of Chester, 24 in all, and a casual collection, called of Coventry, of later and unconnected plays. Of course, these sets only represent a small portion of the Miracle plays of England. It is not improbable that every little town had its own maker of them. Any play that pleased was carried from the town to the castle, from the castle, it may be, to the court. The castle chaplain sometimes composed them : the king kept players of them and scenery for them. On the whole this irregular drama lasted, if we take in its Anglo-Norman beginnings in French and Latin, for nearly 500 years, from 1110, when we first hear at St. Albans of the Miracle play of St. Catherine, to the reign of Henry III., when *The Harrowing of Hell*, our first extant religious drama in English, was acted, and then to 1580, when we last hear of the representation of a Miracle play at Coventry.

76. Separate plays preceded and existed alongside of these large series. Not only on the days of Christ-

mas, Easter, and Corpus Christi were plays acted, but
plays were made for separate feasts, saints' days, and
the turns of the year, and these had the character of
the counties where they were made. The villages took
them up, and soon began to ask for secular as well as
religious representations at their fairs and merry-mak-
ings. The strolling players answered the demand, and
secular subjects began to be treated with romantic or
comic aims, and with some closeness to natural life.
We have a play about Robin Hood of the sixteenth
century, acted on May Day; the *Play of St. George;*
the *Play of the Wake* on St. John's Eve. Some of the
farcical parts of the Miracle plays, isolated from the
rest, were acted, and we have a dramatic fragment
taken from the very secular romance of *Dame Siriz,*
which dates from the time of Edward I. We may be
sure it was not the only one.

77. **The Morality** begins as we come to the reign
of Edward III. We hear of the *Play of the Paternoster,* and of one of its series, the *Play of Laziness.*
But the oldest extant are of the time of Henry VI.
*The Castle of Constancy; Humanity; Spirit, Will, and
Understanding* — these titles partly explain what the
Morality was. It was a play in which the characters
were the Vices and Virtues, with the addition afterwards of allegorical personages, such as Riches, Good
Deeds, Confession, Death, and any human condition or
quality needed for the play. These characters were
brought together in a rough story, at the end of which

Virtue triumphed, or some moral principle was established. The later dramatic *fool* grew up in the Moralities out of a personage called "The Vice," and the humorous element was introduced by the retaining of "The Devil" from the Miracle play and by making *The Vice* torment him. We draw nearer then in the Morality to the regular drama. Its story had to be invented, a proper plot had to be conceived, a clear end fixed upon, to produce which the allegorical characters acted on one another. We are on the very verge of the natural drama; and so close was the relation that the acting of Moralities did not die out till about the end of Elizabeth's reign. A certain transition to the regular drama may be observed in them when historical characters, celebrated for a virtue or vice, were introduced instead of the virtue or the vice, as when Aristides took the place of Justice. Moreover, as the heat of the struggle of the Reformation increased, the Morality was used to support a side. Real men and women were shown under the thin cloaks of its allegorical characters. The stage was becoming a living power when this began.

78. **The Interludes** must next be noticed. There had been interludes in the Miracle plays, short, humorous pieces, interpolated for the amusement of the people. These were continued in the Moralities, and were made closer still to popular life. It occurred to JOHN HEYWOOD to identify himself with this form of drama, and to raise the Interludes into a place in literature. In his

hands, from 1520 to 1540, the Interlude became a kind
of farce, and he wrote several for the amusement of the
court of Henry VIII. He drew the characters from real
life ; in many cases he gave them the names of men and
women, but he retained " the Vice " as a personage.

79. **The Regular Drama: its First Stage.** — These
were the beginnings of the English Drama. To trace
the many and various windings of the way from the
Interludes of Heywood to the regular drama of Elizabeth
were too long and too involved a work for this book.
We need only say that the first pure English comedy
was *Ralph Roister Doister*, written by NICHOLAS UDALL,
master of Eton, known to have been acted before 1551,
but not published till 1566. It is our earliest picture of
London manners ; it is divided into regular acts and
scenes, and is made in rhyme. The first English tragedy
is *Gorboduc*, or *Ferrex and Porrex*, written by Sackville
and Norton, and represented in 1561. The story was
taken from British legend ; the method followed that of
Seneca. A few tragedies on the same classical model followed, but before long this classical type of plays died out.

For twenty years or so, from 1560 to 1580, the drama
was learning its way by experiments. Moralities were
still made, comedies, tragi-comedies, farces, tragedies ;
and sometimes tragedy, farce, comedy, and morality were
rolled into one play. The verse of the drama was as
unsettled as its form. The plays were written in dog-
gerel, in the fourteen-syllable line, in prose, and in a ten-
syllable verse, and these were sometimes mixed in the

K

same play. They were acted chiefly at the Universities, the Inns of Court, the Court, and after 1576 by players in the theatres. Out of this confusion arose 1580–8 (1) two sets of dramatic writers, the "University Wits" and the theatrical playwrights; (2) a distinct dramatic verse, the blank verse destined to be used by Marlowe, Peele, and Greene; and (3) the licensed theatre.

80. **The Theatre.** — A patent was given in 1574 to the Earl of Leicester's servants to act plays in any town in England, and they built in 1576 the Blackfriars Theatre. In the same year two others were set up in the fields about Shoreditch — "The Theatre" and "The Curtain." The Globe Theatre, built for Shakespeare and his fellows in 1599, may stand as a type of the rest. In the form of a hexagon outside, it was circular within, and open to the weather, except above the stage. The play began at three o'clock; the nobles and ladies sat in boxes or in stools on the stage, the people stood in the pit or yard. The stage itself, strewn with rushes, was a naked room, with a blanket for a curtain. Wooden imitations of animals, towers, woods, houses, were all the scenery used, and a board, stating the place of action, was hung out from the top when the scene changed. Boys acted the female parts. It was only after the Restoration that movable scenery and actresses were introduced. No "pencil's aid" supplied the landscape of Shakespeare's plays. The forest of Arden, the castle of Macbeth, were "seen only by the intellectual eye."

81. **The Second Stage of the Drama** ranges from

1580 to 1596. It includes the plays of Lyly, Peele, Greene, Lodge, Marlowe, Kyd, Nash, and the earliest works of Shakespeare. During this time we know that more than 100 different plays were performed by four out of the eleven companies; so swift and plentiful was their production. They were written in prose, and in rhyme, and in blank verse mixed with prose and rhyme. Prose and rhyme prevailed before 1587, when Marlowe in his play of *Tamburlaine* made blank verse so new and splendid a thing that it overcame all other dramatic vehicles. JOHN LYLY, however, wrote so much of his eight plays in prose, that he established, we may say, the use of prose in the drama — an innovation which Gascoigne introduced, and which Shakespeare carried to perfection. Some beautiful little songs scattered through Lyly's plays are the forerunners of the songs with which Shakespeare and his fellows illumined their dramas, and the witty "quips and cranks," repartees and similes of Lyly's fantastic prose dialogue were the school of Shakespeare's first prose dialogue. PEELE, GREENE, and MARLOWE, the three important names of the period, belong to the University men. So do Lodge and Nash, and perhaps Kyd. They are the first in whose hands the play of human passion and action is expressed with any true dramatic effect. GEORGE PEELE's *Arraignment of Paris*, 1584, and his *David and Bethsabe* are full of passages of new and delightful poetry, and when the poetry is good, his blank verse and his heroic couplet are smooth and tender. ROBERT

GREENE, of whose prose in pamphlet and tale much
might be said, spent ten years in writing, and died in
1592. There is little poetry in his plays, but he could
write a charming song. KYD's best play is the *Spanish
Tragedy*. None of these men had the power of working out a play by the development of their " characters "
to a natural conclusion. They anticipate the poetry,
but not the art, of Shakespeare. CHRISTOPHER MARLOWE
as dramatist surpassed, as poet rose far above, them,
and as metrist is almost as great as Shakespeare. The
difference between the unequal action and thought of
his *Doctor Faustus*, and the quiet and orderly progres-
sion to its end of the play of *Edward II.*, is all the more
remarkable when we know that he died at thirty. As
he may be said to have made the verse of the drama, so
he created the English tragic drama. His best plays
are wrought with a new skill to their end, his characters
are outlined with strength and developed with fire.
Each play illustrates one ruling passion, in its growth,
its power, and its extremes. *Tamburlaine* paints the
desire of universal empire ; the *Jew of Malta*, the married passions of greed and hatred; *Doctor Faustus*, the
struggle and failure of man to possess all knowledge and
all pleasure without toil and without law ; *Edward II.*, the
misery of weakness and the agony of a king's ruin. His
knowledge of human nature was neither extensive nor
penetrative, but the splendour of his imagination, and
the noble surging of his verse, make us forget his want
of depth and of variety. Every one has dwelt on his

intemperance in phrases and of images, but the spirit of
poetry moves in them ; we even enjoy the natural faults
of fiery youth in a fiery time. He had no humour, and
his farcical fun is like the boisterous play of a clumsy
animal. In nothing is the difference between Shakespeare and him and his fellows more infinite than in this
point of humour. And indeed he had little pathos.
His sorrows are too loud. Nevertheless, by force of
poetry, not of dramatic art, Marlowe made a noble
porch to the temple which Shakespeare built. That temple, however, in spite of all the preceding work, seems to
spring out of nothing, so astonishing it is in art, in
beauty, in conception. He himself was his only worthy
predecessor, and *the third stage of the drama* includes
his work, that of Ben Jonson's, and of a few others. It
is the work, moreover, not of University men who did
not know the stage, but of men who were not only men
of genius, but also playwrights who understood what a
play should be, and how it was to be staged.

82. **William Shakespeare** in twenty-eight years made
the drama represent almost the whole of human life. He
was baptised April 26, 1564, and was the son of a com-
fortable burgess of Stratford-on-Avon. While he was
still young his father fell into poverty, and an interrupted
education left him an inferior scholar. "He had small
Latin and less Greek ;" but he had a vast store of English.[1]

---

[1] He uses 15,000 words, and he wrote pure English. Out of every
five verbs, adverbs, and nouns (*e.g.* in the last act of *Othello*), four are
Teutonic ; and he is more Teutonic in comedy than in tragedy.

However, by dint of genius and by living in a society in which every kind of information was attainable, he became an accomplished man. The story told of his deer-stealing in Charlecote woods is without proof, but it is likely that his youth was wild and passionate. At nineteen he married Anne Hathaway, more than seven years older than himself, and was probably unhappy with her. For this reason, or from poverty, or from the driving of the genius that led him to the stage, he left Stratford about 1586–7, and came to London at the age of twenty-two years, and falling in with Marlowe, Greene, and the rest, became an actor and playwright, and may have lived their unrestrained and riotous life for some years. It is convenient to divide his work into periods, and to state the order in which it is now supposed his plays were written. But we must not imagine that the periods and the order are really settled. We know something, but not all we ought to know, of this matter.

83. **His First Period.** — It is probable that before leaving Stratford he had sketched a part at least of his *Venus and Adonis*. It is full of the country sights and sounds, of the ways of birds and animals, such as he saw when wandering in Charlecote woods. Its rich and overladen poetry and its warm colouring made him, when it was published, 1593, at once the favourite of men like Lord Southampton, and lifted him into fame. But before that date he had done work for the stage by touching up old plays, and writing new ones. We seem to trace his "prentice hand" in some dramas of the time, but the

first he is usually thought to have fully retouched is *Ti-
tus Andronicus*, and some time after the *First Part of
Henry VI. Love's Labour's Lost*, supposed to be written
1589 or 1590, the first of his original plays, in which he
quizzed and excelled the Euphuists in wit, was followed
by the involved and rapid farce of the *Comedy of Errors*.
Out of these frolics of intellect and action he passed
into pure poetry in the *Midsummer Night's Dream*, and
mingled into fantastic beauty the classic legend, the
mediæval fairyland, and the clownish life of the English
mechanic. Italian story laid its charm upon him about
the same time, and the *Two Gentlemen of Verona* preceded the southern glow of passion in *Romeo and Juliet*,
in which he first reached tragic power. They are said to
complete, with *Love's Labour's Won*, afterwards recast as
All's Well that Ends Well, the love plays of his early
period. We should read along with them, as belonging
to the same period, the *Rape of Lucrece*, a poem finally
printed in 1594, one year later than the *Venus and Adonis*, which was probably finished, if not wholly written,
at this passionate time.

The same poetic succession we have traced in the poets,
is now found in Shakespeare. The patriotic feeling of
England, also represented in Marlowe and Peele, had
seized on him, and he began his great series of historical
plays with *Richard II.* and *Richard III.* To introduce
Richard III. or to complete the subject, he recast the
Second and Third Parts of Henry VI., and ended what
we have called his first period by *King John* about 1596.

84. His Second Period, 1596-1601. — In the *Merchant of Venice* Shakespeare reached entire mastery over his art. A mingled woof of tragic and comic threads is brought to its highest point of colour when Portia and Shylock meet in court. Pure comedy followed in his retouch of the old *Taming of the Shrew*, and all the wit of the world mixed with noble history met in the first and second *Henry IV.*, 1597-8; while Falstaff was continued in the *Merry Wives of Windsor*. The historical plays were then closed with *Henry V.*, 1599; a splendid dramatic song to the glory of England. The Globe Theatre of which he was one of the proprietors, was built in 1599. In the comedies he wrote for it, Shakespeare turned to write of love again, not to touch its deeper passion as before, but to play with it in all its lighter phases. The flashing dialogue of *Much Ado About Nothing* was followed by the far-off forest world of *As You Like It*, 1599, where "the time fleets carelessly," and Rosalind's character is the play. Amid all its gracious lightness steals in a new element, and the melancholy of Jaques is the first touch we have of the older Shakespeare who had "gained his experience, and whose experience had made him sad." As yet it was but a touch; *Twelfth Night* shows no trace of it, though the play that followed, *All's Well that Ends Well*, 1601? again strikes a sadder note. We find this sadness fully grown in the later *Sonnets*, which are said to have been finished about 1602. We know that some of the *Sonnets* existed in 1598, but they were all printed together for the first time in 1609. They form together the most deep, ardent, subtle, and varied representation of love in our language, and their emotion is mingled with so great a wealth of simple and complex thought that they seem to be written out of the experience, not of one but of many men.

Shakespeare's life changed now, and his mind changed with it. He had grown wealthy during this period, famous, and loved by society. He was the friend of the Earls of Southampton and Essex, and of William Herbert, Lord Pembroke. The queen patronised him; all the best literary society was his own. He had rescued his father from poverty, bought the best house in Stratford and much land, and was a man of wealth and comfort. Suddenly all his life seems to have grown dark. His best friends fell into ruin, Essex perished on the scaffold, Southampton went to the Tower, Pembroke was banished from the court; he may himself, some have thought, have been slightly involved in the rising of Essex. Added to this, we may conjecture, from the imaginative pageantry of the sonnets, that he had unwisely loved, and been betrayed in his love by a dear friend. Public and private ill then weighed heavily upon him; he seems to even have had disgust for his profession as an actor; and in darkness of spirit, though still clinging to the business of the theatre, he passed from comedy to write of the sterner side of the world, to tell the tragedy of mankind.

85. **His Third Period, 1601–1608,** begins with the last days of Queen Elizabeth. It opens with *Julius*

Cæsar, and we may have, scattered through the telling
of the great Roman's fate, the expression of Shakespeare's sorrow for the ruin of Essex. *Hamlet* followed,
1601–3? for the poet felt, like the Prince of Denmark,
that "the time was out of joint." *Hamlet*, the dreamer,
may well represent Shakespeare as he stood aside from
the crash that overwhelmed his friends, and thought on
the changing world. The tragi-comedy of *Measure for
Measure*, 1603? may have now been written, and is tragic
in thought throughout. *Othello*, 1604, *Macbeth*, *Lear*,
Troilus and Cressida, *Antony and Cleopatra*, *Coriolanus*,
1608? *Timon* (only in part his own), were all written in
these five years. The darker sins of men ; the unpitying
fate which slowly gathers round and falls on mistakes
and crimes, on ambition, luxury, and pride ; the aveng-
ing wrath of conscience ; the cruelty and punishment of
weakness ; the treachery, lust, jealousy, ingratitude, mad-
ness of men ; the follies of the great and the fickleness
of the mob, are all, with a thousand other varying
moods and passions, painted, and felt as his own while
he painted them, during this stern time.

86. **His Fourth Period, 1608–1613.** — As Shakespeare
wrote of these things he passed out of them, and his last
days are full of the gentle and loving calm of one who
has known sin and sorrow and fate, but has risen above
them into peaceful victory. Like his great contemporary
Bacon, he left the world and his own evil time behind
him, and with the same quiet dignity sought the innocence and stillness of country life. The country breathes

through all the dramas of this time. The flowers Perdita gathers in *Winter's Tale*, the frolic of the sheep-shearing, he may have seen in the Stratford meadows; the song of Fidele in *Cymbeline* is written by one who already feared no more the frown of the great, nor slander, nor censure rash, and was looking forward to the time when men should say of him —

> Quiet consummation have ;
> And renownèd be thy grave !

Shakespeare probably left London in 1609, and lived in the house he had bought at Stratford-on-Avon. He was reconciled, it is said, to his wife, and the plays now written dwell on domestic peace and forgiveness. The story of *Marina*, which he left unfinished, and which it is supposed two later writers expanded into the play of *Pericles*, is the first of his closing series of dramas. *Cymbeline*, 1609? *The Tempest*, 1610? *Winter's Tale*, bring his history up to 1611, and in the next year he may have closed his poetic life by writing, with Fletcher, *Henry VIII.*, 1612? The *Two Noble Kinsmen* of Fletcher, part of which is attributed to Shakespeare, and in which the poet sought the inspiration of Chaucer, would belong to this period. For some three years he kept silence, and then, on the 23d of April, 1616, it is supposed on his fifty-second birthday, he died.

87. **His Work.** — We can only guess with regard to Shakespeare's life and character. It has been tried to find out what he was from his sonnets, and from his plays,

but every attempt seems to be a failure. We cannot lay
our hand on anything and say for certain that it was
spoken by Shakespeare out of his own personality. He
created men and women whose dramatic action on each
other, and towards a chosen end, was intended to please
the public, not to reveal himself. Frequently failing in
fineness of workmanship, having, but far less than the
other dramatists, the faults of the art of his time, he was
yet in all other points—in creative power, in impassioned
conception and execution, in truth to universal human
nature, in intellectual power, in intensity of feeling, in
the great matter and manner of his poetry, in the welding together of thought, passion, and action, in range, in
plenteousness, in the continuance of his romantic feeling
— the greatest poet our modern world has known. Like
the rest of the greater poets, he reflected the noble things
of his time, but refused to reflect the base. Fully influenced, as we see in Hamlet he was, by the graver and
more philosophic cast of thought of the latter time of
Elizabeth ; passing on into the reign of James I., when
pedantry took the place of gaiety. and sensual the place
of imaginative love in the drama, and artificial art the
place of that art which itself is nature ; he preserves to
the last the natural passion, the simple tenderness, the
sweetness, grace, and fire of the youthful Elizabethan
poetry. The *Winter's Tale* is as lovely a love-story as
Romeo and Juliet, the *Tempest* is more instinct with imagination and as great in fancy as the *Midsummer Night's
Dream*, and yet there are fully twenty years between

them. The only change is in the increase of power and in a closer, graver, and more ideal grasp of human nature. In the unchangeableness of this joyful and creative art-power Shakespeare is almost alone. It is true that in these last plays his art is more self-conscious, less natural, and the greater glory is therefore lost, but the power is not less nor the beauty.

88. **The Decline of the Drama** begins while Shakespeare is alive. At first we can scarcely call it decline, it was so superb in its own qualities. For it began with "rare BEN JONSON." With him are connected by associated work, by quarrels, and by date, Dekker, Marston, and Chapman. They belong with Shakespeare to the days of Elizabeth and the days of James I. Ben Jonson's first play, in its very title, *Every Man in his Humour*, 1596, enables us to say in what the first step of this decline consisted. The drama in Shakespeare's hands had been the painting of the whole of human nature, the painting of characters as they were built up by their natural bent, and by the play of circumstance upon them. The drama, in Ben Jonson's hands, was the painting of particular phases of human nature, especially of his own age ; and his characters are men and women as they may become when they are completely mastered by a special bias of the mind or *Humour*. "The Manners, now called Humours, feed the stage," says Jonson himself. *Every Man in his Humour* was followed by *Every Man out of his Humour*, and by *Cynthia's Revels*, written to satirise the courtiers. The

fierce satire of these plays brought the town down upon
him, and he replied to their "noise" in the *Poetaster*,
in which Dekker and Marston were satirised. Dekker
answered with the *Satiro-Mastix*, a bitter parody on
the *Poetaster*, in which he did not spare Jonson's bodily
defects. Silent then for two years, he reappeared with
the tragedy of *Sejanus*, and then quickly produced
three splendid comedies in James I.'s reign, *Volpone the
Fox*, the *Silent Woman*, and the *Alchemist*, 1605-9-10.
The first is the finest thing he ever did, as great in
power as it is in the interest and skill of its plot; the
second is chiefly valuable as a picture of English life
in high society; the third is full of Jonson's obscure
learning, but its character of Sir Epicure Mammon is
done with Jonson's keenest power. In 1611 his *Catiline*
appeared, and then *Bartholomew Fair*. Eight years
after he was made Poet Laureate. Soon he became
poor and palsy-stricken, but his genius did not decay.
His tender and imaginative pastoral drama, the *Sad
Shepherd*, proves that, like Shakespeare, Jonson grew
gentler as he grew near to death, and death took him
in 1637. He was a great man. The power and copi-
ousness of the young Elizabethan age belonged to him;
and he stands far below, for he had no passion, but
still worthily by, Shakespeare, "a robust, surly, and observing dramatist." THOS. DEKKER. whose lovely lyrics
are well known, and whose copious prose occupies five
volumes, "had poetry enough," Lamb said, "for anything." His light comedies of manners are excellent

pictures of the time. But his romantic poetry is better felt in such dramas as *Patient Grissil, Old Fortunatus,* and *The Witch of Edmonton,* in which, though others worked them along with Dekker, the women are all his own by tenderness, grace, subtlety, and pathos. JOHN MARSTON, whose chief plays were written between 1602 and 1605, needs little notice here. He is best known by certain noble and beautiful passages, and his finest plays were *Antonio and Mellida* and the *Malcontent.* Of the three GEO. CHAPMAN was the most various genius, and the most powerful. He illuminated the age of Elizabeth by the first part of his translation of Homer; he lived on into the reign of Charles I. His poems (of which the best are his continuation of Marlowe's *Hero and Leander,* and *The Tears of Peace*) are extreme examples of the gnarled, sensuous, formless, and obscure poetry of which Dryden cured our literature. His plays are of a finer quality, especially the five tragedies taken from French history. They are weighty with thought, but the thought devours their action, and they are difficult and sensational. Inequality pervades them. His mingling of intellectual violence with intellectual imagination, of obscurity with a noble exultation and clearness of poetry, is a strange compound of the earlier and later Elizabethans. He, like Marlowe, but with less of beauty, "hurled instructive fire about the world." With these three I may mention Cyril Tourneur and John Day, the one as ferocious in the *Atheist's Tragedy* as the other was graceful in his *Parliament of Bees.*

Both were poets, and both were more truly Elizabethan than Beaumont, Fletcher, or Webster.

89. **Masques.** — Rugged as Jonson was, he could turn to light and graceful work, and it is with his name that we connect the *Masques*. He wrote them delightfully. Masques were dramatic representations made for a festive occasion, with a reference to the persons present and the occasion. Their personages were allegorical. They admitted of dialogue, music, singing, and dancing, combined by the use of some ingenious fable into a whole. They were made and performed for the court and the houses of the nobles, and the scenery was as gorgeous and varied as the scenery of the playhouse proper was poor and unchanging. Arriving for the first time at any repute in Henry VIII.'s time, they reached splendour under James and Charles I. Great men took part in them. When Ben Jonson wrote them, Inigo Jones made the scenery and Lawes the music; and Lord Bacon, Whitelock, and Selden sat in committee for the last great masque presented to Charles. Milton himself made them worthier by writing *Comus*, and their scenic decoration was soon introduced into the regular theatres.

90. **Beaumont and Fletcher** worked together, and belong not only in date, but in spirit, to the reign of James. In two plays, *Henry VIII.* and *The Two Noble Kinsmen*, Fletcher has been linked to Shakespeare. With Beaumont as fellow-worker and counsellor, he wrote about a third of the more than fifty plays which go under

their names. Beaumont died, aged thirty, in 1616, Fletcher, aged fifty, in 1625. The creative power of the Elizabethan time has no more striking example than in their vast production. The inventiveness of the plays is astonishing, and their plots are almost always easily connected and well supported. Far the greater part of the work was done by Fletcher, but it has been tried to trace Beaumont's hand chiefly in such fine tragedies as *The Maid's Tragedy* and *Philaster*. In comedy Fletcher is gay, and quick, and interesting. In tragedy and comedy alike, his level of goodness is equal, but then we have none of those magnificent outbursts of imaginative passion to which, up to this time, we have been accustomed. *The Faithful Shepherdess* of Fletcher is a lovely pastoral, and the lyrics which diversify his plays have even some of the charm of Shakespeare.

He and his fellows represent a distinct change, and not for the better, in the drama — a kind of *fourth stage*. Its poetry is on the whole less masculine. Its blank verse is rendered smoother and sweeter by the incessant addition of an eleventh syllable, but it is also enfeebled. This weak ending, by the additional freedom and elasticity it gave to the verse, was suited to the rapid dialogue of comedy, but the dignity of tragedy was lowered by it. The change is also seen in other matters. In the previous plays moral justice is done. The good are divided from the bad. Fletcher seems quite indifferent to this. In the previous plays,

L

men and women, save in Shakespeare, are coarse and foul enough at times, but they are so by nature or under furious passion. In Fletcher, there is a natural indecency, an every-day foulness of thought, which belongs to the good and the bad alike. The women are, when good, beyond nature, and, when bad, below it. The situations invented tend to be studiously out of the way, beyond the natural aspects of humanity. The aim of art has changed for the worse. It strives for the strange and the sensational. Even JOHN WEBSTER lost some of the power his genius gave him by the ghastly situations he chose to dwell upon. Yet he all but redeemed the worst of them by the intensity of his imagination, and by the soul-piercing power with which, in a few words, he sounds the depths of the human heart when it is wrought by remorse, by sorrow, by fear, or by wrath to its greatest point of passion. Moreover, in his worst characters there is some redeeming touch, and this poetic pity saves his sensationalism from weariness, and brings him nearer to Shakespeare than others of his time. His two greatest plays, things which will be glorious forever in poetry, are *The Duchess of Malfi*, acted in 1616, and the *White Devil, Vittoria Corrombona*, printed in 1612. One other play of the time is held to approach them in poetic quality, *The Changeling*, by Thomas Middleton, but it does so only in parts.

91. **Decay of the Drama.** — In the next dramatists, in the followers, if I may thus class them, of MASSINGER

and FORD, the change for the worse in the drama is more marked than in the work of those of whom we have been speaking. The poetic and creative qualities are both less, the sensationalism is greater, the foulness of language increases, the situations are more out of nature, the verse is clumsier and more careless, the composition and connexion of the plots are tumbled and confused. But these statements are only moderately true of Massinger and Ford. They stand at the head of the rapid decay of the drama, but they still retain a predominant part of that which made the Elizabethans great. Massinger's first dated play was the *Virgin Martyr*, 1620. He lived poor, and died "a stranger," in 1639. In these twenty years he wrote thirty-seven plays, of which the *New Way to Pay Old Debts* is the best known by its character of Sir Giles Overreach. His versification and language are flexible and strong, "and seem to rise out of the passions he describes." He speaks the tongue of real life. He is greater than he seems to be. Like Fletcher, there is a steady equality in his work. Coarse, even foul as he is in speech, he is the most moral of the secondary dramatists. Nowhere is his work so forcible as when he represents the brave man struggling through trial to victory, the pure woman suffering for the sake of truth and love; or when he describes the terrors that conscience brings on injustice and cruelty. JOHN FORD, his contemporary, published his first play, the *Lover's Melancholy*, in 1629, and five years after, *Perkin War-*

beck, one of the best historical dramas after Shake-speare. Between these dates appeared others, of which the best are the *Broken Heart* and *'Tis Pity She's a Whore*. He carried to an extreme the tendency of the drama to unnatural and horrible subjects, but he did so with great power. He has no comic humour, but few men have described better the worn and tortured human heart. A crowd of dramatists carried on the production of plays till the Commonwealth. Some names alone we can mention here — Thomas Heywood, Henry Glapthorne, Richard Broome, William Rowley, Thomas Randolph, Nabbes, and Davenport. Of these "all of whom," says Lamb, "spoke nearly the same language, and had a set of moral feelings and notions in common," James Shirley is the best and last. He lived till 1666. In him the fire and passion of the old time pass away, but some of the delicate poetry remains, and in him the Elizabethan drama dies. Sir John Suckling and Davenant, who wrote plays before the Commonwealth, can scarcely be called even decadent Elizabethans. In 1642 the theatres were closed during the calamitous times of the Civil War. Strolling players managed to exist with difficulty, and against the law, till 1656, when Sir William Davenant had his opera of the *Siege of Rhodes* acted in London. It was the beginning of a new drama, in every point but impurity different from the old, and four years after, at the Restoration, it broke loose from the prison of Puritanism to indulge in a shameless license.

In this rapid sketch of the drama in England we have been carried on beyond the death of Elizabeth to the date of the Restoration. It was necessary, because it keeps the whole story together. We now return to the time that followed the accession of James I.

CHAPTER V

FROM ELIZABETH'S DEATH TO THE RESTORATION, 1603–1660

92. **The Literature of this Period** may fairly be called Elizabethan, but not so altogether. The prose retained the manner of the Elizabethan time and the faults of its style, but gradually grew into greater excellence, spread itself over larger fields of thought, and took up a greater variety of subjects. The poetry, on the whole, declined. It exaggerated the vices of the Elizabethan art, and lessened its virtues. But this is not the whole account of the matter. We must add that a new prose, of greater force of thought and of a simpler style than the Elizabethan, arose in the writings of a theologian like Chillingworth, an historian like Clarendon, and a philosopher like Hobbes: and that a new type of poetry, distinct from the poetry of fantastic wit into which Elizabethan poetry had descended, was written by some of the lyrical writers. It was Elizabethan in its lyric note, but it was not obscure. It had grace, simplicity, and smoothness. In its greater art and clearness it tells us that the critical school is at hand.

93. **Prose Literature.   James I.** — The greatest prose triumph of this time was the *Authorised Version* of the Bible.   There is no need to dwell on it, nor on all it has done for the literature of England.   It lives in almost every book of worth and imagination, and its style, especially when the subject soars, is inspired by the spirits of fitness and beauty and melody.   Philosophy passed from Elizabeth into the reign of James I. with Francis Bacon.   The splendour of the form and of the English prose of the *Advancement of Learning,* two books of which were published in 1605, raises it into the realm of pure literature.   It was expanded into nine Latin books in 1623, and with the *Novum Organon,* finished in 1620, and the *Historia Naturalis et Experimentalis,* 1622, formed the *Instauratio Magna.*   The impulse these books gave to research, and to the true method of research, awoke scientific inquiry in England; and before the Royal Society was constituted in the reign of Charles II., our science, though far behind that of the Continent, had done some good work.   William Harvey lectured on the circulation of the blood in 1615, and during the Civil War and the Commonwealth men like Robert Boyle, the chemist, John Wallis, the mathematician, and others, met in William Petty's rooms at Brazenose, and prepared the way for Newton.

94. **History,** except in the publication of the earlier *Chronicles* of Archbishop Parker, does not appear in the later part of Elizabeth's reign, but under James I. Camden, Spelman, Selden, and Speed continued the anti-

quarian researches of Stow and Grafton. Bacon wrote
a dignified *History of Henry VII.*, and Daniel the poet,
in his *History of England to the Time of Edward III.*,
1613–18, was one of the first to throw history into such a
literary form as to make it popular. KNOLLES's *History
of the Turks*, 1603, and SIR WALTER RALEIGH's vast
sketch of the *History of the World*, show how for the
first time history spread itself beyond English interests.
Raleigh's book, written in the peaceful evening of a
stormy life, and in the quiet of his prison, is not only
literary from the impulsive passages which adorn it, but
from its still spirit of melancholy thought. In 1614,
John Selden's *Titles of Honour* added to the accurate
work he had done in Latin on the English Records,
and his *History of Tithes* was written with the same
careful regard for truth in 1618.

95. **Miscellaneous Literature.** — The pleasure of Travel,
still lingering among us from Elizabeth's reign, found a
quaint voice in Thomas Coryat's *Crudities*, which, in
1611, describes his journey through France and Italy;
and in George Sandys' book, 1615, which tells his
journey in the East; while Henry Wotton's *Letters from
Italy* are pleasant reading. The care with which Samuel
Purchas embodied (1613) in *Purchas his Pilgrimage*
("his own in matter, though borrowed") and in *Hakluyt's Posthumus, or Purchas his Pilgrimes* (1625), the
great deeds, sea voyages, and land travels of adventurers,
brings us back to the time when England went out to
win the world. The painting of short "Characters"

was begun by Sir Thomas Overbury's book in 1614, and
carried on in the following reign by John Earle and
Joseph Hall, who became bishops. This kind of literature marks the interest in individual life which now began
to arise, and which soon took form in Biography.

96. **In the Caroline Period and the Commonwealth,
Prose** grew into a nearer approach to the finished instrument it became after the Restoration. History was
illuminated, and its style dignified, by the work of Clarendon — the *History of the Rebellion* (begun in 1641) and
his own *Life*. Thomas May wrote the *History of the
Parliament* of 1640, a book with a purpose. Thomas
Fuller's *Church History of Britain*, 1656, may in style
and temper be put alongside of his *Worthies of England*
in 1662.

In Theology and Philosophy the masters of prose at
this time were Jeremy Taylor and Thomas Hobbes. It
is a comfort amidst the noisy war of party to breathe the
calm spiritual air of *The Great Exemplar* and the *Holy
Living and Dying* which Taylor published at the close
of the reign of Charles I. They had been preceded in
1647 by the *Liberty of Prophesying*, in which, agreeing
with his contemporaries, John Hales and William Chillingworth, he pleaded the cause of religious toleration,
and of rightness of life as more important than correct
theology. Taylor was the most eloquent of men, and
the most facile of orators. Laden with thought, his
books are read for their sweet and deep devotion (a
quality which also belonged to his fellow-writer, Lancelot

Andrewes), even more than for their impassioned and
convoluted outbreaks of beautiful words. On the Puritan
side, the fine sermons of Richard Sibbes converted Richard Baxter, whose manifold literary work only ended in
the reign of James II. One little thing of his, written
at the close of the Civil War, became a household book
in England. There used to be few cottages which did
not possess a copy of the *Saints' Everlasting Rest.* The
best work of Hobbes belonged to Charles I. and the
Commonwealth, but will better be noticed hereafter.
The other great prose writer is one of a number of
men whose productions may be classed under the title
of Miscellaneous Literature. He is Sir Thomas Browne,
who, born in 1605, died in 1682. In 1642 his *Religio
Medici* was printed, and the book ran over Europe.
The *Enquiry into Vulgar Errors* followed in 1646, and
the *Hydriotaphia, or Urn-Burial,* in 1658. These books,
with other happy things of his, have by their quaintness,
their fancy, and their special charm always pleased the
world, and often kindled weary prose into fresh production. We may class with them Robert Burton's *Anatomy
of Melancholy,* a book of inventive wit and scattered learning, and Thomas Fuller's *Holy and Profane State* and
Worthies of England, in which gaiety and piety, good
sense and whimsical fancy meet. This kind of writing
was greatly increased by the setting up of libraries,
where men dipped into every kind of literature. It
was in James I.'s reign that Sir Thomas Bodley established the Bodleian at Oxford, and Sir Robert Cotton

a library now in the British Museum. A number of
writers took part in the Puritan and Church controversies, among whom for graphic force William Prynne
stands out clearly. But the great controversialist was
Milton. His prose is still, under the Commonwealth,
Elizabethan in style. It has the fire and violence, the
eloquence and diffuseness of the earlier literature, but in
spite of the praise its style has received, it can in reality
be scarcely called a style. It has all the faults a prose
style can have except obscurity and the commonplace.
Its magnificent storms of eloquence ought to be in
poetry, and it never charms, though it amazes, except
when Milton becomes purposely simple in personal
narrative. It has no humour, but it has almost unex-
ampled individuality and ferocity. Among this tem-
pestuous pamphleteering one pamphlet is almost singular
in its masterly and uplifted thought, and the style only
rarely loses its dignity. This is the *Areopagitica*. In
pleasant contrast to these controversies arises the gentle
literature of Izaak Walton's *Compleat Angler*, 1653, a
book which resembles in its quaint and garrulous style
the rustic scenery and prattling rivers that it celebrates,
and marks the quiet interest in country life which had
now arisen in England. Prose, then, in the time of
James and Charles I., and of the Commonwealth, had
largely developed its powers.

97. **The Poetry of the Reign of James I.** — It is said
that during this reign and the following one, poetry
declined. On the whole that is true, but it is true with

many modifications. We must remember that Shakespeare and many of the Elizabethan poets, like Drayton and Daniel, did their finest work in the reign of James I. Yet there was decline. The various elements which we have noticed in the poetry of Elizabeth's reign, without the exception even of the slight Catholic element, though opposed to each other, were filled with one spirit — the love of England and the queen. Nor were they ever sharply divided; they are found interwoven, and modifying one another in the same poet, as for instance Puritanism and Chivalry in Spenser, Catholicism and Love in Constable : and all are mixed together in Shakespeare and the dramatists. This unity of spirit in poetry became less and less after the queen's death. The elements remained, but they were separated. The cause of this was that the strife in politics between the Divine Right of Kings and Liberty, and in religion between the Church and the Puritans, grew so defined and intense that England ceased to be at one, and the poets represented the parties, not the whole, of England. Then, too, that general passion and life which inflamed everything Elizabethan lessened, and as it lessened, the faults of the Elizabethan work became more prominent ; they were even supposed to be excellences. Hence the fantastic, far-fetched, involved style, which was derived from the *Euphues* and the *Arcadia*, grew into favour and was developed in verse, till it ended by greatly injuring good sense and clearness in English poetry. In the reaction from this the critical and classical school began. Again,

when passion lessens, original work lessens, and imitation
begins. The reign of James is marked by a class of
poets who imitated Spenser. Giles Fletcher in his
Christ's Victory and Triumph, 1610, owned Spenser as
his master. So did his brother Phineas Fletcher, whose
Purple Island, an allegory of the human body, 1633, has
both grace and sweetness. We may not say that William Browne imitated, but only that he was influenced
by Spenser. His *Britannia's Pastorals* in two parts,
1613–16, followed by the seven eclogues of the *Shepherd's
Pipe*, are an example in true poetry of the ever-recurring
element in English poetry, pleasure in country life and
scenery, which from this time forth grew through Milton,
Wither, Marvell, and then, after an apparent death, through
Thomson, Gray, and Collins, into its wonderful flower in
our own century. These, if we include the poetry of the
Dramatists, especially the *Underwoods* of Ben Jonson,
and the poems already mentioned of Drummond and
Stirling, are the poets of the reign of James I. They
link back to Elizabeth's time and its temper, and it may
be said of them that they have no special turn, save that
which arises from their own individuality. *That* cannot
be said of the poets of Charles I.'s reign, even though
they may be classed as writing under the influence of
Ben Jonson and of Donne.

98. **The Caroline Poets**, as they are called, are love
poets or religious poets. Often, as in the case of Herrick
and Crashaw, they combined both kinds into a single
volume. Sometimes they were only religious like Her-

bert, sometimes only love poets like Lovelace and Suckling. But whatever they were, they were as individual as
Botticelli, with whose position and whose contemporaries
in painting they may, with much justice, be compared.
The greatest of these was ROBERT HERRICK. The gay
and glancing charm of *The Hesperides*, 1648, in which
Horace and Tibullus seem to mingle ; their peculiar art
which never misses its aim, nor fails in exquisite execution ;
the almost equal power of *The Noble Numbers*, published
along with the *Hesperides*, in which the spiritual side of
Herrick's nature expressed itself, make him, within his
self-chosen and limited range, the most remarkable of
those who at this time sat below the mountain top on
which Milton was alone. Close beside him, but more
unequal, was THOMAS CAREW, whose lyrical poems, well
known as they are, do not prevent our pleasure in his
graver work like the *Elegy on Donne*. Greater in imagination, but more unequal still, was RICHARD CRASHAW.
One of his poems, *The Flaming Heart*, expresses in its
name his religious nature and his art. He does not
burn with a steady fire, he flames to heaven ; and when
he does, he is divine in music and in passion. At other
times he is one of the worst of the fantasticals, of those
lovers of the quaint for quaintness' sake, among whom the
exclusively *religious poets* of the time are sadly to be
classed. There is GEORGE HERBERT, whose *Temple*,
1631, is, by the purity and devotion of its poems, dear
to all. It is his quiet religion, his quaint, contemplative,
vicarage-garden note of thought and scholarship which

pleases most, and will always please, the calm piety of
England.   He also is individual, and so is HENRY
VAUGHAN, whose *Sacred Poems*, 1651, unequal as a whole,
love nature dearly, and leap sometimes into a higher air
of poetry than Herbert could attain; "transcend our
wonted themes, and into glory peep." Nor must we
forget WILLIAM HABINGTON, who mingled his devotion to
Roman Catholicism with the praises of his wife under the
name of *Castara*, 1634; nor GEORGE WITHER, who sent
forth, just before the Civil War began, when he left the
king for the Parliament, his *Hallelujah*, 1641, a noble
series of religious poems; nor FRANCIS QUARLES, whose
Divine Emblems, 1635, is still read in the cottages of
England.   These poets, with Henry More, the Platonist,
and Joseph Beaumont, the friend of Crashaw and the
rival of More, are far below (Wither's work being ex-
cepted) both Herbert and Vaughan, and bring to an end
the religious poetry of this curious transition time.   I
have omitted some poems of Cowley and of Edmund
Waller, which appeared during the Commonwealth, because both these poets belong to a new class of poetry,
the classical poetry of the Restoration.   Between this
new kind of poetry, which rose to full power in Dryden,
and the dying poetry of the transition, stands alone the
majestic work of a great genius who touches the great
Elizabethan time with one hand and our own time with
the other.   But before we speak of Milton, a word must
be said of the lyrics.

99. **The Songs and other Lyrical Poetry.** — All through

the period between James I. and the Restoration, Song-writing went on, and was more natural and less "meta-physical" than the other forms of poetry. The elements of decay attacked it slowly ; those of brightness and pas-sion, nature and gaiety, continued to live in it. Moreover, the time was remarkable for no small number of lyrical poems, other than songs, of a strange loveliness, in which the Elizabethan excellences were enhanced by a special, particular grace, due partly to the more isolated life some of the poets led, and partly to the growth among them of a more artistic method.

With regard to the Songs, a distinct set of them, on the most various subjects, are to be found in the Dramatists, from Ben Jonson to Shirley. Another set has been collected out of the many Song-books which appeared with music and words. Many arose in the court of Charles I. and among the Royalists in the country, — Cavalier songs — on love, on constancy, on dress, on fleeting fancies of every kind. Others were on battle and death for the king ; and a few, sterner and more ideal, on the Puritan side. The same power of song-writing went on for a brief time after the Restoration, but finally perished in the political ballad which was sung about the streets by the political parties of the Revolution. Then the song-lyric of love was almost silent till the days of Burns.

With regard to the Lyrical poems, it is impossible to mention all that are worthy, but an age which produced the masques, the poems, and the *Sad Shepherd* of Ben

Jonson ; which heard the lyrical measures of Fletcher's
Faithful Shepherdess; which read with joy Herrick's
Corinna and his country lyrics ; which wished, while it
had its delight in Wither's *Philarete,* that it was not so
long ; which felt a finer thrill than usual of the imagination in Marvell's *Emigrants in the Bermudas* and *The
Thoughts in a Garden;* which was caught, as it were into
another world, by the *Allegro,* the *Penseroso,* the songs
in *Comus* and the *Arcades,* and by the *Lycidas* of Milton
—can scarcely be called an age of decay. There was
decline, on the whole. We feel what had passed away
when we come to the days of the Restoration. But the
Elizabethan lyrical day died in a lovely sunset. And as
if to make this clear, we meet with Milton who bore the
passion, the force, and the beauty of the past along with
his own grandeur into the age of Dryden.

100. **John Milton** was the last of the Elizabethans, and,
except Shakespeare, far the greatest of them all. Born in
1608, in Bread Street (close by the Mermaid Tavern), he
may have seen Shakespeare, for he remained till he was
sixteen in London. His literary life may be said to begin
with his entrance into Cambridge, in 1625, the year of the
accession of Charles I. Nicknamed the " Lady of Christ's "
from his beauty, delicate taste, and moral life, he soon
attained a reputation by his Latin poems and discourses,
and by his English poems which revealed as clear and
original a genius as that of Chaucer and Spenser. Of
Milton even more than of the two others, it may be said
that he was " whole in himself, and owed to none." The

M

Ode to the Nativity, 1629, the third poem he composed, while it went back to the Elizabethan age in beauty, in instinctive fire, went forward into a new world of art, the world where the architecture of the lyric is finished with majesty and music. The next year heard the noble sounding strains of *At a Solemn Music;* and the sonnet, *On Attaining the Age of Twenty-three*, reveals in dignified beauty that intense personality which lives, like a force, through every line he wrote. He left the university in 1632, and went to live at Horton, near Windsor, where he spent five years, steadily reading the Greek and Latin writers, and amusing himself with mathematics and music. Poetry was not neglected. The *Allegro* and *Penseroso* were written in 1633 and probably the *Arcades;* *Comus* was acted in 1634, and *Lycidas* composed in 1637. They prove that though Milton was Puritan in heart his Puritanism was of that earlier type which disdained neither the arts nor letters. But they represent a growing revolt from the Court and the Church. The *Penseroso* prefers the contemplative life to the mirthful, and *Comus*, though a masque, rose into a celestial poem to the glory of temperance, and under its allegory attacked the Court. Three years later, *Lycidas* interrupts its exquisite stream of poetry with a fierce and resolute onset on the greedy shepherds of the Church. Milton had taken his Presbyterian bent.

In 1638 he went to Italy, the second home of so many of the English poets, visited Florence where he saw Galileo, and then passed on to Rome. At Naples he

heard the sad news of civil war, which determined him
to return; "inasmuch as I thought it base to be travelling at my ease for amusement, while my fellow-country-
men at home were fighting for liberty." At the meeting
of the Long Parliament we find him in a house in Alders-
gate, where he lived till 1645. He had projected while
abroad a great epic poem on the subject of Arthur, but
in London his mind changed, and among a number of
subjects, tended at last to *Paradise Lost*, which he meant
to throw into the form of a Greek Tragedy with lyrics
and choruses.

101. **Milton's Prose. The Commonwealth.** — Suddenly
his whole life changed, and for twenty years — 1640–60
— he was carried out of art into politics, out of poetry
into prose. Most of the *Sonnets*, however, belong to
this time. Stately, rugged, or graceful, as he pleased to
make them, some with the solemn grandeur of Hebrew
psalms, others having the classic ease of Horace, some
of his own grave tenderness, they are true, unlike those
of Shakespeare and Spenser, to the correct form of this
difficult kind of poetry. But they were all he could now
do of his true work. Before the Civil War began in
1642, he had written five vigorous pamphlets against
Episcopacy. Six more pamphlets appeared in the next
two years. One of these was the *Areopagitica; or,
Speech for the Liberty of Unlicensed Printing*. 1644, a
bold and eloquent attack on the censorship of the press
by the Presbyterians. Another, remarkable, like the
Areopagitica, for its finer prose, was a tract *On Educa-*

tion. The four pamphlets in which he advocated conditional divorce made him still more the horror of the Presbyterians. In 1646 he published his poems, and in that year the sonnet *On the Forcers of Conscience* shows that he had wholly ceased to be Presbyterian. His political pamphlets begin when his *Tenure of Kings and Magistrates* defended in 1649 the execution of the king. The *Eikonoclastes* answered the *Eikon Basilike* (a portraiture of the sufferings of the king); and his famous Latin *Defence for the People of England*, 1651, replied to Salmasius's *Defence of Charles I.*, and inflicted so pitiless a lashing on the great Leyden scholar that Milton's fame went over the whole of Europe. In the next year he wholly lost his sight. But he continued his work (being Latin secretary since 1649) when Cromwell was made Protector, and wrote another *Defence for the English People*, 1654, and a further *Defence of Himself* against scurrilous charges. This closed the controversy in 1655. In the last year of the Protector's life he began the *Paradise Lost*, but the death of Cromwell threw him back into politics, and three more pamphlets on the questions of a Free Church and a Free Commonwealth were useless to prevent the Restoration. It was a wonder he was not put to death in 1660, and he was in hiding and also in custody for a time. At last he settled in a house near Bunhill Fields. It was here that *Paradise Lost* was finished, before the end of 1665, and then published in 1667.

102. **Paradise Lost.** — We may regret that Milton was

shut away from his art during twenty years of controversy. But it may be that the poems he wrote when the
great cause he fought for had closed in seeming defeat
but real victory, gained from its solemn issues and from
the moral grandeur with which he wrought for its ends
their majestic movement, their grand style, and their
grave beauty. During the struggle he had never forgotten his art. "I may one day hope," he said, speaking of his youthful studies, "to have ye again, in a still
time, when there shall be no chiding. Not in these
Noises," and the saying strikes the note of calm sublimity which is kept in *Paradise Lost.*

As we read the great epic, we feel that the lightness of
heart of the *Allegro*, that even the quiet classic philosophy
of the *Comus*, are gone. The beauty of the poem is like
that of a stately temple, which, vast in conception, is
involved in detail. The style is the greatest in the whole
range of English poetry. Milton's intellectual force sup-
ports and condenses his imaginative force, and his art is
almost too conscious of itself. Sublimity is its essential
difference. The subject is one phase of the great and
universal subject of high poetic thought and passion, that
struggle of Light with Darkness, of Evil with Good,
which, arising in a hundred myths, keeps its undying
attraction to the present day. But its great difficulty in
his case was that he was obliged to interest us, for a
great part of the poem, in two persons, who, being inno-
cent, were without any such play of human passion and
trouble as we find in Œdipus, Æneas, Hamlet, or Alceste.

In the noble art with which this is done Milton is supreme. The interest of the story collects at first round the character of Satan, but he grows meaner as the poem develops, and his second degradation after he has destroyed innocence is one of the finest and most consistent motives in the poem. This at once disposes of the view that Milton meant Satan to be the hero of the epic. His hero is Man. The deep tenderness of Milton, his love of beauty, the passionate fitness of his words to his work, his religious depth, fill the scenes in which he paints Paradise, our parents and their fall, and at last all thought and emotion centre round Adam and Eve, until the closing lines leave us with their lonely image on our minds. In every part of the poem, in every character in it, as indeed in all his poems, Milton's intense individuality appears. It is a pleasure to find it. The egotism of such a man, said Coleridge, is a revelation of spirit.

103. **Milton's Later Poems.** — *Paradise Lost* was followed by *Paradise Regained* and *Samson Agonistes*, published together in 1671. *Paradise Regained* opens with the journey of Christ into the wilderness after his baptism, and its four books describe the temptation of Christ by Satan, and the answers and victory of the Redeemer. The speeches in it overwhelm the action, and their learned argument is only relieved by a few descriptions; but these, as in that of Athens, are done with Milton's highest power. Its solemn beauty of quietude, and a more severe style than that of *Paradise Lost*, make us feel in it that Milton has grown older.

In *Samson Agonistes* the style is still severer, even to the verge of a harshness which the sublimity alone tends to modify. It is a choral drama, after the Greek model. Samson in his blindness is described, is called on to make sport for the Philistines, and overthrows them in the end. Samson represents the fallen Puritan cause, and Samson's victorious death Milton's hopes for the final triumph of that cause. The poem has all the grandeur of the last words of a great man in whom there was now "calm of mind, all passion spent." It is also the last word of the music of the Elizabethan drama long after its notes seemed hushed, and its deep sound is strange in the midst of the shallow noise of the Restoration. Soon afterwards, November, 1674, blind and old and fallen on evil days, Milton died; but neither blindness, old age, nor evil days could lessen the inward light, nor impair the imaginative power with which he sang, it seemed with the angels, the "undisturbed song of pure concent," until he joined himself, at last, with those "just spirits who wear victorious palms."

104. **His Work.** — To the greatness of the artist Milton joined the majesty of a clear and lofty character. His poetic style was as stately as his character, and proceeded from it. Living at a time when criticism began to purify the verse of England, and being himself well acquainted with the great classical models, his work is seldom weakened by the false conceits and the intemperance of the Elizabethan writers, and yet is as imaginative as theirs, and as various. He has not their naturalness, nor all

their intensity, but he has a larger grace, a lovelier colour, a closer eye for nature, a more finished art, and a sublime dignity they did not possess. All the kinds of poetry which he touched he touched with the ease of great strength, and with so much energy, that they became new in his hands. He put a fresh life into the masque, the sonnet, the elegy, the descriptive lyric, the song, the choral drama; and he created the epic in England. The lighter love poem he never wrote, and we are grateful that he kept his coarse satirical power apart from his poetry. In some points he was untrue to his descent from the Elizabethans, for he had no dramatic faculty, and he had no humour. He summed up in himself the learned and artistic influences of the English Renaissance, and handed them on to us. His taste was as severe, his verse as polished, his method and language as strict as those of the school of Dryden and Pope that grew up when he was old. A literary past and present thus met in him, nor did he fail, like all the greatest men, to make a cast into the future. He established the poetry of pure natural description. Lastly, he did not represent in any way the England that followed the Stuarts, but he did represent Puritan England, and the whole spirit of Puritanism from its cradle to its grave.

105. **The Pilgrim's Progress.** — We might say that Puritanism said its last great words with Milton, were it not that its spirit continued in English life, were it not also that four years after his death, in 1678, JOHN BUNYAN, who had previously written religious poems, and in

1665 the *Holy City*, published the *Pilgrim's Progress*. It is the journey of Christian the Pilgrim from the City of Destruction to the Celestial City. The *second part* was published in 1684. In 1682 he had written the allegory of the *Holy War*, and in 1680 *The Life and Death of Mr. Badman*, a curious little story. I class the *Pilgrim's Progress* here, because in its imaginative fervour and imagery, and in its quality of naturalness, it belongs to the spirit of the Elizabethan times. Written by a man of the people, it is a people's book ; and its simple form grew out of passionate feeling, and not out of self-conscious art. The passionate feeling was religious, and in painting the pilgrim's progress towards Heaven, and his battle with the world and temptation and sorrow, the book touched those deep and universal interests which belong to poor and rich. Its language, the language of the Bible, and its allegorical form, initiated a plentiful prose literature of a similar kind. But none have equalled it. Its form is almost epic : its dramatic dialogue, its clear types of character, its vivid descriptions, as of Vanity Fair, and of places, such as the Valley of the Shadow of Death and the Delectable Mountains, which represent states of the human soul, have given an equal but a different pleasure to children and men, to the villager and the scholar.

CHAPTER VI

FROM THE RESTORATION TO THE DEATH OF POPE AND SWIFT, 1660–1745

106. **Poetry. Change of Style.** — We have seen the natural style as distinguished from the artificial in the Elizabethan poets. Style became not only natural but artistic when it was made by a great genius like Chaucer, Shakespeare, or Spenser, for a first-rate poet creates rules of art : his work is filled with laws which other men see, collect, and obey. Art, which is the just and lovely arrangement of nature to fulfil a nobly chosen aim, is then born. But when the art of poetry is making, the second-rate poets, inspired only by their feelings, will write in a natural style unrestrained by rules, that is, they will put their feelings into verse without caring much for the form in which they do it. As long as they live in the midst of a youthful national life, and feel an ardent sympathy with it, their style will be fresh and im-passioned, and give pleasure because of the strong feel-ing that inspires it. But it will also be extravagant and unrestrained in its use of images and words because of its want of art. This is the general history of the style

of the second-class poets of the middle period of Elizabeth's reign, and even Shakespeare affords examples of
this want of art.   (2) Afterwards the national life grew
chill, and the feelings of the poets also chill.   Then the
want of art in the style made itself felt.   The far-fetched
images, the hazarded meanings, the over-fanciful way of
putting thoughts, the sensational expression of feeling,
in which the Elizabethan poets indulged, not only appeared in all their ugliness when they were inspired by
no ardent feeling, but were indulged in far more than before.   Men tried to produce by extravagant use of words
the same results that a passionate sense of life had produced, and the more they failed the more extravagant and
fantastic they became, till at last their poetry ceased to
have clear meaning.   This is the general history of the
style of the poets from the later days of Elizabeth till the
Civil War.   (3) The natural style, unregulated by art,
had thus become unnatural.   When it had reached that
point, men began to feel how necessary it was that the
work of poetry should be subjected to the rules of art,
and two influences partly caused and partly supported this
desire.   One was the influence of Milton.   Milton, first
by his superb genius, which, as I said, creates of itself
rules of art, and secondly by his knowledge and imitation
of the great classical models, was able to give the first
example in England of a pure, grand, and finished style ;
and in blank verse, in the lyric and the sonnet, wrote for
the first time with absolute correctness.   Another influence
was that of the movement all over Europe towards inquiry

into the right way of doing things, and into the truth of
things, a movement we shall soon see at work in science,
politics, and religion. In poetry it produced a school
of criticism which first took form in France, and the
influence of Boileau, La Fontaine, and others who were
striving after greater finish and neatness of expression,
told on England now. It is an influence which has been
exaggerated. It is absurd to place the "creaking lyre"
of Boileau side by side with Dryden's "long resounding
march and energy divine." Our critical school of poets
have few French qualities in them even when they imitate the French. (4) Further, our own poets had
already, before the Restoration, begun the critical work,
and the French influence served only to give it a greater
impulse. We shall see the growth of a colder and more
correct phrasing and versification in Waller, Denham, and
Cowley. Vigour was given to this new method in art by
Dryden, and perfection of artifice added to it by Pope.
The *artificial* style succeeded to and extinguished the
natural, or to put it otherwise, a merely intellectual
poetry finally overcame a poetry in which emotion always
accompanied thought.

107. **Change of Poetic Subject.** — The subject of the
Elizabethan poets was Man as influenced by the Passions, and it was treated from the side of natural feeling.
This was fully and splendidly done by Shakespeare. But
after a time this subject followed, as we have seen in
speaking of the drama, the same career as the style. It
was treated in an extravagant and sensational manner,

and the representation of the passions tended to become unnatural or fantastic.   Milton redeemed the subject from this vicious excess.   He wrote in a grave and natural manner of the passions of the human heart ; he made strong in English poetry the religious passions of love of God, of sorrow for sin, and he raised in song the moral passions into a solemn splendour.   But with him the subject of man as influenced by the great passions died for a time.   Dryden, Pope, and their followers turned to another subject.   They left, except in Dryden's Dramas and Fables, the passions aside, and wrote of the things in which the intellect and the casuistical conscience, the social and political instincts in man, were interested.   In this way the satiric, didactic, philosophical, and party poetry of a new school arose.

108. **The Poems in which the New School began** belong in date to the age before the Restoration, but in spirit and form they were the sources of the poetry which is called classical or critical, or artificial.   EDMUND WALLER, SIR JOHN DENHAM, and ABRAHAM COWLEY are the precursors of Dryden.   Waller remodelled the heroic couplet of Chaucer, and gave it the precise character which made it for nearly a century and a half the prevailing form of verse.   He wrote his earliest poems about 1623, in precisely the same symmetrical manner as Dryden and Pope.   His new manner was not followed for many years, till Denham published in 1642 his *Cooper's Hill.*   "The excellence and dignity of rhyme were never fully known," said Dryden, "till Mr. Waller taught it, but this

sweetness of his lyric poetry was afterwards followed in the epic of Sir John Denham in his *Cooper's Hill.*" The chill stream of this poem, which is neither "lyric" nor "epic," has the metrical cadence, but none of the grip and force of Dryden's verse. Cowley's earlier poems belong to the Elizabethan phantasies, but the later were, with the exception of some noble poems of personal feeling, cold and exact enough for the praise of the new school. He invented that curious misnomer — the Pindaric Ode — which, among all its numerous offspring, had but one splendid child in Dryden's *Alexander's Feast.* When Gray took up the ode again, Cowley was not his master. Sir W. Davenant's *Gondibert,* 1651, also an heroic poem, is another example of this transition. Worthless as poetry, it represents the new interest in political philosophy and in science that was arising, and preludes the intellectual poetry. Its preface discourses of rhyme and the rules of art, and embodies the critical influence which came over with the exiled court from France. The critical school had therefore begun even before Dryden's poems were written. The change was less sudden than it seemed.

Satiric poetry, soon to become a greater thing, was made during this transition time into a powerful weapon by two men, each on a different side. Andrew Marvell's *Satires,* after the Restoration, exhibit the Puritan's wrath with the vices of the court and king, and his shame for the disgrace of England among the nations. The *Hudibras* of SAMUEL BUTLER, in 1663, represents the fierce

reaction which had set in against Puritanism. It is
justly famed for wit, learning, good sense, and ingenious
drollery, and, in accordance with the new criticism, it is
absolutely without obscurity. It is often as terse as
Pope's best work. But it is too long, its wit wearies us
at last, and it undoes the force of its attack on the Puritans by its exaggeration. Satire should have at least the
semblance of truth ; yet Butler calls the Puritans cow-
ards. We turn now to the greatest of these poets in
whom poetry is founded on intellect rather than on feeling, and whose verse is mostly devoted to argument and
satire.

109. **John Dryden** was the first of the new, as Milton
was the last of the elder, school of poetry. It was late in
life that he gained fame. Born in 1631, he was a Crom-
wellite till the Restoration, when he began the changes
which mark his life. His poem on the death of the Protector was soon followed by the *Astræa Redux*, which
celebrated the return of Justice to the realm in the person of Charles II. The *Annus Mirabilis* appeared in
1667, and in this his metrical ease was first clearly marked.
But his power of exact reasoning expressing itself with
powerful and ardent ease in a rapid succession of condensed thoughts in verse, was not shown (save in drama)
till he was fifty years old, in the first part of *Absalom and
Achitophel*, the foremost of English satires. He had been
a playwriter for fourteen years, till its appearance in 1681,
and the rhymed plays which he had written enabled him
to perfect the versification which is now so remarkable

in his work. The satire itself, written in mockery of the Popish Plot and the Exclusion Bill, attacked Shaftesbury as Achitophel, was kind to Monmouth as Absalom, and in its sketch of Buckingham as Zimri the poet avenged himself for the *Rehearsal*. It was the first fine example of that party poetry which became still more bitter and personal in the hands of Pope. It was followed by the *Medal*, a new attack on Shaftesbury, and the *Mac Fleck-noe*, 1682, in which Shadwell, a rival poet, who had sup-ported Shaftesbury's party, was made the witless successor of Richard Flecknoe, a poet of all kinds of poetry, and master of none. Then in the same year, after the arrest of Monmouth, the second part of *Absalom and Achito-phel* appeared, all of which, except two hundred lines, was written by Nahum Tate. These were four terrible masterpieces of ruthless wit and portraiture. Then he turned to express his transient theology in verse, and the *Religio Laici*, 1682, defends and states the argument for the Church of England. It was perhaps poverty that led him to change his religion, and the *Hind and Panther*, 1687, is a model of melodious reasoning in behalf of the milk-white hind of the Church of Rome. The Dissenters are mercilessly treated under the image of the baser beasts; while at first the Panther, the Church of Eng-land, is gently touched, but in the end lashed with sever-ity. However, Hind and Panther tell, at the close, two charming stories to one another. It produced in reply one of the happiest burlesques in English poetry, *The Country Mouse and the City Mouse*, the work of Charles

Montague (Lord Halifax), and Mat Prior. Deprived of
his offices at the Revolution, Dryden turned again to the
drama and to prose, but the failure of the last of his good
plays in 1694, drove him again from the stage, and he
gave himself up to his *Translation of Virgil* which he
published in 1697. As a narrative poet his *Fables,
Ancient and Modern,* finished late in life, in 1699, give
him a high rank in this class of poetry. They sin from
coarseness, but in style, in magnificent march of verse,
in intellectual but not imaginative fire, in ease but not
in grace, they are excellent. As a lyric poet his fame
rests on the animated *Song for St. Cecilia's Day,* 1687,
and on *Alexander's Feast,* 1697. From Milton's death,
1674, till his own in 1700, Dryden reigned undisputed,
and round his throne in Will's Coffeehouse, where he sat
as " Glorious John," we may place the names of the lesser
poets, the Earls of Dorset, Roscommon, and Mulgrave,
Sir Charles Sedley, and the Earl of Rochester. The
lighter poetry of the court lived on in the two last. John
Oldham won a short fame by his *Satire on the Jesuits,*
1679 ; and Bishop Ken, 1668, established, in his *Morning and Evening Hymns,* a new type of religious poetry.

110. **Prose Literature of the Restoration and Revolution. Criticism.** — As Dryden was now first in poetry, so
he was in prose. No one can understand the poetry of
this time, in its relation to the past, to the future, and
to France, who does not read the Critical Essays pre-
fixed to his dramas, *On the Historical Poem,* on dramatic
rhyme, on *Heroic Plays,* on the classical writers, and his

N

Essay on Dramatic Poetry. He is in these essays, not only the leader of modern literary criticism, but the leader of that modern prose in which the style is easy, unaffected, moulded to the subject, and in which the proper words are put in the proper places. Dryden was a great originator.

III. **Science.** During the Civil War the religious and political struggle absorbed the country, but yet, apart from the strife, a few men who cared for scientific matters met at one another's houses. Out of this little knot, after the Restoration, arose the Royal Society, embodied in 1662. Astronomy, experimental chemistry, medicine, mineralogy, zoölogy, botany, vegetable physiology, were all founded as studies, and their literature begun, in the age of the Restoration. One man's work was so great in science as to merit his name being mentioned among the literary men of England. In 1671 Isaac Newton laid his *Theory of Light* before the Royal Society; in the year before the Revolution his *Principia* established, by its proof of the theory of gravitation, the true system of the universe.

It was in political and religious knowledge, however, that the intellectual inquiry of the nation was most shown. When the thinking spirit succeeds the active and adventurous in a people, one of the first things they will think upon is the true method and grounds of government, both divine and human. Two sides will be taken: the side of authority and the side of reason in Religion; the side of authority and the side of individual liberty in Politics.

112. **The Theological Literature** of those who declared that reason was supreme as a test of truth, arose with some men who met at Lord Falkland's just before the Civil War, and especially with John Hales and William Chillingworth. The same kind of work, though modified towards more sedateness of expression, and less rationalistic, was now done by Archbishop Tillotson, and Bishop Burnet. In 1678, Cudworth's *Intellectual System of the Universe* is perhaps the best book on the controversy which then took form against those who were called Atheists. A number of divines in the English Church took sides for Authority or Reason, or opposed the growing Deism during the latter half of the seventeenth century. It was an age of preachers, and Isaac Barrow, Newton's predecessor in the chair of mathematics at Cambridge, could preach, with grave and copious eloquence, for three hours at a time. Theological prose was strengthened by the publication of the sermons of Edward Stillingfleet and William Sherlock, and their adversary, Robert South, was as witty in rhetoric as he was fierce in controversy.

113. **Political Literature.** — The resistance to authority in the opposition to the theory of the Divine Right of Kings did not much enter into literature till after the severe blow that theory received in the Civil War. During the Commonwealth and after the Restoration the struggle took the form of a discussion on the abstract question of the Science of Government, and was mingled with an inquiry into the origin of society and the ground

of social life. THOMAS HOBBES, during the Commonwealth, was the first who dealt with the question from
the side of abstract reason, and he is also, before Dryden,
the first of all our prose writers whose style may be said
to be uniform and correct, and adapted carefully to the
subjects on which he wrote. His treatise, the *Leviathan*,
1651, declared (1) that the origin of all power was in
the people, and (2) that the end of all power was the
commonweal. It destroyed the theory of a Divine
Right of Kings and Priests, but it created another kind
of Divine Right when it said that the power lodged in
rulers by the people could not be taken away by the
people. Sir R. Filmer supported the side of Divine
Right in his *Patriarcha*, published 1680. Henry Nevile,
in his *Dialogue concerning Government*, and James Harrington in his romance, *The Commonwealth of Oceana*,
published at the beginning of the Commonwealth, con-
tended that all secure government was to be based on
property, but Nevile supported a monarchy, and Harrington -- with whom I may class Algernon Sidney, whose
political treatise on government is as statesmanlike as it
is finely written — a democracy, on this basis. I may
here mention that it was during this period, in 1667, that
the first effort was made after a Science of Political
Economy by Sir William Petty in his *Treatise on Taxes*.
The *political pamphlet* was also begun at this time by Sir
Roger L'Estrange, and George Savile, Lord Halifax.

114. **John Locke,** after the Revolution, in 1690, followed the two doctrines of Hobbes in his treatises on

Civil Government, but with these important additions —
(1) that the people have a right to take away the power
given by them to the ruler, (2) that the ruler is respon-
sible to the people for the trust reposed in him, and (3)
that legislative assemblies are Supreme as the voice of
the people. This was the political philosophy of the
Revolution. Locke carried the same spirit of free inquiry into the realm of religion, and in his *Letters on
Toleration* laid down the philosophical grounds for liberty of religious thought. He finished by entering the
realm of metaphysical inquiry. In 1690 appeared his
Essay concerning the Human Understanding, in which
he investigated its limits, and traced all ideas, and therefore all knowledge, to experience. In his clear statement of the way in which the Understanding works, in
the way in which he guarded it and Language against
their errors in the inquiry after truth, he did almost as
much for the true method of thinking as Bacon had done
for the science of nature.

115. The intellectual stir of the time produced, apart
from the great movement of thought, a good deal of
Miscellaneous Literature. The painting of short " characters " was carried on after the Restoration by Samuel
Butler and W. Charleton. These " characters " had no
personality, but as party spirit deepened, names thinly
disguised were given to characters drawn of living men,
and Dryden and Pope in poetry, and all the prose wits
of the time of Queen Anne and George I., made personal and often violent sketches of their opponents a

special element in literature. On the other hand, Izaak Walton's *Lives*, in 1670, are examples of kind, agreeable, and careful Biography. Cowley's small volume, written shortly before his death in 1667, gave richness to the Essay, and its prose almost anticipated the prose of Dryden. John Evelyn's multitudinous writings are themselves a miscellany. He wrote on painting, sculpture, architecture, timber (the *Sylva*), on gardening, commerce, and he illustrates the searching spirit of the age. In William III.'s time Sir William Temple's pleasant *Essays* bring us in style and tone nearer to the great class of essayists of whom Addison was chief. Lady Rachel Russell's Letters begin the Letter-writing literature of England. Pepys (1660–9), and Evelyn, whose Diary grows full after 1640, gave rise to that class of gossiping Memoirs which has been of so much use in giving colour to history. History itself at this time is little better than memoirs, and such a name may be fairly given to Bishop Burnet's *History of his Own Time* and to his *History of the Reformation*. Finally Classical Criticism, in the discussion on the genuineness of the *Letters of Phalaris*, was created by Richard Bentley in 1697–9. Literature was therefore plentiful. It was also correct, but it was not inventive.

116. **The Literature of Queen Anne and the First Georges.** — With the closing years of William III. and the accession of Queen Anne (1702) a literature arose which was partly new and partly a continuance of that of the Restoration. The conflict between those who

took the oath to the new dynasty and the Nonjurors who
refused, the hot blood that it produced, the war between
Dissent and Church, and between the two parties which
now took the names of Whig and Tory, produced a mass
of political pamphlets, of which Daniel Defoe's and
Swift's were the best; of songs and ballads, like *Lillibul-
lero*, which were sung in every street; of squibs, reviews,
of satirical poems and letters. Every one joined in it,
and it rose to importance in the work of the greater men
who mingled literary studies with their political excitement. In politics, all the abstract discussions we have
mentioned ceased to be abstract, and became personal
and practical, and the spirit of inquiry applied itself more
closely to the questions of every-day life. The whole of
this stirring literary life was concentrated in London,
where the agitation of society was hottest; and it is
round this vivid city life that the literature of Queen
Anne and the two following reigns is best grouped.

117. It was, with a few exceptions, a **Party Literature.**
The Whig and Tory leaders enlisted on their sides the
best poets and prose writers, who fiercely satirised and
unduly praised them under names thinly disguised. Our
" Augustan Age " was an age of unbridled slander. Per-
sonalities were sent to and fro like shots in battle. Those
who could do this work well were well rewarded, but the
rank and file of writers were left to starve. Literature
was thus honoured not for itself, but for the sake of party.
The result was that the abler men lowered it by making
it a political tool, and the smaller men, the fry of Grub

Street, degraded it by using it in the same way, only in a
baser manner. Their flattery was as abject as their abuse
was shameless, and both were stupid. They received and
deserved the merciless lashing which Pope was soon to
give them in the *Dunciad.* Being a party literature, it
naturally came to study and to look sharply into human
character and into human life as seen in the great city.
It debated subjects of literary and scientific inquiry and
of philosophy with great ability, but without depth. It
discussed all the varieties of social life, and painted town
society more vividly than has been done before or since ;
and it was so wholly taken up with this, that country life
and its interests, except in the writings of Addison, were
scarcely touched by it at all. Criticism being so active,
the *form* in which thought was expressed was now especially dwelt on, and the result was that the style of English
prose became even more simple than in Dryden's hands ;
and English verse, leaving Dryden's power behind it,
reached a neatness of expression as exquisite as it was
artificial. At the same time, and for the same reasons,
Nature, Passion, and Imagination decayed in poetry.

118. **Alexander Pope** absorbed and reflected all these
elements. Born in 1688, he wrote tolerable verse at
twelve years old ; the *Pastorals* appeared in 1709, and
two years afterwards he took full rank as the critical poet
in the *Essay on Criticism* (1711). The next year saw
the first cast of his *Rape of the Lock,* the most brilliant
occasional poem in our language. This closed what we
may call his first period. In 1712 his sacred pastoral,

The Messiah, appeared, and in 1713, when he published *Windsor Forest*, he became known to Swift and to Henry St. John, Lord Bolingbroke. When these, with Gay, Parnell, Prior, Arbuthnot, and others, formed the Scriblerus Club, Pope joined them, and soon rose into great fame by his Translation of the *Iliad* (1715–20), and by the Translation of the *Odyssey* (1723–5), in which he was assisted by Fenton and Broome. Being now at ease, for he received fully 9000*l*. for this work, he published from his retreat at Twickenham, and in bitter scorn of the poetasters and of all the petty scribblers who annoyed him, the *Dunciad*, 1728. Its original hero was Lewis Theobald, but when the fourth book was published, under Warburton's influence, in 1742, Colley Cibber was enthroned as the King of Dunces instead of Theobald. The fiercest and finest of Pope's satires, it closes his second period which breathes the savageness of Swift. The third phase of Pope's literary life was closely linked to his friend Bolingbroke. It was in conversation with him that he originated the *Essay on Man* (1732–4) and the *Imitations of Horace*. The *Moral Essays*, or Epistles to men and women, were written to praise those whom he loved, and to satirise the bad poets and the social follies of the day, and all who disliked him or his party. Among these, who has not read the *Epistle to Dr. Arbuthnot?* In the last few years of his life, Bishop Warburton, the writer of the *Legation of Moses* and editor of Shakespeare, helped him to fit the *Moral Essays* into the plan of which the *Essay on Man* formed part. Warburton was Pope's last great friend; but almost his only old friend. By 1740 nearly all the members of his literary circle were dead, and a new race of poets and writers had grown up. In 1744 he died. His *Elegy on an Unfortunate Lady* and the Epistle of *Eloisa to Abelard* show how he once tried to handle the passions of sorrow and love. The masterly form into which he threw the philosophical principles he condensed into didactic poetry make them more impressive than they have a right to be. The *Essay on Man*, though its philosophy is poor and not his own, is crowded with lines that have passed into daily use. The *Essay on Criticism* is equally full of critical precepts put with exquisite skill. The *Satires* and *Epistles* are didactic, but their excellence is in the terse and finished types of character, in the almost creative drawing of which Pope remains unrivalled, even by Dryden. His translation of Homer resembles Homer as much as London resembled Troy, or Marlborough Achilles, or Queen Anne Hecuba. It is done with great literary art, but for that very reason it does not make us feel the simplicity and directness of his original. It has neither the manner nor the spirit of the Greek, just as Pope's descriptions of nature have neither the manner nor the spirit of nature. The *heroic couplet*, in which he wrote nearly all his work, he used with a correctness that has never been surpassed, but its smooth perfection, at length, wearies the ear. It wants the breaks that passion and imagination naturally make. Finally, he had the spirit of an artist, hating those who degraded his art, and at a time when men followed it for money, and place, and the applause of the club and of the town, he loved it faithfully to the end, for its own sake.

119. **The Minor Poets** who surrounded Pope in the first two-thirds of his life did not approach his genius. Richard Blackmore endeavoured to restore the epic in his *Prince Arthur*, 1695, and Samuel Garth's mock heroic poem of the *Dispensary* appeared along with John Pomfret's poems in 1699. In 1701, Defoe's *Trueborn Englishman* defended William III. against those who said he was a foreigner, and Prior's finest ode, the *Carmen Seculare*, took up the same cause. John Philips is known by his Miltonic burlesque of *The Splendid Shilling*, and his *Cyder* was a Georgic of the apple. Matthew Green's *Spleen* and Ambrose Philip's *Pastorals* were contemporary with Pope's first poetry ; and John Gay's *Shepherd's Week*, six pastorals, 1714, were as lightly wrought as his famous *Fables*. He had a true vein of happy song, and *Black-eyed Susan* remains with the *Beggars' Opera* to please us still. The political poems of Swift were coarse, but always hit home. Addison celebrated the Battle of Blenheim in the *Campaign*, and his cultivated grace is found in some devotional pieces. On his death Thomas Tickell made a noble elegy. Prior's charming ease is best shown in the light narrative poetry which we may say began with him in the reign of William III. In Pope's later life a new and quickening impulse came upon poetry, and changed it root and branch. It arose in Ramsay's

Gentle Shepherd, 1725, and in Thomson's *Seasons*, 1730, and it rang the knell of the manner and the spirit of the critical school.

120. **The Prose Literature** of Pope's time collects itself round four great names, Swift, Defoe, Addison, and Bishop Berkeley, and they all exhibit those elements of the age of which I have spoken. JONATHAN SWIFT was the keenest of political partisans, for his fierce and earnest personality made everything he did impassioned. But he was far more than a partisan. He was the most original prose writer of his time — the man of genius among many men of talent. It was not till he was thirty years old, 1697, that he wrote the *Battle of the Books*, concerning the so-called *Letters of Phalaris*, and the *Tale of a Tub*, a satire on the Dissenters, the Papists, and even the Church of England. These books, published in 1704, made his reputation. He soon became the finest and most copious writer of pamphlets England had ever known. At first he supported the Whigs, but left them for the new Tory party in 1710, and his tracts brought him court favour, while his literary fame was increased by many witty letters, poems, and arguments. On the fall of the Tory party at the accession of George I., 1714, he retired to the Deanery of St. Patrick in Ireland, an embittered man, and the *Drapier's Letters*, 1724, written against Wood's halfpence, gained him popularity in a country that he hated. In 1726 his inventive genius, his savage satire, and his cruel indignation with life were all shown in *Gulliver's Travels*. The voyage to Lilliput

and Brobdingnag satirised the politics and manners of
England and Europe; that to Laputa mocked the philosophers; and the last, to the country of the Houyhnhnms,
lacerated and defiled the whole body of humanity.   No
English is more robust than Swift's, no life in private
and public more sad and proud, no death more pitiable.
He died in 1745 hopelessly insane.   DANIEL DEFOE's
vein as a pamphleteer seems to have been inexhaustible,
and the style of his tracts was as roughly persuasive as
it was popular.   Above all he was the journalist.   His
Review, published twice a week for a year, was wholly
written by himself; but he "founded, conducted, and
wrote for a host of other newspapers," and filled them
with every subject of the day.   His tales grew out of
matters treated of in his journals, and his best art lay
in the way he built up these stories out of mere sug-
gestions.   "The little art he is truly master of," said one
of his contemporaries, "is of forging a story and impos-
ing it on the world for truth."   His circumstantial invention, combined with a style which exactly fits it by its
simplicity, is the root of the charm of the great story
by which he chiefly lives in literature.   *Robinson Crusoe*,
1719, equalled *Gulliver's Travels* in truthful representation, and excelled them in invention.   The story lives
and charms from day to day.   But none of his stories
are real novels; that is, they have no plot to the working
out of which the characters and the events contribute.
They form the transition, however, from the slight tale
and the romance of the Elizabethan time to the finished
novel of Richardson and Fielding.

121. **Metaphysical Literature**, which drifted into theology, was enriched by the work of BISHOP BERKELEY.
The Platonic dialogue of *Hylas and Philonous*, 1713,
charms us even more than his subtle and elastic *Siris*,
1744. These books, with *Alciphron, the Minute Philosopher*, 1732, questioned the real existence of matter, —
"no idea can exist," he said, "out of the mind," — and
founded on the denial of it an answer to the English
Deists, round whom in the first half of the eighteenth
century centred the struggle between the claims of natural and revealed religion. The influence of Shaftesbury's *Characteristics*, 1711, was far more literary than
metaphysical. He condemned metaphysics, but his philosophy, such as it was, inspired Pope, and his cultivated
thinking on several subjects made many writers in the
next generation care for beauty and grace. He, like
Bolingbroke, and Wollaston, Tindal, Toland, and Collins,
on the Deists' side, were opposed by Samuel Clark, by
Bentley, by Bishop Butler, and by Bishop Warburton.
BISHOP BUTLER'S acute and solid reasoning treated in
his *Sermons* the subject of Morals, inquiring what was
the particular nature of man, and hence determining the
course of life correspondent to this nature. His *Analogy
of Religion, Natural and Revealed, to the Constitution and
Course of Nature*, 1736, endeavours to make peace between authority and reason, and has become a standard
book. I may mention here a social satire, *The Fable of
the Bees*, by Mandeville, half-poem, half-prose dialogue,
and finished in 1729. It tried to prove that the vices

of society are the foundation of civilisation, and is one
of the first of a new set of books which marked the rise
in England of the bold speculations on the nature and
ground of society to which the French Revolution gave
afterwards so great an impulse.

122. **The Periodical Essay** is connected with the
names of JOSEPH ADDISON and SIR RICHARD STEELE.
The gay, light, graceful, literary Essay, differing from
such Essays as Bacon's as good conversation about a
subject differs from a clear analysis of all its points, was
begun in France by Montaigne in 1580. Charles Cotton, a wit of Charles II.'s time, retranslated Montaigne's
Essays, and they soon found imitators in Cowley and
Sir W. Temple. But the periodical Essay was created
by Steele and Addison. It was at first published three
times a week, then daily, and it was anonymous, and
both these characters necessarily changed its form from
that of an essay by Montaigne. Steele began it in the
Tatler, 1709, and it treated of everything that was going
on in the town. He paints as a social humourist the
whole age of Queen Anne — the political and literary
disputes, the fine gentlemen and ladies, the characters
of men, the humours of society, the new book, the new
play ; we live in the very streets and drawing-rooms of
old London. Addison soon joined him, first in the *Tatler*, afterwards in the *Spectator*, 1711. His work is more
critical, literary, and didactic than his companion's. The
characters he introduces, such as Sir Roger de Coverley,
are finished studies after nature. The humour is very

fine and tender; and, like Chaucer's, it is never bitter.
The style adds to the charm: in its varied cadence and
subtle ease it has not been surpassed within its own
peculiar sphere in England; and it seems to grow out
of the subjects treated of. Addison's work was a great
one, lightly done. The *Spectator*, the *Guardian*, and the
Freeholder, in his hands, gave a better tone to manners,
and hence to morals, and a gentler one to political and
literary criticism. The essays published every Friday
were chiefly on literary subjects, the Saturday essays
chiefly on religious subjects. The former popularised
literature, so that culture spread among the middle
classes and crept down to the country; the latter popularised religion. "I have brought," he says, "philosophy
out of closets and libraries, schools and colleges, to dwell
in clubs and assemblies, at tea-tables and in coffee-houses."

THE DRAMA, FROM THE RESTORATION TO 1780

123. **The Drama** after the Restoration took the tone
of the court both in politics and religion, but its partisan-
ship decayed under William III., and died in the reign
of Queen Anne. The court of Charles II., which the
plays now written represented much more than they did
the national life, gave the drama the "genteel" ease
and the immorality of its society. and encouraged it
to find new impulses from the tragedy and comedy of
Spain and of France. The French romances of the
school of Calprenède and Scudéry furnished plots to
the playwriters. The great French dramatists, Corneille,

Racine, and Molière, were translated and borrowed from
again and again. The "three unities" of Corneille, and
rhyme instead of blank verse as the vehicle of tragedy,
were adopted, but "the spirit of neither the serious nor
the comic drama of France could then be transplanted
into England."

Two acting companies were formed on Charles II.'s
return, under Thomas Killigrew and Davenant ; actresses
came on the stage for the first time, the ballet was introduced, and scenery began to be largely used.   Dryden,
whose masterly force was sure to strike the key-note that
others followed, began his comedies in 1663, but turned
to tragedy in the *Indian Queen*, 1664.   This play, with
the *Indian Emperour*, established for fourteen years the
rhymed couplet as the dramatic verse.   His defence of
rhyme in the *Essay on Dramatic Poesy* asserted the
originality of the English school, and denied that it followed the French.   *The Maiden Queen*, 1667, brought
him new fame, and then *Tyrannic Love* and the *Conquest of Granada*, 1672, induced the burlesque of the
Rehearsal, written by the Duke of Buckingham, in which
the bombastic extravagance of these heroic plays was
ridiculed.   Dryden now changed, in 1678, his dramatic
manner, and following Shakespeare, "disencumbered
himself from rhyme" in his fine tragedy of *All for Love*,
and showed what power he had of low comedy in the
Spanish Friar. After the Revolution, his tragedy of
Don Sebastian ranks high, but not higher than his brill-
iantly written comedy of *Amphitryon*, 1690.   Dryden is

o

the representative dramatist of the Restoration. Among
the tragedians who followed his method and possessed
their own, those most worthy of notice are Nat Lee,
whose *Rival Queens*, 1667, deserves its praise; Thomas
Otway, whose two pathetic tragedies, the *Orphan* and
Venice Preserved, still keep the stage; Thomas Southerne
whose *Fatal Marriage*, 1694, was revived by Garrick;
and Congreve who once turned from comedy to write
The Mourning Bride.

It was in comedy, however, that the dramatists excelled. Sir George Etherege originated with great skill
the new comedy of England with *She Would if She
Could*, 1668. Sedley, Mrs. Behn, Lacy, and Shadwell
carry on to the Revolution that light Comedy of Manners which William Wycherley's gross vigour and natural
plots lifted into an odious excellence in such plays as the
Country Wife and the *Plain Dealer*. Three great come-
dians followed Wycherley — William Congreve, whose
well-bred ease is almost as remarkable as his brilliant
wit; Sir John Vanbrugh, and George Farquhar, both of
whom have quick invention, gaiety, dash, and sincerity.
The indecency of all these writers belongs to the time,
but it is partly forgotten in their swift and sustained
vivacity. This immorality produced Jeremy Collier's
famous attack on the stage, 1698; and the growth of
a higher tone in society, uniting with this attack, began
to purify the drama, though Mrs. Centlivre's comedies,
during the reign of Queen Anne, show no love of purity.
Steele, at this time, whose *Lying Lover* makes him the

father of Sentimental comedy, wrote all his plays with
a moral purpose. Nicholas Rowe, whose melancholy
tragedies "are occupied with themes of heroic love," is
dull, but never gross ; while Addison's ponderous tragedy
of *Cato*, 1713, praised by Voltaire as the first *tragédie
raisonnable*, marks, in its total rejection of the drama of
nature for the classical style, "a definite epoch in the
history of English tragedy, an epoch of decay, on which
no recovery has followed." Comedy, however, had still
a future. The *Beggars' Opera* of Gay, 1728, revived an
old form of drama in a new way. Colley Cibber carried
on into George II.'s time the light and the sentimental
comedy ; Fielding made the stage the vehicle of criticism
on the follies, literature, and politics of his time ; and Foote
and Garrick did the same kind of work in their farces.

The influence of the Restoration drama continues, past
this period, in the manner of Goldsmith and Sheridan
who wrote between 1768 and 1778 ; but the lambent
humour of Goldsmith's *Good-natured Man* and *She
Stoops to Conquer*, and the wit, almost as brilliant and
more epigrammatic than Congreve's, of Sheridan's *Rivals*
and the *School for Scandal*, are not deformed by the
indecency of the Restoration. Both were Irishmen, but
Goldsmith has more of the Celtic grace and Sheridan
of the Celtic wit. The sentimental comedy was carried
on into the next age by Macklin, Murphy, Cumberland,
the Colmans, and many others, but we may say that with
Sheridan the history of the elder English Drama closes.
That which belongs to our century is a different thing.

CHAPTER VII

PROSE LITERATURE FROM THE DEATH OF POPE AND OF
SWIFT TO THE FRENCH REVOLUTION, AND FROM THE
FRENCH REVOLUTION TO THE DEATH OF SCOTT

1745-1789-1832

124. **Prose Literature.** — The rapid increase of manu-
factures, science, and prosperity which began with the
middle of the eighteenth century is paralleled by the
growth of Literature. The general causes of this growth
were —

1st, That *a good prose style had been perfected*, and
the method of writing being made easy, production increased. Men were born, as it were, into a good school
of the art of composition.

2ndly, The *long peace* after the accession of the House
of Hanover had left England at rest, and given it wealth.
The reclaiming of waste tracts, the increased population
and trade, made better communication necessary; and
the country was soon covered with a network of high-
ways. The leisure gave time to men to think and
write; the quicker interchange between the capital and
the country spread over England the literature of the
capital, and stirred men everywhere to express their

thoughts. The coaching services and the post carried the new book and the literary criticism to the villages, and awoke the men of talent there, who might otherwise have been silent.

3rdly, *The Press* sent far and wide the news of the day, and grew in importance till it contained the opinions and writings of men like Johnson. Such seed produced literary work in the country. *Newspapers* now began to play a larger part in literature. They rose under the Commonwealth, but became important when the censorship which reduced them to a mere broadsheet of news was removed after the Revolution of 1688. The political sleep of the age of the two first Georges hindered their progress ; but in the reign of George III., after a struggle with which the name of John Wilkes and the author of the *Letters of Junius* are connected, and which lasted from 1764 to 1771, the press claimed and obtained the right to criticise the conduct and measures of ministers and the king ; and the further right to publish and comment on the debates in the two Houses.

4thly, *Communication with the Continent* had increased during the peaceable times of Walpole, and the wars that followed made it still more common. With its increase two new and great outbursts of literature told upon England. France sent the works of Montesquieu, of Voltaire, Rousseau, Diderot, D'Alembert, and the rest of the liberal thinkers who were called the Encyclopædists, to influence and quicken English literature on all the great subjects that belong to the social and political life of man. Afterwards, the fresh German movement, led by Lessing and others, and carried on by Goethe and Schiller, added its impulse to the poetical school that arose in England along with the French Revolution. These were the general causes of the rapid growth of literature from the time of the death of Swift and of Pope.

125. **Prose Literature between 1745 and the French Revolution** may be said to be bound up with the literary lives of one man and his friends. SAMUEL JOHNSON, born in 1709, and whose first important prose work, the *Life of Savage*, appeared in 1744, was the last representative of the literary king, who, like Dryden and Pope, held a court in London. Poor and unknown, he worked his way to fame, and his first poem, the *London*, 1738, satirised the town where he loved to live. His longer and better poem, *The Vanity of Human Wishes*, was published in 1749, and his moral power was never better shown than in its weighty verse. His one play, *Irene*, was acted in the same year. He carried on the periodical essays in the *Rambler*, 1750-2, but in it, as afterwards in the *Idler*, grace and lightness, the essence of this kind of essay, were lost. Driven by poverty, Johnson undertook a greater work: the *Dictionary of the English Language*, 1755, and his celebrated letter to Lord Chesterfield. concerning its publication, gave the death-blow to patronage, and makes Johnson the first of the modern literary men who, independent of patrons, live by their pen and find

in the public their only paymaster. He represents thus
a new class. In 1759 he set on foot the Didactic Novel
in *Rasselas*. For a time he was one of the political
pamphleteers, from 1770 to 1776. As he drew near to
his death his *Lives of the Poets* appeared as prefaces
to his edition of the poets in 1781, and lifted biography
into a higher place in literature. But he did even more
for literature as a converser, as the chief talker of a
literary club, than by writing, and we know exactly what
a power he was by the vivid *Biography*, the best in our
language, which James Boswell, with fussy devotedness,
made of his master in 1791. Side by side with Johnson
stands OLIVER GOLDSMITH, whose graceful and pure
English is a pleasant contrast to the loaded Latinism of
Johnson's style. The *Vicar of Wakefield*, the *History
of Animated Nature*, are at one in charm, and the
latter is full of that love of natural scenery, the sentiment of which is absent from Johnson's *Journey to
the Western Isles*. Both these men were masters of
Miscellaneous Literature, and in that class, I mention
here, as belonging to the latter half of the eighteenth
century, EDMUND BURKE'S *Vindication of Natural Society*, a parody of Bolingbroke; and his *Inquiry into
the Origin of our Ideas of the Sublime and Beautiful*,
a book which in 1757 introduced him to Johnson. Nor
ought we to forget Sir Joshua Reynolds, another of
Johnson's friends, who first made English art literary
in his *Discourses on Painting;* nor Horace Walpole,
whose *Anecdotes of Painting*, 1762-71, still please;

and whose familiar *Letters*, malicious, light as froth, but amusing, retail with liveliness all the gossip of the time. Among all these books on the intellectual subjects of life arose to delight the lovers of quiet and the country the *Natural History of Selborne*, by Gilbert White. His seeing eye and gentle heart are imaged in his fresh and happy style.

126. **The Novel.** — " There is more knowledge of the heart," said Johnson, " in one letter of Richardson's than in all *Tom Jones*," and the saying introduces SAMUEL RICHARDSON and HENRY FIELDING, the makers of the modern novel. Wholly distinct from merely narrative stories like Defoe's, the true novel is a story wrought round the passion of love to a tragic or joyous conclusion. But the name is applied now to any story of human life which is woven by the action of characters or of events on characters to a chosen conclusion. Its form, far more flexible than that of the drama, admits of almost infinite development. The whole of human life, at any time, at any place in the world, is its subject, and its vast sphere accounts for its vast production. *Pamela*, 1741, appeared while Pope was yet alive, and was the first of Richardson's novels. Like *Clarissa Harlowe*, 1748, it was written in the form of letters. The third of these books was *Sir Charles Grandison*. They are novels of Sentiment, and their purposeful morality and religion mark the change which had taken place in the morals and faith of literature since the preceding age.

Clarissa Harlowe is a masterpiece in its kind. Rich-

ardson himself is mastered day by day by the passionate
creation of his characters : and their variety and the
variety of their feelings are drawn with a slow, diffusive,
elaborate intensity which penetrates into the subtlest
windings of the human heart. But all the characters are
grouped round and enlighten Clarissa, the pure and
ideal star of womanhood. The pathos of the book, its
sincerity, its minute reality, have always, but slowly, impassioned its readers, and it stirred as absorbing an
interest in France as it did in England. "Take care,"
said Diderot, " not to open these enchanting books, if
you have any duties to fulfil." HENRY FIELDING followed
Pamela with *Joseph Andrews*, 1742, and Clarissa with
Tom Jones, 1749. At the same time, in 1748, appeared
TOBIAS SMOLLETT's first novel, *Roderick Random*. Both
wrote many other stories, but in the natural growth and
development of the story, and in the infitting of the
characters and events towards the conclusion, Tom
Jones is said to be the English model of the novel. The
constructive power of Fielding is absent from Smollett,
but in inventive tale-telling and in cynical characterisation, he is not easily equalled. Fielding, a master of
observing and of recording what he observed, draws
English life both in town and country with a coarse and
realistic pencil : Smollett is led beyond the truth of
nature into caricature. Ten years had thus sufficed to
create a wholly new literature.

LAURENCE STERNE published the first part of *Tristram
Shandy* in the same year as *Rasselas*, 1759. *Tristram*

Shandy and the *Sentimental Journey* are scarcely novels. They have no plot, they can scarcely be said to have any story. The story of *Tristram Shandy* wanders like a man in a labyrinth, and the humour is as labyrinthine as the story. It is carefully invented, and whimsically subtle; and the sentiment is sometimes true, but mostly affected. But a certain unity is given to the book by the admirable consistency of the characters. A little later, in 1766, Goldsmith's *Vicar of Wakefield* was the first and, perhaps, the most charming, of all those novels which we may call idyllic, which describe in a pure and gentle style the simple loves and lives of country people. Lastly, but still in the same circle of Johnson's friends, Miss Burney's *Evelina*, 1778, and her *Cecilia*, in which we detect Johnson's Roman hand, were the first novels of society.

127. **History** shared in the progress made after 1745 in prose writing, and was raised into the rank of literature by three of Johnson's contemporaries. All of them were influenced by the French school, by Montesquieu and Voltaire. DAVID HUME'S *History of England*, finished in 1761, is, in the writer's endeavour to make it a philosophic whole, in its clearness of narrative and purity of style, our first literary history. But he is neither exact, nor does he care to be exact. He does not love his subject, and he wants sympathy with mankind and with his country. His manner is the manner of Voltaire, passionless, keen, and elegant. DR. ROBERTSON, Hume's friend, was a careful and serious but also a cold writer. His histories of Scotland, of Charles V., and of America

show how historical interest again began to reach beyond
England. EDWARD GIBBON, whose *Decline and Fall of
the Roman Empire*, completed in 1788, gave a new impulse and a new model to historical literature, had no
more sympathy with humanity than Hume, and his irony
lowers throughout the human value of his history. But
he had creative power, originality, and the enjoyment and
imagination of his subject. It was at Rome in 1764, while
musing amid the ruins of the Capitol, that the idea of
writing his book arose in his mind, and his conception
of the work was that of an artist. Rome, eastern and
western, was painted in the centre of the world, dying
slowly like a lion in his cave. Around it and towards it he
drew all the nations and hordes and faiths that wrought
its ruin ; told their stories from the beginning, and the results on themselves and on the world of their victories over
Rome. This imaginative conception, together with the
collecting and use of every detail of the arts, literature,
customs, and manners of the times he described, the reading and use of all the contemporary literature, the careful
geographical detail, the marshalling of all this information
into his narration and towards his conclusion, the power
with which he moved over this vast arena, and the use of
a full if too grandiose a style to give importance to his
subject, makes him the one historian of the eighteenth
century whom modern research recognises as its master.

128. **Philosophical and Political Literature.** — Hutch-
eson, Hartley, and Reid were inferior as philosophers
to DAVID HUME, who inquired, while he followed Locke,

into the nature of the human understanding, and based philosophy upon psychology. He constructed a science of man; and finally limited all our knowledge to the world of phenomena revealed to us by experience. In morals he made utility the only measure of virtue. The first of his books, the *Treatise of Human Nature*, 1739, was written in France, and was followed by the *Inquiry concerning the Principles of Morals* in 1751. The *Dialogues on Natural Religion* were not published till after his death. These were his chief philosophical works. But in 1741–2, he had published two volumes of *Essays Moral and Political*, from which we might infer a political philosophy; and in 1752 the *Political Discourses* appeared, and they have been fairly said to be the cradle of political economy. But that subject was afterwards taken up by ADAM SMITH, a friend of Hume's, whose book on the *Moral Sentiments*, 1759, classes him also with the philosophers of Scotland. In his *Wealth of Nations*, 1776, by its theory that labour is the source of wealth, and that to give the labourer absolute freedom to pursue his own interest in his own way is the best means of increasing the wealth of the country; by its proof that all laws made to restrain, or to shape, or to promote commerce, were stumbling-blocks in the way of the wealth of a state, he created the Science of Political Economy, and brought the theory of Free Trade into practice. All the questions of labour and capital were now placed on a scientific basis, and since that time the literature of the whole of the subject has engaged great thinkers. As the

immense increase of the industry, wealth, and commerce
of the country from 1720 to 1770 had thus stirred inquiry
into the laws which regulate wealth, so now the Methodist movement, beginning in 1738, awoke an interest in
the poor, and gave the first impulse to popular education.
Social Reform became a literary subject, and fills a large
space until 1832, when political reform brought forward
new subjects, and the old subjects under new forms.
This new philanthropy was stirred into further growth
by the theories of the French Revolution, and these
theories, taking violent effect in France, roused into
opposition the genius of Edmund Burke.   Unlike Hume,
whose politics were elaborated in the study, Burke wrote
his political tracts and speeches face to face with events
and upon them.   Philosophical reasoning and poetic
passion were wedded together in them on the side of
Conservatism, and every art of eloquence was used with
the mastery that imagination gives.   In 1766 he defended
Lord Rockingham's administration ; he was then wrongly
suspected of the authorship of the *Letters of Junius*,
political invectives (1769–72), whose trenchant style has
preserved them to this day.   Burke's *Thoughts on the
Cause of the Present Discontents*, 1770, maintained an
aristocratic government ; and the next year appeared his
famous *Speech on American Taxation*, while that on
American Conciliation, 1774, was answered by his friend
Johnson in *Taxation no Tyranny*.   The most powerful
of his works were the *Reflections on the French Revolution*, 1790, the *Letter to a Noble Lord*, and the *Letters*

on a Regicide Peace, 1796-7. The first of these, answered by Thomas Paine's *Rights of Man*, and by
James Mackintosh's *Vindiciæ Gallicæ*, spread over all
England a terror of the principles of the Revolution ; the
third doubled the eagerness of England to carry on the
war with France. As a writer he needed more temperance, but, if he had possessed it, we should probably have
not had his magnificence. As an orator he ended by
wearying his hearers, but the very men who slept under
him in the House read over and over again the same
speech when published with renewed delight. Goldsmith's praise of him — that he "wound himself into
his subject like a serpent" — gives the reason why he
sometimes failed as an orator, why he generally succeeded as a writer.

129. **Prose from 1789-1832. Miscellaneous.** — The
death of Johnson marks a true period in our later prose
literature. London had ceased then to be the only literary
centre. Books were produced in all parts of the country,
and Edinburgh had its own famous school of literature.
The doctrines of the French Revolution were eagerly
supported and eagerly opposed, and stirred like leaven
through a great part of the literary work of England.
Later on, through Coleridge, Scott, Carlyle, and others,
the influence of Lessing, Goethe, of all the new literature
of Germany, began to tell upon us, in theology, in philosophy, and even in the novel. The great English
Journals, the *Morning Chronicle*, the *Times*, the *Morning
Post*, the *Morning Herald*, were all set on foot between

1775 and 1793, between the war with America and the
war with France; and when men like Coleridge and
Canning began to write in them the literature of journal-
ism was started.   A literature especially directed towards
education arose in the *Cyclopædias*, which began in 1778,
and rapidly developed into vast dictionaries of knowledge.   Along with them were the many series issued
from Edinburgh and London of *Popular Miscellanies*.   A
crowd of literary men found employment in writing about
books rather than in writing them, and the literature of
Criticism became a power.   The *Edinburgh Review* was
established in 1802, and the *Quarterly*, its political op-
ponent, in 1809, and these were soon followed by *Fraser's*
and *Blackwood's Magazine*.   Jeffrey, Professor Wilson,
Sydney Smith, and a host of others wrote in these reviews
on contemporary events and books.   Interest in contemporary stimulated interest in past literature, and Coleridge, Charles Lamb, Thomas Campbell, Hazlitt, Southey,
and Savage Landor carried on that study of the Elizabethan and earlier poets to which Warton had given so
much impulse in the eighteenth century.   Literary quarrels concerning the nature of poetry produced books like
Coleridge's *Biographia Literaria*; and Wordsworth's
Essays on his own art are in admirable prose.   DE
QUINCEY, one of the Edinburgh School, is, owing to the
over-lapping and involved melody of his style, one of our
best, as he is one of our most various miscellaneous
writers : and with him for masculine English, for various
learning and forcible fancy, and, not least, for his vigor-

ous lyrical work and poems, we may rank WALTER
SAVAGE LANDOR, who deepened an interest in English
and classic literature and made a literature of his own.
CHARLES LAMB's inimitable fineness of perception was
shown in his criticisms on the old dramatists, but his
most original work was the *Essays of Elia*, in which he
renewed the lost grace of the Essay, and with a humour
not less gentle, more surprising, more self-pleased than
Addison's.

130. **Theological Literature** had received a new impulse in 1738–91 from the evangelising work of John
Wesley and Whitfield; and their spiritual followers,
Thomas Scott, Newton, and Cecil, made by their writings the Evangelical School. William Paley, in his
Evidences, defended Christianity from the common-sense
point of view; while the sermons of Robert Hall and of
Dr. Chalmers are, in different ways, fine examples of
devotional and philosophical eloquence.

131. The eloquent intelligence of Edinburgh con-
tinued the **Literature of Philosophy** in the work of
Dugald Stewart, Reid's successor, and in that of Dr.
Browne, who for the most part opposed Hume's funda-
mental idea that Psychology is a part of the science of
life. Coleridge brought his own and German philosophy
into the treatment of theological questions in the *Aids to
Reflection*, and into various subjects of life in the *Friend*.
The utilitarian view of morals was put forth by Jeremy
Bentham with great power, but his chief work was in the
province of law. He founded the philosophy of juris-

prudence, he invented a scientific legal vocabulary, and we
owe to him almost every reform that has improved our law.
He wrote also on political economy, but that subject was
more fully developed by Malthus, Ricardo, and James Mill.

132. **Biography** and **travel** are linked at many points
to history, and the literature of the former was enriched
by Hayley's *Cowper*, Southey's *Life of Nelson*, McCrie's
Life of Knox, Moore's *Life of Byron*, and Lockhart's
Life of Scott. As to travel, it has rarely produced books
which may be called literature, but the works of biog-
raphers and travellers have brought together the materials of literature. Bruce left for Africa in 1762, and in
the next seventy years Africa, Egypt, Italy, Greece,
the Holy Land, and the Arctic Regions were made the
common property of literary men.

133. **The Historical School** produced Mitford's *History of Greece* and Lingard's *History of England;* but
it was Henry Hallam who for the first time wrote history
in this country without prejudice. His *Europe during
the Middle Ages*, 1818, is distinguished by its exhaustive
and judicial summing-up of facts, and his *Constitutional
History of England* opened a new vein of history in the
best way. Since his time, history has become more
and more worthy of the name of fine literature, and the
critical schools of our own day, while making truth the
first thing, and the philosophy of history the second, do
not disdain but exact the graces of literature. But of all
the forms of prose literature, the novel was the most
largely used and developed.

P

134. **The Novel.** — The stir of thought made by the French Revolution had many side influences on novel-writing. The political stories of Thomas Holcroft and William Godwin disclosed a new realm to the novelist. The *Canterbury Tales* of Sophia and Harriet Lee, and the wild and picturesque tales of Mrs. Radcliffe introduced the romantic novel. Mrs. Inchbald's *Simple Story*, 1791, started the novel of passion, whilst Mrs. Opie made domestic life the sphere of her graceful and pathetic stories, 1806. Miss Edgeworth in her Irish stories gave the first impulse to the novel of national character, and in her other tales to the novel with a moral purpose, 1800–47. Miss Austen, "with an exquisite touch which renders commonplace things and characters interesting from truth of description and sentiment," produced the best novels we have of everyday society, 1811–17. With the peace of 1815 arose new forms of fiction; and travel, now popular, gave birth to the tale of foreign society and manners; of these, Thomas Hope's *Anastasius* (1819) was the first. The classical novel arose in Lockhart's *Valerius*, and Miss Ferrier's humorous tales of Scottish life were pleasant to Walter Scott.

It was WALTER SCOTT, however, who raised the whole of the literature of the novel into one of the great influences that bear on human life. Men are still alive who remember the wonder and delight with which *Waverley* (1814) was welcomed. The swiftness of work combined with vast diligence which belongs to very great

genius belonged to him. *Guy Mannering* was written
in six weeks, and the *Bride of Lammermoor*, as great in
fateful pathos as *Romeo and Juliet*, but more solemn,
was done in a fortnight. There is then a certain *abandon*
in his work which removes it from the dignity of the
ancient writers, but we are repaid for this loss by the intensity, and the animated movement, the clear daylight,
and the inspired delight in and with which he invented
and wrote his stories. It is not composition ; it is Scott
actually present in each of his personages, doing their
deeds and speaking their thoughts. His national tales
—and his own country was his best inspiration—are
written with such love for the characters and the scenes,
that we feel his living joy and love underneath each of
the stories as a completing charm, as a spirit that en-
chants the whole. And in these tales and in his poems
his own deep kindliness, his sympathy with human
nature, united, after years of enmity, the Highlands to
the Lowlands. In the vivid portraiture and dramatic
reality of such tales as *Old Mortality* and *Quentin Dur-
ward* he created the historical novel. " All is great,"
said Goethe, speaking of one of these historical tales, "in
the Waverley Novels ; material, effect, characters, execution." In truth, so natural is Scott's invention, that it
seems creation — even the landscape is woven through
the events and in harmony with them. His comprehensive power, which drew with the same certainty so many
characters in so many various classes, was the direct result of his profound sympathy with the simpler feelings

of the human heart, and of his pleasure in writing so as to make human life more beautiful and more good in the eyes of men. He was always romantic, and his personal romance did not fail him when he came to be old. Like Shakespeare he kept that to the very close. The later years of his life were dark, but the almost unrivalled nobleness of his battle against ill fortune proves that he was as great-hearted as he was great. "God bless thee, Walter, my man," said his uncle, "thou hast risen to be great, but thou wast always good." His last long tale of power was the *Fair Maid of Perth*, 1828, and his last effort, in 1831, was made the year before he died. That year, 1832, which saw the deaths of Goethe and Scott, is the close of an epoch in literature.

CHAPTER VIII

POETRY FROM 1730 TO 1832

135. The Elements and Forms of the New Poetry. —
The poetry we are now to study may be divided into two
periods. The first dates from about the middle of
Pope's life, and closes with the publication of Cowper's
Task, 1785; the second begins with the *Task* and closes
in 1832. The first is not wrongly called a time of transition. The influence of the poetry of the past lasted;
new elements were added to poetry, and new forms of it
took shape. There was a change also in the style and
in the subject of poetry. Under these heads I shall
bring together the various poetical works of this period.

(1) The influence of the didactic and satirical poetry
of the critical school lingered among the new elements
which first modified and then changed poetry altogether.
It is found in Johnson's two satires on the manners of
his time, the *London*, 1738, and the *Vanity of Human
Wishes*, 1749; in Robert Blair's dull poem of *The
Grave*, 1743; in Edward Young's *Night Thoughts*, 1743,
a poem on the immortality of the soul, and in his satires
on *The Universal Passion* of fame; in the tame work of

Richard Savage, Johnson's poor friend ; and in the short-lived but vigorous satires of Charles Churchill, who died in 1764, twenty-one years after Savage. The *Pleasures of the Imagination*, 1744, by Mark Akenside, belongs also in spirit to the time of Queen Anne, and was suggested by Addison's essays in the *Spectator* on Imagination.

(2) The study of the Greek and Latin classics revived, and with it a more artistic poetry. Men like Thomas Gray and William Collins attempted to "revive the just designs of Greece," not only in fitness of language, but in perfection of form. They are commonly placed together, but the genius of each was essentially different. What they had in common belonged to the age in which they lived, and one of these elements was a certain artificial phrasing from which they found it difficult to escape. Both sought beauty more than their fellows, but Collins found it more than Gray. He had the greater grace and the sweeter simplicity, and his *Ode to Simplicity* tells us the direction in which poetry was going. His best work, like *The Ode to Evening*, is near to Keats, and recalls that poet's imaginative way. His inferior work is often rude and his style sometimes obscure, but when he is touched by joy in "ecstatic trial," or when he sits with Melancholy in love of peace and gentle musing, he is indeed inspired by truth and loveliness. He died too young to do much in a perfect way. Gray was different. All is clear light in his work. There is no gradual dusky veil such as Collins threw with so much

charm over his expression. Out of his love of Greek
work he drew his fine lucidity. Out of the spirit of his
own time and from his own cultivated experience he
drew the moral criticism of human life which gives his
poetry its weight, even its heaviness. It is true the
moral criticism, even in the *Elegy*, shares in the commonplace, but it was not so commonplace in his time,
and it is so full of a gentle charity that it transcends his
time. He moved with easy power over many forms of
poetry, but there is naturalness and no rudeness in the
power. It was adorned by high ornament and finish.
The *Odes* are far beyond their age, especially *The
Progress of Poesy*, and each kind has its own appropri-
ate manner. The *Elegy* will always remain one of the
beloved poems of Englishmen. It is not only a piece of
exquisite work; it is steeped in England. It is contemplative and might have been cold. On the contrary,
even when it is conventional, it has a certain passion in
its contemplation which is one of the marks of the work
of Gray. Had he had more imagination he would have
been greater, but the spirit of his age repressed nature in
him. But he stands clear and bright, along with his
brother, on the ridge between the old and the new.
Having ascended through the old poetry, he saw the new
landscape of song below him, felt its fresher air, and sent
his own power into the men who arose after him.

(3) The study of the Elizabethan and the earlier
poets like Chaucer, and of the whole course of poetry in
England, was taken up with great interest. Shakespeare

and Chaucer had engaged both Dryden and Pope; but the whole subject was now enlarged. Gray, like Pope, projected a history of English poetry, and his *Ode on the Progress of Poesy* illustrates this new interest. Thomas Warton wrote his *History of English Poetry*, 1774-81, and brought the lovers of poetry into closer contact with Chaucer. Pope's, Theobald's, Sir Thomas Hanmer's, and Warburton's editions of Shakespeare were succeeded by Johnson's in 1765; and Garrick began the restoration of the genuine text of Shakespeare's plays for the stage. Spenser formed the spirit and work of some poets, and Thomas Warton wrote an essay on the *Faerie Queene*. William Shenstone's *Schoolmistress*, 1742, was one of these Spenserian poems, and so was Thomson's delightful *Castle of Indolence*, 1748. James Beattie, in the *Minstrel*, 1771, also followed the stanza and manner of Spenser.

(4) A new element — interest in the romantic past — was aided by the publication of Dr. Percy's *Reliques of Ancient English Poetry*, 1765. The narrative ballad and the narrative romance, afterwards taken up and perfected by Sir Walter Scott, had already begun to strike their roots afresh in English poetry. *The Braes of Yarrow* and Mallet's *William and Margaret* were written before 1725. Men now began to seek among the ruder times of history for wild, natural stories of human life; and the pleasure in these increased and accompanied the growing love of lonely, even of savage scenery. Even before the *Reliques* were published, Gray's power of

seeing into the right thing is seen in this matter. He
entered the new paths, and in a new atmosphere, when
he wrote of the Norse legends, or studied what he could
learn of the poetry of Wales. The *Ossian*, 1762, of
James Macpherson, which imposed itself on the public
as a translation of Gaelic epic poems, is an example of
this new element. Still more remarkable in this way
were the poems of Thomas Chatterton,

> " That sleepless soul who perished in his pride."

He pretended to have discovered, in a muniment room
at Bristol, the *Death of Sir Charles Bawdin*, and other
poems, by an imaginary monk named Thomas Rowley,
1768. Written with quaint spelling, and with a great
deal of lyrical invention, they raised around them a great
controversy. His early death, at seventeen, has, by the
pity of it, lifted his lyric poetry, romantic as it is, into
more repute than it deserves.

136. **Change of Style.** — We have seen how the natural
style of the Elizabethan poets had passed into a style
which erred against the simplicity of natural expression.
In reaction from this the critical poets set aside natural
feeling, and wrote according to intellectual rules of art.
Their style lost life and fire; and losing these, lost art
and gained artifice. Unwarmed by natural feeling, it became as unnatural a style, though in a different way,
as that of the later Elizabethan poets. But out of the
failure of nature without art, and of art without nature,

and out of the happy union of both in scattered and
particular examples, the way was now ready for a style
in which the art should itself be nature, and it found
its first absolute expression in a few of Cowper's lyrics.
His style, in such poems as the *Lines to Mary Unwin*,
and in *The Castaway*, arises out of the simplest pathos,
and yet is almost as pure in expression as a Greek elegy.
The work was then done; but the element of fervent
passion did not enter into poetry till the poems of Robert
Burns appeared in 1786.

137. **Change of Subject. Nature.** — The Poets have
always worked on two great subjects — man and nature.
Up to the age of Pope the subject of man was chiefly
treated, and we have seen how many phases it went
through.   There remained the subject of nature and of
man's relation to it; that is, of the visible landscape, sea,
and sky, and all that men feel in contact with them.
Natural scenery had been hitherto chiefly used as a background to the picture of human life.   It now began to
occupy a much larger space in poetry, and after a time
grew to occupy a distinct place of its own apart from
man.   Much of this was owing to the opening out of the
wild country by new roads and to the increased safety of
travel.   It is the growth of this new subject which will
engage us now.

138. **The Poetry of Natural Description.** — We have
already found in the poets, but chiefly among the lyrical
poets, a pleasure in rural scenery and the emotions it
awakened.   But nature is only, as in the work of Shake-

speare, Marvell, Milton, Vaughan, or Herrick, incident-
ally introduced. The first poem devoted to natural
description appeared while Pope was yet alive, in the
very midst of the town poetry. It was the *Seasons*,
1726–30; and it is curious, remembering what I have
said about the peculiar turn of the Scots for natural description, that it was the work of JAMES THOMSON, a Scotsman. It described the landscape and country life of
Spring, Summer, Autumn, and Winter. He wrote with
his eye upon their scenery, and even when he wrote of
it in his room, it was with "a recollected love." The
descriptions were too much like catalogues, the very
fault of the previous Scottish poets, and his style was
heavy and cold, but he was the first poet who deliber-
ately led the English people into that separated world of
natural description which has enchanted us in the work
of modern poetry. The impulse he gave was soon followed. Men left the town to visit the country and
record their feelings. John Dyer's *Grongar Hill*, 1726,
a description of a journey in South Wales, and his *Fleece*,
1757, are full of country sights and scenes: and even
Akenside mingled his spurious philosophy with pictures
of the solitudes of nature.

Foreign travel now enlarged the love of nature. The
wilder country of England was eagerly visited. Gray's
letters, some of the best in the English language, describe the landscape of Yorkshire and Westmoreland with
a minuteness quite new in English literature. In his
poetry he used the description of nature as " its most

graceful ornament," but never made it the subject. It was interwoven with reflections on human life, and used to point its moral. Collins observes the same method in his *Ode on the Passions* and the *Ode to Evening*. There is as yet but little love of nature entirely for its own sake. A further step was made by Oliver Goldsmith in his *Traveller*, 1764, a sketch of national manners and governments, and in his *Deserted Village*, 1770. He describes natural scenery with less emotion than Collins, but does not moralise it like Gray. The scenes he paints are pure pictures, and he has no personal interest in them. The next step was made a few years later by some fourth-rate men like the two Wartons. Their poems do not speak of nature and human life, but of nature and themselves. They see the reflection of their own passions in the woods and streams, and this self-conscious pleasure with lonely nature grew slowly into a main subject of poetry. These were the steps towards that love of nature for its own sake which we shall find in the poets who followed Cowper. One poem of the time almost anticipates it. It is the *Minstrel*, 1771, of JAMES BEATTIE. This poem represents a young poet educated almost altogether by solitary communion with nature, and by love of her beauty; and both in the spirit and treatment of the first part of the story resembles very closely Wordsworth's description of his own education by nature in the beginning of the *Prelude*.

139. **Further Change of Subject. Man.** — During this time the interest in mankind, that is, in man inde-

pendent of nation, class, and caste, which we have seen
in prose, began to influence poetry. One form of it
appeared in the pleasure the poets began to take in
men of other nations than England; another form of it
— and this was increased by the Methodist revival — was
a deep feeling for the lives of the poor. Thomson
speaks with sympathy of the Siberian exile and the
Mecca pilgrim, and the *Traveller* of Goldsmith enters
into foreign questions. His *Deserted Village*, Shenstone's
Schoolmistress, Gray's *Elegy* celebrate the annals of the
poor. Michael Bruce in his *Lochleven* praises the " secret
primrose path of rural life," and Dr. John Langhorne in
his *Country Justice* pleads the cause of the poor and
paints their sorrows. Connected with this new element
is the simple ballad of simple love, such as Shenstone's
Jemmy Dawson, Mickle's *Mariner's Wife*, Goldsmith's
Edwin and Angelina, poems which started afresh a delightful type of poetry, afterwards worked out more completely in the *Lyrical Ballads* of Wordsworth. In a class
apart stands the *Song to David*, a long poem written by
Christopher Smart, a friend of Johnson's. Its power of
metre and imaginative presentation of thoughts and
things, and its mingling of sweet and grand religious
poetry ought to make it better known.

140. **Scottish Poetry** illustrates and anticipates the
poetry of the poor and the ballad. We have not mentioned it since Sir David Lyndsay, for with the exception
of stray songs its voice was almost silent for a century
and a half. It revived in ALLAN RAMSAY, a friend of

Pope and Gay. His light pieces of rustic humour were followed by the *Tea Table Miscellany* and the *Ever-Green*, collections of existing Scottish songs mixed up with some of his own. Ramsay's pastoral drama of the *Gentle Shepherd*, 1725, is a pure, tender, and genuine picture of Scottish life and love among the poor and in the country. ROBERT FERGUSON deserves to be named because he kindled the muse of Burns, but his occasional pieces, 1773, are chiefly concerned with the rude and humorous life of Edinburgh. One man, Michael Bruce, illustrates the English transition of which I have spoken. The Ballad, Scotland's dear companion, took a more modern but pathetic form in some Yarrow poems, in *Auld Robin Gray* and the *Lament for Flodden*. The peculiarities I have dwelt on already continue in this Scottish revival. There is the same nationality, the same rough wit, the same love of nature, but the love of colour has lessened.

141. **The Second Period of the New Poetry.** — The new elements and the changes on which I have dwelt are expressed by three poets — Cowper, Crabbe, and Burns. But before these we must mention the poems of WILLIAM BLAKE, the artist, and for three reasons. (1) They represent the new elements. *The Poetical Sketches*, written in 1777, illustrate the new study of the Elizabethan poets. Blake imitated Spenser, and in his short fragment of *Edward III.* we hear again the note of Marlowe's violent imagination. A short poem *To the Muses* is a cry for the restoration to English poetry of the old poetic passion it had lost. In some ballad poems

we trace the influence represented by *Ossian* and quickened by the publication of Percy's *Reliques*. (2) We
find also in his work certain elements which belong to
the second period of which I shall soon speak. The
love of animals is one. A great love of children and
the poetry of home is another. He also anticipated in
1789 and 1794, when his *Songs of Innocence* and *Experience* were written, the simple natural poetry of ordinary
life which Wordsworth perfected in the Lyrical Ballads,
1798. Moreover, the democratic element, the hatred of
priestcraft, and the cry against social wrongs which came
much later into English poetry spring up in his poetry.
Then, he was a full Mystic, and through his mysticism
appears that search after the true aims of life and after a
freer theology which characterise our poetry after 1832.
(3) He cast back as well as forward, and reproduced in
his songs the spirit, movement, and music of the Elizabethan songs. The little poems in the *Songs of Innocence*, on infancy and first motherhood, and on subjects
like the *Lamb*, are without rival in our language for simplicity, tenderness, and joy. The *Songs of Experience*
give the reverse side of the *Songs of Innocence*, and they
see the evil of the world as a child with a man's heart
would see it — with exaggerated horror. This small but
predictive work of Blake, coming where it did, between
1777 and 1794, going back to Elizabethan lyrics and forward to those of Wordsworth, is very remarkable.

142. **William Cowper's** first poems were some of the
Olney Hymns, 1779, and in these the religious poetry of

Charles Wesley was continued. The profound personal religion, gloomy even to insanity as it often became, which fills the whole of Cowper's poetry, introduced a theological element into English poetry which continually increased till it died out with Browning and Tennyson. His didactic and satirical poems in 1782 link him backwards to the last age. His translation of Homer, 1791, and of shorter pieces from the Latin and Greek, connects him with the classical influence, his interest in Milton with the revived study of the English poets. The playful and gentle vein of humour which he showed in *John Gilpin* and other poems, opened a new kind of verse to poets. With this kind of humour is connected a simple pathos of which Cowper is a great master. The *Lines to Mary Unwin* and to his *Mother's Picture* prove, with the work of Blake, that pure natural feeling wholly free from artifice had returned to English song. A new element was also introduced by him and Blake — the love of animals and the poetry of their relation to man, a vein plentifully worked by after poets. His greatest work was the *Task*, 1785. It is mainly a description of himself and a life in the country, his home, his friends, his thoughts as he walked, the quiet landscape of Olney, the life of the poor people about him, mixed up with disquisitions on political and social subjects, and at the end, a prophecy of the victory of the Kingdom of God. The change in it in relation to the subject of nature is very great. Cowper loves nature entirely for her own sake. The change in relation to the subject of man is equally

great. The idea of mankind as a whole which we have
seen growing up is fully formed in Cowper's mind. And
though splendour and passion were added by the poets
who succeeded him to the new poetry, yet they worked
on the thoughts he had begun to express, and he is so
far their forerunner.

143. **George Crabbe** took up the side of the poetry of
man which had to do with the lives of the poor in the
Village, 1783, and in the *Parish Register*, 1807. In the
short tales related in these books we are brought face to
face with the sacrifices, temptations, love, and crimes of
humble life, and the effect of these poems in widening
human sympathies was great among his readers. His
work wanted the humour of Cowper, and though often
pathetic and always forcible, was perhaps too unrelenting
for pure pathos. He did much better work afterwards
in his *Tales of the Hall*. His work on nature is as minute and accurate, but as limited in range of excellence,
as his work on man. ROBERT BLOOMFIELD, himself a
poor shoemaker, added to this poetry of the poor. The
Farmer's Boy, finished in 1798, and the *Rural Tales*,
are poems as cheerful as Crabbe's were stern, and his
descriptions of rural life are not less faithful. The poetry
of the poor, thus started, long continued in our verse.
Wordsworth added to it new features, and Thomas Hood
in short pieces like the *Song of the Shirt* gave it a direct
bearing on social evils.

144. One element, the passionate treatment of love,
had been on the whole absent from our poetry since the

Q

Restoration. It was restored by **Robert Burns.** In his love songs we hear again, even more simply, more directly, the same natural music which in the age of Elizabeth enchanted the world. It was as a love-poet that he began to write, and the first edition of his poems appeared in 1786. But he was not only the poet of love, but also of the new excitement about mankind. Himself poor, he sang the poor. He did the same work in Scotland in 1786 which Crabbe began in England in 1783 and Cowper in 1785, and it is worth remarking how the dates run together. As in Cowper, so also in Burns, the further widening of human sympathies is shown in his tenderness for animals. He carried on also the Celtic elements of Scottish poetry, but the rattling fun of the *Jolly Beggars* and of *Tam o' Shanter* is united to a life-like painting of human character which is peculiarly English. A large gentleness of feeling often made his wit into that true humour which is more English than Celtic, and the passionate pathos of such poems as *Mary in Heaven* is connected with this vein of English humour. The special nationality of Scottish poetry is as strong in Burns as in any of his predecessors, but it is also mingled with a larger view of man than the merely national one. Nor did he fail to carry on the Scottish love of nature, though he shows the English influence in using natural description not for the love of nature alone, but as a background for human love. It was the strength of his passions and the weakness of his moral will which made his poetry and spoilt his life.

145. **The French Revolution and the Poets.** — Certain ideas relating to mankind considered as a whole had been growing up in Europe for some centuries, and we have seen their influence on the work of Cowper, Crabbe, and Burns. These ideas spoke of a return to nature, and of the best life being found in the country rather than in the town, so that the simple life of the poor and the scenery of the country were idealised into subjects for poetry. They spoke also of natural rights that belonged to every man, and which united all men to one another. All men were equal, and free, and brothers. There was therefore only one class, the class of man ; only one nation, the nation of man, of which all were citizens. The divisions therefore which wealth and rank and caste and national boundaries had made were theo- retically put aside as wrong. Such ideas had been growing into the political, moral, and religious life of men ever since the Renaissance, and they brought with them their own emotions. France, which does much of the formative work of Europe, had for some time past expressed them constantly in her literature. She now expressed them in the action which overthrew the Bastille in 1789 and proclaimed the new Constitution in the fol- lowing year. They passed then from an abstract to a concrete form, and became active powers in the world, and it is round the excitement they kindled in England that the work of the poets from 1790 to 1832 can best be grouped. Wordsworth, Coleridge, and Southey ac- cepted them at first with joy, but receded from them

when they ended in the violence of the Reign of Terror, and in the imperialism of Napoleon. Scott turned from them with pain to write of the romantic past which they destroyed. Byron did not express them themselves, but he expressed the whole of the revolutionary spirit in its action against old social opinions. Shelley took them up after the reaction against them had begun to die away, and in half his poetry re-expressed them. Two men, Rogers and Keats, were wholly untouched by them. One special thing they did for poetry. They brought back, by the powerful feelings they kindled in men, passion into its style, into all its work about man, and through that, into its work about nature.

But, in giving the French Revolution its due weight, we must always remember that these ideas existed already in England and were expressed by the poets. The French outburst precipitated them, and started our new poetry with a rush and a surprise. But the enthusiasm soon suffered a chill, and a great part of our new poetry was impelled, not by the Revolution, but by the indignant revolt against what followed on it. Moreover, I have already shown that fully half of the new lines of thought and feeling on which the poetry of England ran in the nineteenth century had been laid down in the century which preceded it, and they were completed now.

146. **Robert Southey** began his political life with the revolutionary poem of *Wat Tyler*, 1794; and between 1801 and 1814 wrote *Thalaba*, *Madoc*, *The Curse of*

Kehama, and *Roderick the Last of the Goths*. *Thalaba* and *Kehama* are stories of Arabian and of Indian mythology. They are real poems, and have the interest of good narrative and the charm of musical metre, but the finer spirit of poetry is not in them. *Roderick* is the most human and the most poetical. His *Vision of Judgment*, written on the death of George III., and ridiculed by Byron in another *Vision*, proves him to have become a Tory of Tories. SAMUEL T. COLERIDGE could not turn round so completely, but the stormy enthusiasm of his early poems was lessened when in 1796 he wrote the *Ode on the Departing Year* and *France, an Ode*, 1798. His early poems are transitional, partly based on Gray, violent and obscure in style. But when he came to live with Wordsworth, he gained simplicity, and for a short time his poetic spirit was at the height of joy and production. But his early disappointment about France was bitter, and then, too, he injured his own life. The noble ode to *Dejection* is instinct not only with his own wasted life, but with the sorrow of one who has had golden ideals and found them turn in his hands to clay. His best work is but little, but unique of its kind. For exquisite metrical movement and for imaginative phantasy, there is nothing in our language to be compared with *Christabel* and *Kubla Khan*. The *Ancient Mariner*, published as one of the *Lyrical Ballads* in 1798, belongs to the dim country between earth and heaven, where the fairy music is heard. sometimes dreadful, sometimes lovely, but always lonely. All that he did excellently might be bound up in twenty pages, but it should be bound in pure gold.

147. Of all the poets misnamed Lake Poets, **William Wordsworth** was the greatest. Born in 1770, educated on the banks of Esthwaite, he loved the scenery of the Lakes as a boy, lived among it in his manhood, and died in 1850 at Rydal Mount, close to Rydal Lake. He took his degree in 1791 at Cambridge. The year before, he had made a short tour on the Continent, and stepped on the French shore at the very time when the whole land was "mad with joy." The end of 1791 saw him again in France and living at Orleans. He threw himself eagerly into the Revolution, joined the "patriot side," and came to Paris just after the September massacre of 1792. Narrowly escaping the fate of his friends the Brissotins, he got home to England before the execution of Louis XVI. in 1793, and published his *Descriptive Sketches* and the *Evening Walk*. His sympathy with the French continued, and he took their side against his own country. He was poor, but his friend Raisley Calvert left him 900*l.* and enabled him to live the simple life he had then chosen —the life of a retired poet. At first we find him at Racedown, where in 1797 he made friendship with Coleridge, and then at Alfoxden, in Somerset, where he and Coleridge planned and published in 1798 the first volume of the *Lyrical Ballads*. After a winter in Germany with Coleridge, where the *Prelude* was begun, he took a small cottage at Grasmere, and the

first book of *The Recluse* tells of his settlement in that
quiet valley. It tells also of the passion and intensity
of the young man who saw infinite visions of work
before him, and who lived poor, in daily and unbroken
joy. It was in this irradiated world that he wrote the
best of his poems. There in 1805–6 he finished the
Prelude. Another set of the *Lyrical Ballads* appeared
in 1800, and in 1807 other poems. The *Excursion*
belongs to 1814. From that time till his death he
produced from his home at Rydal Mount a long succession of poems.

148. **Wordsworth and Nature.** — The *Prelude* is the
history of Wordsworth's poetical growth from a child
till 1806. It reveals him as the poet of Nature and
of Man. His view of nature was entirely different from
that which up to his time the poets had held. Wordsworth conceived, as poet, that nature was alive. It had,
he imagined, one living soul which, entering into flower,
stream, or mountain, gave them each a soul of their
own. Between this Spirit in nature and the mind of
man there was a prearranged harmony which enabled
nature to communicate its own thoughts to man, and
man to reflect upon them, until an absolute union between them was established. This was, in fact, the
theory of the Florentine Neo-Platonists of the Renaissance. They did not care for nature, but when Wordsworth either reconceived or adopted this idea, it made
him the first who loved nature with a personal love,
for she, being living, and personal, and not only his

reflection, was made capable of being loved as a man loves a woman. He could brood on her character, her ways, her words, her life, as he did on those of his wife or sister. Hence arose his minute and loving observation of her and his passionate description of all her life. This was his poetic philosophy with regard to nature, and bound up as it was with the idea of God as the Thought which pervaded and made the world, it rose into a poetic religion of nature and man.

149. **Wordsworth and Man.** — The poet of nature in this special way, Wordsworth is even more the poet of man. It is by his close and loving penetration into the realities and simplicities of human life that he himself makes his claim on our reverence as a poet. He relates in the *Prelude* how he had been led through his love of nature to honour man. The shepherds of the Lake hills, the dalesmen, had been seen by him as part of the wild scenery in which he lived, and he mixed up their life with the grandeur of nature and came to honour them as part of her being. The love of nature led him to the love of man. It was exactly the reverse order to that of the previous poets. At Cambridge, and afterwards, in the crowd of London and in his first tour on the Continent, he received new impressions of the vast world of man, but nature still remained the first. It was only during his life in France and in the excitement of the new theories and their activity that he was swept away from nature and found himself thinking of man as distinct from her and first

in importance. But the hopes he had formed from the
Revolution broke down. All his dreams about a new
life for mankind were made vile when France gave up
liberty for Napoleon; and he was left without love of
nature or care for man. It was then that his sister
Dorothy, herself worthy of mention in a history of literature, led him back to his early love of nature and restored
his mind. Living quietly at Grasmere, he sought in the
simple lives of the dalesmen round him for the foundations of what he felt to be a truer view of mankind than
the theories of the French Revolution afforded. And
in thinking and writing of the common duties and faith,
kindnesses and truth of lowly men, he found in man once
more

> an object of delight,
> Of pure imagination and of love.

With that he recovered his interest in the larger movements of mankind. His love of liberty and hatred of
oppression revived. He saw in Napoleon the enemy of
the human race. A series of sonnets followed the events
on the Continent. One recorded his horror at the attack
on the Swiss, another mourned the fate of Venice, another the fate of Toussaint the negro chief; others celebrated the struggle of Hofer and the Tyrolese, others
the struggle of Spain. Two thanksgiving odes rejoiced in
the overthrow of the oppressor at Waterloo. He became
conservative in his old age, but his interest in social
and national movements did not decay. He wrote, and

badly, on Education, the Poor Laws, and other subjects. When almost seventy he took the side of the
Carbonari and sympathised with the Italian struggle.
He was truly a poet of mankind. But his chief work
was done in his own country and among his own folk ;
and he is the foremost singer of those who threw around
the lives of homely men and women the glory and sweetness of song. He made his verse "deal boldly with sub-
stantial things" ; his theme was "no other than the very
heart of man" ; and his work has become what he desired it to be, a force to soothe and heal the weary soul
of the world, a power like one of nature's, to strengthen
or awaken the imagination in mankind. He lies asleep
now among the people he loved, in the green churchyard
of Grasmere, by the side of the stream of Rothay, in a
place as quiet as his life. Few spots on earth are more
sacred than his grave.

150. **Sir Walter Scott** was Wordsworth's dear friend,
and his career as a poet began with the *Lay of the Last
Minstrel*, 1805. But before that he had collected,
inspired by his revolt from the Revolution to the re-
gretted past, the songs and ballads of the Border.
Marmion was published in 1808, and the *Lady of the
Lake* in 1810. These were his best poems ; the others,
with the exception of some lyrics which touch the sadness and exultation of life with equal power, do not
count in our estimate of him. He brought the narrative
poem into a new and delightful excellence. In *Marmion* and the *Lady of the Lake* his wonderful inventiveness

in story and character is at its height, and it is matched
by the vividness of his natural description. No poet,
and in this he carries on the old Scottish quality, is a
finer colourist. Nearly all his natural description is of
the wild scenery of the Highlands and the Lowland
moorland. He touched it with a pencil so light, graceful, and true, that the very names are made forever
romantic ; while his faithful love for the places he describes fills his poetry with the finer spirit of his own
tender humanity.

151. Scotland produced another poet in **Thomas
Campbell**. His earliest poem, the *Pleasures of Hope*,
1799, belonged in its formal rhythm and rhetoric, and
in its artificial feeling for nature, to the time of Thomson
and Gray rather than to the newer time. He will chiefly
live by his lyrics. *Hohenlinden*, the *Battle of the Baltic*,
the *Mariners of England*, are splendid specimens of the
war poetry of England ; and the *Song to the Evening Star*
and *Lord Ullin's Daughter*, full of tender feeling, mark
the influence of the more natural style that Wordsworth
had brought to excellence.

152. **Rogers and Moore.** —The *Pleasures of Memory*,
1792, and the *Italy*, 1822, of Samuel Rogers, are the
work of a slow and cultivated mind, and contain some
laboured but fine descriptions. The curious thing is that,
living apart in a courtly region of culture, there is not a
trace in all his work that Europe and England and
society had passed during his life through a convulsion
of change. To that convulsion the best poems of THOMAS

MOORE may be referred. They are the songs he wrote
to the Irish airs collected in 1796. The best of them
have for their hidden subject the struggle of Ireland
against England. Many of them have lyrical beauty and
soft melody. At times they reach true pathos, but their
lightly lifted gaiety is also delightful. He sang them
himself in society, and it is not too much to say that they
helped by the interest they stirred to further Catholic
Emancipation.

153. We turn to very different types of men when we
come to **Byron, Shelley,** and **Keats.** Of the three, LORD
BYRON had most of the quality we call force. Born in
1788, his *Hours of Idleness*, a collection of short poems,
in 1807, was mercilessly lashed in the *Edinburgh Review*.
The attack only served to awaken his genius, and he
replied with astonishing vigour in the satire of *English
Bards and Scotch Reviewers* in 1809. Eastern travel
gave birth to the first two cantos of *Childe Harold*, 1812,
to the *Giaour* and the *Bride of Abydos* in 1813, to the
Corsair and *Lara* in 1814. The *Siege of Corinth, Par-
isina*, the *Prisoner of Chillon, Manfred*, and *Childe
Harold* were finished before 1819. In 1818 he began
a new style in *Beppo*, which he developed fully in the
successive issues of *Don Juan*, 1819-24. During this
time he published a number of dramas, partly historical,
as his *Marino Faliero*, partly imaginative, as the *Cain*.
His life had been wild and useless, but he died in trying
to redeem it for the sake of the freedom of Greece. At
Missolonghi he was seized with fever, and passed away
in April, 1824.

154. The Position of Byron as a Poet is a curious one.
He is partly of the past and partly of the present. Something of the school of Pope clings to him ; yet no one so
completely broke away from old measures and old manners to make his poetry individual, not imitative. At
first, he has no interest whatever in the human questions
which were so strongly felt by Wordsworth and Shelley.
His early work is chiefly narrative poetry, written that
he might talk of himself and not of mankind. Nor has
he any philosophy except that which centres round the
problem of his own being. *Cain*, the most thoughtful
of his productions, is in reality nothing more than the
representation of the way in which the doctrines of
original sin and final reprobation affected his own soul.
We feel naturally great interest in this strong personality,
put before us with such obstinate power, but it wearies
us at last. Finally it wearied himself. As he grew in
power, he escaped from his morbid self, and ran into
the opposite extreme in *Don Juan*. It is chiefly in it
that he shows the influence of the revolutionary spirit.
It is written in bold revolt against all the conventionality
of social morality and religion and politics. It claimed
for himself and for others absolute freedom of individual
act and thought in opposition to that force of society
which tends to make all men after one pattern. This
was the best result of his work, though the way in which
it was done can scarcely be approved. As the poet of
nature he belongs also to the old and the new school.
Byron's sympathy with nature is a sympathy with himself

reflected in her moods. But he also escapes from this position of the later eighteenth century poets, and looks on nature as she is, apart from himself; and this escape is made, as in the case of his poetry of man, in his later poems. Lastly, it is his colossal power and the ease that comes from it, in which he resembles Dryden, as well as his amazing productiveness, which mark him specially. But it is always more power of the intellect than of the imagination.

155. **In Percy Bysshe Shelley,** on the contrary, the imagination is first and the intellect second. He produced while yet a boy some worthless tales, but soon showed in *Queen Mab*, 1813, the influence of the revolutionary era, combined in him with a violent attack on the existing forms of religion. One half of Shelley's poetry, and of his heart, was devoted to help the world towards the golden year he prophesied in *Queen Mab*, and to denounce and overthrow all that stood in its way. The other half was personal, an outpouring of himself in his seeking after the perfect ideal he could not find, and, sadder still, could not even conceive. *Queen Mab* is an example of the first, *Alastor* of the second. The hopes for man with which *Queen Mab* was written grew cold, and he turned from writing about mankind to describe in *Alastor* the life and wandering and death of a lonely poet. But the *Alastor* who isolated the poet from mankind was, in Shelley's own thought, a spirit of evil, and his next poem, the *Revolt of Islam*, 1817, unites him again to the interests of humanity. He wrote it with the

hope that men were beginning to recover from the apathy
and despair into which the failure of the revolutionary
ideas had thrown them, and to show them what they
should strive and hope for, and destroy. The poem
itself has finer passages in it than *Alastor*, but as a whole
it is inferior to it. It is far too formless. The same year
Shelley went to Italy, and never returned to England.
He then produced *Rosalind and Helen* and *Julian and
Maddalo*; but the new health and joy he now gained
brought back his enthusiasm for mankind, and he broke
out into the splendid lyric drama of *Prometheus Unbound*.
Asia, at the beginning of the drama separated from Prometheus, is the all-pervading Love which in loving makes
the universe of nature. When Prometheus is united to
Asia, the spirit of Love in man is wedded to the spirit of
Love in nature, and all the world of man and nature is
redeemed. The marriage of these two, and the distinct
existence of each for that purpose, is the same idea as
Wordsworth's differently expressed; and Shelley and he
are the only two poets who have touched it philosophi-
cally, Wordsworth with most contemplation, Shelley with
most imagination. *Prometheus Unbound* is the finest
example we have of the working out in poetry of the idea
of a regenerated universe, and the fourth act is the
choral song of its emancipation. Then, Shelley, having
expressed this idea with exultant imagination, turned to
try his matured power upon other subjects. Two of
these were neither personal nor for the sake of man.
The first, the drama of the *Cenci*, is as restrained in

expression as the previous poem is exuberant : yet there is no poem of Shelley's in which passion and thought and imagery are so wrought together. The second was the *Adonais*, a lament for the death of John Keats. It is a poem written by one who seems a spirit about a spirit, and belongs in expression, thought, and feeling to that world above the senses in which Shelley habitually lived. Of all this class of poems, to which many of his lyrics belong, *Epipsychidion* is the most impalpable, but, to those who care for Shelley's ethereal world, the finest poem he wrote. Of the same class is the *Witch of Atlas*, the poem in which he has personified divine Imagination in her work in poetry, and imaged all her attendants, and her doings among men.

As a lyric poet, Shelley, on his own ground, is easily great. Some of the lyrics are purely personal ; some, as in the very finest, the *Ode to the West Wind*, mingle together personal feeling and prophetic hope for mankind. Some are lyrics of pure nature ; some are dedicated to the rebuke of tyranny and the cause of liberty ; others belong to the indefinite passion he called love, and others are written on visions of those " shapes that haunt Thought's wildernesses." They form together the most sensitive, the most imaginative, and the most musical, but the least tangible lyrical poetry we possess.

As the poet of nature, he had the same idea as Wordsworth, that nature was alive : but while Wordsworth made the active principle which filled and made nature to be Thought, Shelley made it Love. The natural

world was dear then to his soul as well as to his eye,
but he loved best its indefinite aspects. He wants the
closeness of grasp of nature which Wordsworth and Keats
had, but he had the power in a far greater degree than
they of describing the cloud-scenery of the. sky, the
doings of the great sea, and vast realms of landscape.
He is in this, as well as in his eye for subtle colour, the
Turner of poetry. What he might have been we cannot
tell, for at the age of thirty he left us, drowned in the sea
he loved, washed up and burned on the sandy spits near
Pisa. His ashes lie beneath the walls of Rome, and *Cor*
cordium, "Heart of hearts," written on his tomb, well
says what all who love poetry feel when they think of
him.

156. **John Keats** lies near him, cut off like him before
his genius ripened ; not so ideal, but for that very reason
more naturally at home with nature than Shelley. In
one thing he was entirely different from Shelley — he had
no care whatever for the great human questions which
stirred Shelley ; the present was entirely without interest
to him. He marks the close of that poetic movement
which the ideas of the Revolution had crystallised in
England, as Shelley marks the attempt to revive it.
Keats, seeing nothing to move him in an age which had
now sunk into apathy on these points, went back to
Spenser, and especially to Shakespeare's minor poems,
to find his inspiration ; to Greek and mediæval life to
find his subjects, and established, in doing so, that which
has been called the *literary poetry* of England. Leigh

R

Hunt, his friend and Shelley's, did part of this work. The first subject on which Keats worked, after some minor poems in 1817, was *Endymion*, 1818, his last, *Hyperion*, 1820. These, along with *Lamia*, which is, on the whole, the finest of his longer poems, were poems of Greek life. *Endymion* has all the faults and all the promise of a great poet's early work, and no one knew its faults better than Keats, whose preface is a model of just self-judgment. *Hyperion*, a fragment of a tale of the overthrow of the Titans, is itself like a Titanic torso. Its rhythm was derived from Milton, but its poetry is wholly his own. But the mind of Keats was as yet too luxuriant to support the greatness of his subject's argument, and the poem dies away. It is beautiful, even in death. Both poems are filled with that which was deepest in the mind of Keats, the love of loveliness for its own sake, the sense of its rightful and pre-eminent power; and in the singleness of worship which he gave to Beauty, Keats is especially the ideal poet. Then he took us back into mediæval romance, and in this also he started a new type of poetry. There are two poems which mark this revival — *Isabella*, and the *Eve of St. Agnes*. Mediæval in subject, they are modern in manner; but they are, above all, of the poet himself. Their magic is all his own. In smaller poems, such as the *Ode on a Grecian Urn*, the poem *To Autumn*, to the *Nightingale*, and some sonnets, he is the fairest of all Apollo's children. He knew the inner soul of words. He felt the world where ideas and their forms are one, where nature and

humanity, before they divide, flow from a single source.
In all his poems, his painting of nature is as close as
Wordsworth's, but more ideal; less full of the imagination that links human thought to nature, but more full of
the imagination which broods upon enjoyment of beauty.
He was not much interested in human questions, but as
his mind grew, humanity made a more and more impera-
tive call upon him.   Had he lived, his poetry would have
dealt more closely with the heart of man.   His letters,
some of the most original in the English language, show
this clearly.   The second draft of *Hyperion*, unpublished
in his lifetime, and inferior as poetry to the first, accuses
himself of apartness from mankind, and expresses his
resolve to write of Man, the greatest subject of all.
Whether he could have done this well remains unknown.
His career was short; he had scarcely begun to write
when death took him away from the loveliness he loved
so keenly.   Consumption drove him to Rome, and there
he died, save for one friend, alone.   He lies not far
from Shelley, on the "slope of green access," near the
pyramid of Caius Cestius.   He sleeps apart; he is himself a world apart.

157. **Modern English Poetry.** — Keats marks the ex-
haustion of the impulse which began with Burns and
Cowper.   There was no longer now in England any
large wave of public thought or feeling such as could
awaken the national emotion and life out of which poetry
is naturally born.   We have then, arising after the deaths
of Keats, Shelley, and Byron, a number of pretty little

poems, having no inward fire, no idea, no marked character. They might be written by any versifier at any
time, and express pleasant, indifferent thought in pleasant verse. Such were Mrs. Hemans' poems, and those
of L. E. L., and such were Tennyson's earliest poems, in
1830. There were, however, a few men who, close to
1820 and 1822, had drunk at the fountain of Shelley, and
who, for a very brief time, continued, amid the apathy,
to write with some imagination and fervour. T. L. Beddoes, whose only valuable work was done between 1822
and 1825, was one of these. George Darley, whose *Sylvia*
earned the praise of Coleridge, was another. They represent in their imitation of Shelley, in their untutored
imagination, the last struggles of the poetic phase which
closed with the death of Byron. When Browning imitated
or rather loved Shelley in his first poem, *Pauline*, it was
to bid Shelley farewell; when Tennyson imitated Byron
and was haunted by Keats in his first poems, it was also
to bid them both farewell. Then Tennyson and Browning
passed on to strike unexpected waters out of the rocks
and to pour two rivers of fresh poetry over the world.
For with the Reform agitation, and the twofold religious
movement at Oxford, which was of the same date, a
novel national excitement came on England, and with
it the new tribe of poets arose among whom we have
lived. The elements of their poetry were also new,
though we can trace their beginnings in the previous
poetry. This poetry took up, so far as Art could touch
them, the theological, social, and even the political ques-

tions which disturbed England. It came, before long, moved by the critical and scientific inquiries into the origins of religion and man and the physical world, to represent the scepticism of England and the struggle for faith against doubt. It gave itself to metaphysics, but chiefly under the expression and analysis of the characters of men and women. It played with a vast variety of subjects, and treated them all with a personal passion which filled them with emotion. It worked out, from the point of view of deep feeling, the relation of man to God, and of man to sorrow and immortality. It studied and brought to great excellence the Idyll, the Song, and the short poem on classic subjects with a reference to modern life. It increased, to an amazing extent, the lyrical poetry of England. The short lyric was never written in such numbers and of such excellence since the days of Elizabeth. It recaptured and clothed in a new dress the Arthurian tale, and linked us, back through many poets, to the days of legend and delight. It re-established for us in this new time, as the most natural and most emotional subject of English poetry, England, her history, her people, and her landscape, so that the new poets have described not only the whole land but the natural scenery and historical story, the human and animal life of the separate counties. Our native land, as in the days of Elizabeth, has been idealised.

Nor did this new impulse stay in England only. It went abroad for its subjects, and especially to Italy. It

strove to express the main characteristics of periods of
history and of art, of the origins of religions and of Christianity, of classic and Renaissance thought at critical
times, and of lyric passion in modern life. Indeed, it
aimed at a universal representation of human life and
at a subtle characterisation of individual temperaments.
Thus, it was a poetry of England, and also of the larger
world beyond England.

Apart from the main stream of poetry, there were
separate streams which represented distinct passages in
the general movement. The *Sonnets* of Charles Tennyson Turner, which began in 1830, stand by their grace
and tenderness at the head of a large production of
poetry which describes with him the shy, sequestered,
observant life of the English scholar and lover of nature,
of country piety and country people. One man among
them stands alone, William Barnes, of Dorsetshire. The
time will come when the dialect in which he wrote will
cease to prevent the lovers of poetry from appreciating
at its full worth a poetry which, written in the mother-
tongue of the poor and of his own heart, is as close to
the lives and souls of simple folk as it is to the woods
and streams, the skies and farms of rustic England.
Among them also is Coventry Patmore, who, though
alive, belongs to the past. What Barnes did for the
peasant and the farmer, Patmore did for the cultivated
life which in quiet English counties gathers round the
church, the parsonage, and the hall, the lives and piety
of the English homes that are still the haunts of ancient

peace. His work, with its retired and careful if over-
delicate note, is a true picture of a small part of English
life. But it has the faults of its excellences.

The High Church and Broad Church movements, as
they were called, produced two sets of poetical writers who
also stand somewhat apart from the main line of English
poetry. The first is best represented by John Keble,
whose *Christian Year*, in 1827, with its poetry, so good
within its own range, so weak beyond it, was the source
of many books of poems of a similar but inferior character. On the other hand the impulse towards a wider
theology was combined in some poets with a laxer morality than England is accustomed to maintain, and Bailey's
Festus, 1839, was the first of a number of sensational
poems which painted the struggles of the spirit towards
immortal life, and of the senses towards mortal love with
equal effervescence. A noble translation of *Omar
Khayyám* by Edward Fitzgerald, and the fine ballad-songs
and *Andromeda* of Charles Kingsley, may also be said to
flow apart from the main stream in which poetry flowed.

Alfred Tennyson and Robert Browning (whose wife
will justly share his fame) began to write between 1830
and 1833, and continued their work side by side for fifty
years, when they died, almost together. Both of them
were wholly original, and both of them, differing at every
point of their art, kept with extraordinary vitality their
main powers, and were capable of fresh invention, even
to the very last. They passed through a long period of
change and development, during which all the existing

foundations of faith and knowledge and art were dug out, investigated, tested, and an attempt made to reconstruct them, an attempt which still pursues its work. They lived and wrote in sympathy with the emotions which this long struggle created in the minds of men, and expressed as much of these emotions as naturally fell within their capability and within the sphere of poetry. And this they did with great eagerness and intensity. Their love of beauty and of their art was unbroken, and they had as much power, as they had desire, to shape the thought and the loveliness they saw — great poets who have illuminated, impelled, adorned, and exalted the world in which we live.

At first the great inquiry into the roots of things disturbed the next generation of poets, those who stepped to the front between 1850 and 1860 ; and as Arthur Hugh Clough expressed the trouble of the want of clear light on the fates of men and their only refuge in duty, so Matthew Arnold, more deeply troubled, embodied in his poetry, even in his early book of 1852, the restlessness, the dimness, the hopelessness of a world which had lost the vision of the ancient stars and could cling to nothing but a stoic conduct. But he did this with keen sorrow, and with a vivid interest in the world around him. Then about 1860 the poets grew weary of the whole struggle. Theology, the just aim and ends of life, science, political and social questions, ceased on the whole to awaken the slightest interest in them. Exactly that which took place in the case of Keats now took place. The poets sought

only for what was beautiful, romantic, of ancient heroism,
far from a tossed and wearied world, far from all its
tiresome questions. Dante G. Rossetti, whose sister,
Christina, touched the romantic and religious lyric with
original beauty, was the leader of this school. He, and
others still alive, found their chief subjects in ancient
Rome and Greece, in stories and lyrics of passion, in
mediæval romance, in Norse legends, in the old England
of Chaucer, and in Italy. But this literary poetry has
now almost ceased to be produced, and has been succeeded as in 1825 by a vast criticism of poetry, and by a
multitudinous production, much inspired from France, of
poetry, chiefly lyrical, which has few elements of endur-
ance and little relation to life. What will emerge from
this we cannot tell, but we only need some new human
inspiration, having a close relation to the present, and
bearing with it a universal emotion, to create in England
another school of poetry as great as that which arose in
the beginning of this century, and worthy of the traditions which have made England the creator and lover of
poetry for more than 1200 years.

CHRONOLOGICAL TABLE

A.D.

449 . . . . English History begins in Britain. The Jutes land in Thanet.

597 . . . . Christianity brought into England by Augustine;

627 . . . . And into Northumbria by Paulinus.

635, *et seq.* . The Celtic Missionaries evangelise Northumbria.

664 . . . . The Synod of Whitby.

670–80 . . The poems of Cædmon.

669–71 . . School of Canterbury; Archbishop Theodore. ⎫

680?–709 . The literary work of Ealdhelm. (Born 656.) ⎬ Wessex.

690 (cir.) . The laws of Ine. ⎭

674–82 . . Wearmouth, Jarrow, and their libraries, founded by Benedict Biscop.

673 . . . . Bæda, Benedict's scholar, born.

731 . . . Bæda's Ecclesiastical History. (Death of Bæda, 735.)

735 . . . . Ecgberht, Archbp. of York, establishes the School of York and the Library. (Died 766.)

766–82 . . Æthelbert and Alcuin make York the centre of European learning.

782–92 . . Alcuin carries the learning of York to Europe.

793 . . . . The first Viking raid on Northumbria.
Cynewulf (born about 720) wrote his poems probably in the latter half of this century.

800 . . . . Charles the Great crowned emperor.

830 . . . About this date the "Heliand," an Old Saxon poem, was written.

A.D.

867-76 . . The final destruction of the seats of learning in Northumbria by "the Army."

871 . . . . The accession of Ælfred.

886 (cir.) . Ælfred begins his literary work.   The English Chronicle is first carefully edited in this reign.

901 . . . . Death of Ælfred.

913 . . . . Rolf settles in Normandy.

937 . . . . Song of Battle of Brunanburh, in the Chronicle.

961-88 . . Dunstan, Archbishop of Canterbury.

964, *et seq.* . King Eadgar, with Æthelwold and Oswald, Bishops of Winchester and Worcester, revives English monachism in Wessex and East Anglia.

971 . . . . Blickling Homilies.

991 . . . . Song of the Battle of Maldon.

991-96 . . Ælfric's Homilies; after 1005, his Treatise on the Old and New Testament.   (Died 1020-25.)

1031 . . . Swegen of Denmark becomes King of England.

1042-65 . . Reign of Edward the Confessor.   England's first contact with French Romance.
Latin translation of a late Greek Romance, Apollonius of Tyre, and of two small books belonging to the Alexander Saga.

1066 . . . The Lay of Roland is brought to England.

1066 . . . William I.

1070 . . . Lanfranc, Archbishop of Canterbury.
The "Charlemagne," Norman poem, before the end of the 11th century.

1071 . . . The Exeter Book given by Leofric, Bishop of Exeter, to his Cathedral.

1085 . . . The Domesday Book.

1087 . . . William II. crowned by Lanfranc.

1093 . . . Anselm, Archbishop of Canterbury.

1095 . . . The beginning of the Crusades.   The stories of the East soon come to the West.

1100 . . . Henry I.

1109 . . . University of Paris rises into importance with William of Champeaux and Peter Abelard.

In the middle of the 12th century the troubadour poetry of Southern France rose into its fine flower in the work of Bernart de Ventadorn. He had been preceded by Guilhem de Poitiers, the first troubadour of whom we know. Bertrand de Born, Geoffrey Rudel, Pierre Vidal are famous troubadours of this century. The lyrics of Northern France, those of the trouvères, grew out of this Provençal poetry. No lyrical poetry in England in this century. The chansons de geste of the last century in France were largely added to in this. Great literary activity prevailed in Wales from the middle of this century down to the death of Llewellyn in 1282. The epic of the Cid was shaped about 1160-70 out of ballads that had sung the border battles of Moors and Spaniards. In Germany the Minnelieder arose in the middle of the century, and Wolfram von Eschenbach introduced his new conception of Parzival into the Arthurian legend. Also in the middle of this century the Niebelungen Lied was cast into its form. Italian poetry began with Ciullo d'Alcamo in Sicily, and Folca-chiero of Siena, in the years 1172-78. In this century also the mediæval tales from India were cast into the History of the Seven Sages, and into the Disciplina Clericalis. These materials were moulded into various shapes by the French poets, and afterwards in England.

A.D.

1199 . . . *John.*
>   Chronicle of Richard of Devizes. Annals of Barn-
>   well. Chronicle of Jocelyn of Brakelond, and
>   others.

1150–1200 . Sayings of Alfred.

1200–30 . . Roman de la Rose (Part I.) by Guillaume de Lorris.

1205 . . . Loss of Normandy.

1205 (cir.) . Layamon's Brut.

1215 . . . The Orrmulum. The Great Charter.

1210–50 . . Reign of Frederick II. Italian poetry in Sicily.

1216 . . . *Henry III.*
>   Chronicle of Roger of Wendover at St. Albans.

1235–73 . . Matthew Paris' Greater Chronicle; History of
>   England; Lives of earlier abbots.

A.D.

1220–76 . .	Guido Guinicelli. Father of new national literature in Italy.
1220 (cir.) .	Owl and Nightingale (Dorsetshire).
1220 (cir.) .	Ancren Riwle (Dorsetshire).
1221 . . .	Coming of Black Friars to England (Dominicans).
1224 . . .	Coming of Grey Friars (Franciscans).
1225 . . .	St. Francis of Assisi's Song to the Sun.
1225–35? . .	The Bestiary.
1230–40 (cir.)	King Horn.
1235–53 . .	Robert Grossetete (Bp. of Lincoln). Chastel d'amour.
1250 (cir.) .	Genesis and Exodus.
1258 . . .	Provisions of Oxford, Proclamation of King's adhesion to them — in English as well as French.
1262 . . .	Miracle plays acted by the Town Guilds.
1264 . . .	Battle of Lewes — Ballad.
1264 . . .	Corpus Christi Day appointed; fully observed, 1311.
1268 . . .	Roger Bacon's Opus Majus.

After Lewes and its war-ballad, the Love Lyric begins in such verse as the Throstle and the Nightingale and the Cuckoo Song. Also the religious lyric in such verse as the Sorrows of Christ and the Lullaby, and the Love Song of Thomas de Hales, a Franciscan. Also the satirical lyric, such as the Land of Cockayne. In this reign Adam Marsh (De Marisco) has a famous Franciscan school at Oxford. The Harrowing of Hell, first dramatic piece in English, belongs to this reign. Northumbria begins again to write in second half of century.

1272 . . .	*Edward I.*
	The Alexander Romance in English in this reign. The Tristan Story is also widely spread.
	Romances arise in Northumbria. Many war-ballads.
1280–87 . .	Guido delle Colonne's (a poet of Sicily, born 1250) Historia Destructionis Trojæ. Visited England and wrote Historia de regibus et rebus Angliæ.
1290–93 .	Dante's Vita Nuova.
1300 (cir.) .	Gesta Romanorum.

A.D.

1300 (cir.) . Havelok the Dane.
1303 . . . Robert Manning of Brunne's Handlyng Synne.
               His Chronicle finished 1338.
1300–05 . . Roman de la Rose (Part II.), by Jean de Meung.
1307 . . . *Edward II.*
1303–21 . . Dante's Divine Comedy.
1324 . . . Court of Love at Toulouse.
1320–30 . . Cursor Mundi (Northumbrian). William Shore-
               ham's Poems (Kentish). A Cycle of Homilies,
               Legend Cycle (both Northumbrian) are now
               worked at. Sir Tristrem; Sire Otuel; Guy of
               Warwick; Bevis of Hampton; all now in English.
1327 . . . *Edward III.*
1330 . . . Pilgrimage of Human Life, a French poem by
               Guillaume de Delguileville. Legenda Aurea,
               by Jacobus a Voragine, Bishop of Genoa.
               Guillaume de Machault.(B.1282(cir.); d.1370(cir.).)
1340 (cir.) . Richard Rolle of Hampole's Pricke of Conscience.
1340 . . . Dan Michel of Northgate's Ayenbite of Inwyt.
1341 . . . Petrarca crowned laureate at Rome.
1345 . . . Death of Richard Aungerville, Bishop of Durham,
               writer of Philobiblion; leaves library to Oxford.
1333–52 . . Songs of Laurence Minot on King Edward's wars.
1350, *et seq.* . Collections of books, and University foundations in
               England now begin to serve literature.
1350–53 . . Decameron of Boccaccio. 1341, La Teseide. 1348,
               Filostrato.
1350 (cir.) . Romances are now written on the Welsh marches
               in alliterative Old English verse; subject and
               mise-en-scène French, verse and diction national.
               Among first of these, Joseph of Arimathie and
               two fragments of an Alexander Romance.
1355 . . . William of Palerne. 1350? Tale of Gamelyn.
1355 (cir.) . Anturs of Arthur at the Tarnawathelan.
1360–70 (cir.) Sir Gawayne and the Grene ⎫ Perhaps by the
               Knight, Pearl, Cleanness ⎬ "philosophical
               and Patience.   ⎭ Strode."

A.D.

1362–63 . .	Langland's Vision of Piers the Plowman. (A-Text.)
1366–70 . .	Chaucer's first poems. Book of the Duchess, 1369.
1373 . . .	Petrarca's Griselda.
1375 . . .	Barbour's Bruce.
1377 . . .	*Richard II.*
1377 . . .	B-Text of Piers the Plowman.
1378? . . .	Wyclif's Summa in Theologia.
1379 . . .	New College, Oxford; Latin School at Winchester founded by William of Wykeham.
1380 . . .	Wyclif's translation of the Bible.
1380–83 . .	Chaucer's Troilus and Cressida.
1382–85 . .	Chaucer's Parlement of Foules, Hous of Fame, Legend of Good Women.
1383 (cir.) .	Wyclif's Trialogus. (Died 1384.)
1385–89 . .	Chaucer's Prologue and many of the Canterbury Tales.
1393? . . .	Gower's Confessio Amantis.
1395 . . .	Chrysoloras comes to Florence to teach Greek. Guarino Guarini teaches Greek at Venice, Florence, Ferrara. (Born 1370; died 1460.)
1398? . . .	C-Text of Piers the Plowman.

From Boccaccio to the middle of the 16th century a great mass of Italian Novelle were produced; used in England for plays, stories, &c.

1399 . . .	*Henry IV.*
1400 . . .	Death of Chaucer and Langland.
1411–12 . .	Hoccleve's Gouvernail of Princes.
1413 . . .	*Henry V.*
1415 . . .	Eustache Deschamps dies. Alain Chartier and Christine de Pisan, his contemporaries.
1421 . . .	Lydgate's Troy Book. 1424–25, Story of Thebes.
1422 . . .	*Henry VI.*
1422 . . .	James I. of Scotland : The King's Quair.
1422 . . .	Paston Letters begin; end 1509.
1423 . . .	John Aurispa brings from Greece to Italy more than 200 MSS.
1424–25 . .	Lydgate's Falles of Princes.

S

A.D.

1427 . . . Filelfo, laden with MSS., returns from Greece to Florence.

Pletho, Bessarion, Gaza have diffused the spirit of ancient learning in Italy by 1440. Universities at Pavia, Turin, Ferrara, Florence, &c. Eight hundred MSS. left by Niccolo Niccoli to Florence, in 1436; cradle of the Laurentian Library.

1449 . . . Pecock's Repressor of Overmuch blaming of the Clergy.

1453 . . . Fall of Constantinople.

1450 (cir.) . Invention of Printing.

1460-80 . . Poems of Robert Henryson.

1461 . . . *Edward IV.*

1470 . . . Malory's Morte Darthur.

1474-76 . . Caxton sets up printing press at Westminster.

1481 . . . Luigi Pulci's Morgante Maggiore.

1483 . . . *Edward V. Richard III.*

1485 . . . *Henry VII.*

1495? . . . Boiardo's Orlando Inamorato begun.

1501 . . . Gawin Douglas' Palace of Honour.

1503 . . . Dunbar's Thistle and Rose.

1504 . . Sannazaro's Arcadia.

1506 . . . Hawes' Pastime of Pleasure.

1507 . . . Skelton's Bowge of Court; Boke of Phyllip Sparowe.

1507-08 . . Dunbar's Dance of the Seven Deadly Sins.

1509 . . . *Henry VIII.*

1509 . . . Erasmus: Praise of Folly.

1513 . . . Gawin Douglas: Translation of the Æneid.

1513? . . . Sir Thos. More's Life of Edward V. and History of Richard III. written.

1515 . . . Trissino's Sofonisba; first use of blank verse in Italy.

1516 . . . Ariosto's Orlando Furioso begun; the rest in 1532.

1516 . . . Sir Thos. More's Utopia, written in Latin.

1518? . . . Skelton's Colin Clout.

1518? . . . Amadis de Gaul translated into English.

A.D.

1524 . . . Ronsard born. (Died 1586.)

1527 . . . Tyndale's translation of the New Testament.

1528 . . . Lyndsay's Dreme.

1520-40 . . Heywood's Interludes.

1532, *et seq.* . Rabelais' Gargantua, &c.

1535 . . . Lyndsay's Satire of the Three Estates.

1540 . . . Cranmer's Bible.

1541? . . . Ralph Roister Doister, first English comedy, printed 1566.

1545 . . . Ascham's Toxophilus.

1547 . . . *Edward VI.*

1549 . . . Latimer's Sermon on the Ploughers.

1549-52 . . English Prayer Book.

1551 . . . Ralph Robinson's translation of More's Utopia into English.

1553 . . . *Mary.*

1553 . . . Lyndsay's Monarchie.

1557 . . . Tottel's Miscellany; poems by Wyatt and Surrey.

1558 . . . *Elizabeth.*

1559 . . . Sackville's Mirror for Magistrates.

1561-62 . . Gorboduc, the first English Tragedy. Printed as Ferrex and Porrex, 1571.

1562 . . . Phaer's Virgil. Many other translations of the classics before 1579.

1563 . . . Foxe's Book of Martyrs.

1563 . . . Sackville's Induction to Mirror for Magistrates.

1570 . . . Ascham's Schoolmaster.

1571 . . . R. Edward's Damon and Pithias printed.

1575 . . . Comedy of Gammer Gurton's Needle printed. Play of Apius and Virginia printed.

1576 . . . Paradise of Dainty Devices; 1578, Gorgeous Gallery of Gallant Inventions; 1584, Handfull of Pleasant Delights — all Poetical Miscellanies.

1576 . . . Three theatres built in London ; Blackfriars, the Curtain, the Theatre.

1576 . . . Gascoigne's Steele Glas. (First verse satire.)

1577 . . . Holinshed's Chronicle.

A.D.

1579-80 . . Lyly's Euphues. 1580-1601 (cir.) his dramas.

1579 . . . Spenser's Shepheards Calendar.

1579 . . . North's Plutarch's Lives.

1580-81 . . Sidney's Arcadia and Apologie for Poetrie.

1580-88 . . Montaigne's Essaies.

1581 . . . Tasso's Gerusalemme Liberata.

1582? . . . Watson's Hecatompathia or Passionate Century.

1583-1625? . Pamphleteers: Greene, Lodge, G. Harvey, Nash, Dekker, Breton.

1584-92 . . Dramas of Greene. 1583, *et seq.*, Tales in prose.

1584-98 . . Dramas of Peele.

1586 . . . Warner's Albion's England.

1587 . . . Marlowe's Tamburlaine acted. (Printed 1590.)

1588-90 . . Marlowe's Faustus, Jew of Malta, Edward II.

1588-90 . . Series of Martin Marprelate Tracts.

1588-90? . . Love's Labour's Lost.

1589 . . . Hakluyt's Voyages.

1590 . . . Spenser's Faerie Queene (Books i.-iii. 1596, iv.-vi.).

1591 . . . Harrington's translation of Ariosto's Orlando.

1593 . . Donne's Satires (died 1626).

1593 . . . Shakespeare's Venus and Adonis.

1594 . . . Hooker's Ecclesiastical Polity (Bks. i.-iv. 1597, v.).

1593-96 . . Many collections of Sonnets.

1595 . . . Daniel's Hist. of Civil Wars of York and Lancaster.

1596, *et seq.* . Ben Jonson's Dramas. (Died 1637.)

1594-96 . . Merchant of Venice.

1597 . . . Bacon's Essays. (First set.)

1597-98 . . Hall's Satires.

1598 . . . Chapman's Homer (First part). Sylvester's translation of Du Bartas.

1598-99 . . Marston's Satires.

1596-98 . . Drayton's Barons' Wars and England's Heroical Epistles.

1599 . . . The Globe Theatre built.

1600 . . . England's Helicon; England's Parnassus; Belvedere; all poetical Miscellanies.

1600 . . . Fairfax's translation of Tasso.

A.D.

1600 . . .	Lope de Vega began his dramas about 1590, and continued writing till his death in 1635.
1600–81 . .	Calderon, who had a large influence on the French Drama of the 17th and 18th centuries, on the English Restoration Drama, and on the Italian, German and English poetry of 18th and 19th centuries.
1603 (cir.) ? .	The Return from Parnassus.
1603 . . .	Florio's translation of Montaigne's Essays.
1603 . . .	*James I.*
1603 . . .	Knolles' History of the Turks.
1604 . . .	Authorised Version of the Bible.
1605 . .	Bacon's Advancement of Learning (Books i. and ii.).
1606–16 . .	Cervantes' Don Quixote.
1609 . . .	Shakespeare's Sonnets published.
1610–25 (cir.)	Dramas of Beaumont and Fletcher.
1610 . . .	Giles Fletcher's Christ's Victory.
1611 . . .	Speed's History of Great Britain.
1612 . . .	Webster's first drama, The White Devil (printed).
1612–20 . .	T. Shelton's Translation of Don Quixote.
1613–14 . .	Drayton's Polyolbion.
1613–16 . .	Browne's Britannia's Pastorals; 1614, The Shepherd's Pipe.
1613 . . .	Purchas his Pilgrimage.
1613 . . .	Wither's Abuses Stript and Whipt.
1613 . . .	Drummond of Hawthornden's first poem. (D. 1649.)
1614 . . .	Raleigh's History of the World.
1615 . . .	Sandys' Travels.
1615 . . .	Wither's Shepherd's Hunting.
1616 . .	Chapman's Homer finished. Shakespeare dies.
1621 . .	Burton's Anatomy of Melancholy.
1622 . . .	Massinger's Virgin Martyr. (Died 1639.)
1623 . . .	Webster's Duchess of Malfi (printed).
1623	Waller's first poems.
1623 . . .	The " First Folio " of Shakespeare.
	Chapman, Tourneur, Middleton, and other dramatists wrote during this reign.

A.D.

1625 . . . *Charles I.*
1628 . . . Harvey's De Motu Sanguinis.
1629 . . . Milton's Ode on the Morning of Christ's Nativity.
1631 . . . George Herbert's Temple.
1635? . . . Sir Thos. Browne's Religio Medici (pub. 1642).
1632-37 . . Milton's Allegro, Penseroso, Comus, Lycidas.
1633 . . . Phineas Fletcher's Purple Island.
1634 . . . Ford's historical play of Perkin Warbeck.
1636 . . . Corneille's first tragedy, the Cid. His last play, 1675.
1636 . . . French Academy founded.
1640 . . . Thomas Carew's poems.
1641 . . . Milton's first pamphlet.
1641 . . . Evelyn's Diary begins (ends 1697; published 1818).
1642 . . . Theatres closed.
1642 . . . Fuller's Holy and Profane state.
1642 . . . Denham's Cooper's Hill.
1642 . . . Hobbes' De Cive.
1644 . . . Milton's Areopagitica.
1645 . . . Waller's poems.
1645 . . . Meetings held which lead to formation of the
           Royal Society.
1646 . . . Crashaw's Steps to the Temple.
1647 . . . Jeremy Taylor's Liberty of Prophesying.
1647 . . . Cowley's Mistress. Davideis, 1641 (?).
1647-48 . . Herrick's Noble Numbers; Hesperides.
1648 . . . J. Beaumont's Psyche or Love's Mystery.
1648 . . . Suckling's Fragmenta Aurea.
1649 . . . Lovelace's Lucasta.
1649 . . . *Commonwealth.*
1650 . . . Baxter's Saints' Rest.
1650 . . . Milton's Defensio pro Populo Anglicano.
1650-52 . . Marvell's Garden poems written.
1650-56 . . Vaughan's Silex Scintillans.
1650-57 . . Pascal's Provincial Letters.
1651 . . . Hobbes' Leviathan.
1653 . . . Izaak Walton's Compleat Angler.
1653 . . . Molière's first play.

A.D.

1656 . . .	Harrington's Oceana.
1659 . . .	Dryden's Stanzas on the Death of Cromwell.
1659 . . .	Corneille's Essay on the Three Unities.
1659-60 . .	Pepys' Diary begins (finished 1669; published 1825).
1660 . . .	Boileau's first satire.
1660 . . .	*Charles II.*
1660 . . .	Re-opening of the theatres by Davenant and Killigrew.
1662 . . .	Royal Society incorporated.
1663 . . .	Dryden's first play, the Wild Gallant.
1663 . . .	Butler's Hudibras (Part I.).
1663 . . .	Algernon Sidney's Discourses concerning Government, published 1698.
1663 . . .	The London Public Intelligencer. (Becomes the London Gazette, 1666.)
1663-67 . .	Plays of Racine. Esther, 1689 (?), Athalie, 1690(?).
1664 . . .	La Fontaine's first book of *Contes*.
1667 . . .	Dryden's Annus Mirabilis; Essay on Dramatic Poesy.
1667 . . .	Cowley's Essays.
1667 . . .	Milton's Paradise Lost.
1667 . . .	Petty's Treatise on Taxes.
1668 . . .	La Fontaine's first book of Fables. (Died 1695.)
1670 . . .	Izaak Walton's Lives.
1670 . . .	Pascal's Les Pensées.
1671 . . .	Paradise Regained. Samson Agonistes.
1671-77 . .	Dramas of Wycherley.
1672 . . .	Dryden's Essay on Heroic Plays.
1674 . . .	Boileau's Art of Poetry.
1678 . . .	Bunyan's Pilgrim's Progress. (Part I.)
1678 . . .	Dryden's All for Love. (In blank verse.)
1678 . . .	Cudworth's Intellectual System of the Universe.
1680 . . .	Filmer's Patriarcha.
1681 . . .	Dryden's Absalom and Achitophel. (First part.)
1682 . . .	Dryden's Medal, Macflecknoe, Religio Laici.
1684 . . .	Pilgrim's Progress. (Part II.)
	Clarendon's History of the Great Rebellion written during this reign. (Published 1707.)

A.D.

1685 . . .	*James II.*
1687 . . .	Newton's Principia.
1687 . . .	Defoe's first tract.
1687 . . .	La Bruyère's Les Caractères.
1688-89 . .	*The Revolution.* *William III.*
1690 . . .	Locke's Essay on the Human Understanding.
1692 . . .	Sir Wm. Temple's Miscellanea, Vol. ii.
1693-1700 .	Congreve's dramas.
1694 . . .	Dryden's Last Play.
1697-1705 .	Dramas of Vanbrugh.
1698 . . .	Collier's Short View of the Immorality of the Stage.
1698-1707 .	Dramas of Farquhar.
1700 . . .	Dryden's Fables. (Nov. 1699.)
1700 . . .	Prior's Carmen Seculare.
1702 . . .	*Anne.*
1702-05 . .	Steele's Plays. (1722. Comedy of the Conscious Lovers, his last play.)
1704 . . .	Swift's Tale of a Tub, Battle of the Books. (Written by 1596-97.)
1704 . . .	Addison's Campaign. Rosamond (opera), 1706.
1704-13 . .	Defoe's Review.
1709 . . .	Mat Prior's Poems.
1709-11 . .	The Tatler.
1709-44 . .	Writings of Bishop Berkeley.
1709 . . .	Pope's Pastorals. (Written 1704-05.)
1711-12-14 .	The Spectator.
1712 . . .	Pope's Rape of the Lock. (Final form 1714.)
1713 . . .	Addison's Cato.
1714 . . .	Gay's Shepherd's Week.
1714 . . .	*George I.*
1715-20 . .	Pope's Homer's Iliad.
1715, *et seq.* .	Le Sage's Gil Blas.
1719 . . .	Defoe's Robinson Crusoe. 1720-25, Other novels.
1724-34 . .	Bp. Burnet's History of my own Times published.
1725 . . .	Allan Ramsay's Gentle Shepherd. (First form 1723.)
1726-30 . .	Thomson's Seasons.
1726-27 . .	Swift's Gulliver's Travels.

A.D.

1727 . . .	*George II.*
1727 . . .	Gay's Fables. 1728, Beggar's Opera.
1728 . . .	Pope's Dunciad. (First form. Others in 1729-42-43.)
1728 . . .	Voltaire's Henriade.
1730 . . .	Marivaux: Le jeu de l'amour et du hasard. (D. 1763.)
1732-34 . .	Pope's Essay on Man. Moral Essays, 1732-35.
1735 . . .	Johnson's Translation of Lobo's Voyage to Abyssinia. (His first work.)
1736 . . .	Butler's Analogy of Religion.
1737 . . .	Shenstone's Schoolmistress. (Final form, 1742.)
1738 . . .	Johnson's London.
1739 . . .	Hume's Treatise of Human Nature.
1740 . . .	Richardson's Pamela. 1748, Clarissa Harlowe.
1741 . . .	Warburton's Divine Legation.
1740-41 . .	Hume's Essays.
1742 . . .	Fielding's Joseph Andrews. 1749, Tom Jones.
1744 . . .	Johnson's Life of Savage.
1744 . . .	Akenside's Pleasures of the Imagination.
1746 . . .	Collins' Odes.
1742-69 . .	Gray's Poems. (Collected edition 1768.)
1748 . . .	Smollett's Roderick Random.
1748 . . .	Thomson's Castle of Indolence.
1748 . . .	Montesquieu's Esprit des Lois.
1749 . . .	Diderot's Encyclopédie begun.
1749 . . .	Johnson's Vanity of Human Wishes; Irene.
1750-52 . .	Johnson's Rambler.
1751-52 . .	Hume's Principles of Morals and Political Discourses.
1754 . . .	Richardson's Sir Chas. Grandison.
1754-61 . .	Hume's History of England.
1755 . . .	Johnson's Dictionary.
1756 . . .	Burke's Essay on the Sublime and Beautiful; Vindication of Natural Society.
1757 . . .	Hume's Natural History of Religion.
1758 . .	Robertson's History of Scotland. 1769, Charles V.
1758 . . .	Lessing's Litteraturbriefe.
1759 . .	Johnson's Rasselas.
1759 . . .	Adam Smith's Moral Sentiments.

A.D.

1789 . . . Blake's Songs of Innocence.   1794, Songs of Experience.

1789 . . . White's Natural History of Selborne.

1790 . . . Burke's Reflections on the Revolution in France.

1791-92 . . Paine's Rights of Man.   1794-95, Age of Reason.

1791 . . . Boswell's Life of Johnson.

1792-94 . . Arthur Young's Travels in France.

1793 . . . Godwin's Enquiry concerning Political Justice.

1793 . . . Wordsworth's Evening Walk; Descriptive Sketches.

1794 . . . Coleridge and Southey's Fall of Robespierre.

1796 . . . Poems; by Coleridge and Lamb.

1796 . . . Scott's translation of Bürger's Lenore.

1796-97 . . Burke's Letters on a Regicide Peace.

1797 . . . Poems by Coleridge, Lamb, and Lloyd.

1797 . . . Poetry of the Anti-Jacobin.

1798 . . . Lyrical Ballads; by Coleridge and Wordsworth.

1798 . . . Malthus' Essay on the Principles of Population.

1798 . . . Landor's Gebir and other Poems.

1798 . . . Ebenezer Elliott's Vernal Walk.

1799 . . . Scott's translation of Götz von Berlichingen.

1799 . . . Campbell's Pleasures of Hope.

1800 . . . Coleridge's translation of Schiller's Wallenstein.

1801 . . . Southey's Thalaba. (He continued writing till 1843.)

1802 . . . Scott's Border Minstrelsy.

1802 . . . The Edinburgh Review.

1805 . . . Scott's Lay of the Last Minstrel.

1807 . . . Byron's Hours of Idleness.

1807 . . . Wordsworth's Poems in 2 vols.

1807 . . . T. Moore's Irish Melodies begun.

1807-08 . . Lamb's Specimens of Dramatic Poetry.

1808 . . Scott's Marmion.   1810, Lady of the Lake.

1809 . . . The Quarterly Review.

1809 . . Byron's English Bards and Scotch Reviewers.

1810 . . Allan Cunningham's first published poems. (D.1842.)

1811-18 . Novels of Jane Austen.

1822-33 . . Prof. Wilson's Noctes Ambrosianæ. (In Blackwood.)

1812-18 . Byron's Childe Harold.

A.D.

1813 . . . Shelley's Queen Mab. 1816, Alastor.

1814 . . . Scott's Waverley. (His novels continue till 1831.)

1814 . . . Wordsworth's Excursion.

1814 . . . H. Cary's Translation of Dante.

1816 . . . Coleridge's Christabel; Kubla Khan.

1816? . . . Leigh Hunt's Story of Rimini.

1817 . . . Byron's Manfred. 1818, Beppo; 1819-23, Don Juan.

1817 . . . Coleridge's Biographia Literaria.

1817 . . . Keats' first poems.

1817, *et seq.* . . Hazlitt's Dramatic and Poetical Criticisms. (Died 1830.)

1818 . . . Hallam's View of the State of Europe during the Middle Ages. 1827, Constitutional Hist. of England.

1820 . . . *George IV.*

1820 . . . Keats' Hyperion and other Poems.

1820 . . . Shelley's Prometheus Unbound.

1821 . . . Byron's Cain and other dramas.

1821 . . . DeQuincey's Confessions of an English Opium Eater.

1821 . . . Shelley's Adonaïs and Epipsychidion.

1821-23 . . Lamb's Essays of Elia.

1822 . . . T. L. Beddoes' Bride's Tragedy.

1822 . . . Rogers' Italy.

1824 . . . Carlyle's translation of Goethe's Wilhelm Meister.

1826 . . . Poems by Two Brothers. (Chas. and Alfd. Tennyson.)

1827 . . . Keble's Christian Year.

1830 . . . *William IV.*

1830 . . . Alfred Tennyson: Poems.

1830 . . . Moore's Life of Byron.

1830 . . . Mrs. Hemans' Songs of the Affections.

1831, *et seq.* . . Ebenezer Elliott's Corn Law Rhymes.

1831 . . . Robert Browning's Pauline; published 1833.

1832 . . . Death of Sir Walter Scott. Death of Goethe.

INDEX

———•◦•———

269

T

INDEX TO FOREIGN AUTHORS

———◆◇◆———

THE HISTORY

OF

EARLY ENGLISH LITERATURE.

Being the History of English Poetry from its Beginnings to the Accession of King Ælfred.

BY THE

REV. STOPFORD A. BROOKE.

WITH MAPS.

Large 12mo. Gilt top, $2.50.

NOTICES.

"I had been eagerly awaiting it, and find it on examination distinctly the best treatise on its subject." — Prof. CHARLES F. RICHARDSON, *Dartmouth College.*

"I know of no literary estimate of Anglo-Saxon poetry that in breadth of view and sympathetic appreciation can be compared with this." — Prof. W. E. MEAD, *Wesleyan University.*

"In this work we have the view of a real lover of literature, and we have its utterance in a diction graceful enough to make the reading an intellectual pleasure in itself." — *The Christian Union.*

"No other book exists in English from which a reader unacquainted with Anglo-Saxon may gain so vivid a sense of the literary quality of our earliest poetry." — *The Dial.*

"A delightful exposition of the poetic spirit and achievement of the eighth century" — *Chicago Tribune.*

"In Mr. Stopford Brooke's monumental work he strives with rare skill and insight to present our earliest national poetry as a living literature, and not as a mere material for research." — *London Times.*

"It is a monument of scholarship and learning, while it furnishes an authentic history of English literature at a period when little before was known respecting it." — *Public Opinion.*

"It is a comprehensive critical account of Anglo-Saxon poetry from its beginnings to the accession of King Alfred. A thorough knowledge of the Anglo-Saxon language was needed by the man who undertook such a weighty enterprise, and this knowledge is possessed by Mr. Brooke in a degree probably unsurpassed by any living scholar." — *Evening Bulletin.*

THE MACMILLAN COMPANY,

66 FIFTH AVENUE, NEW YORK.

A HISTORY

OF

ELIZABETHAN LITERATURE.

BY

GEORGE SAINTSBURY.

Price, $1.00, net.

NOTICES.

"The work has been most judiciously done and in a literary style and perfection which, alas, the present era has furnished too few examples." — *Christian at Work.*

"Mr. Saintsbury has produced a most useful, first-hand survey — comprehensive, compendious, and spirited — of that unique period of literary history when 'all the muses still were in their prime.' One knows not where else to look for so well-proportioned and well-ordered conspectus of the astonishingly varied and rich products of the turning English mind during the century that begins with Tortel's Miscellany and the birth of Bacon, and closes with the restoration."
— *The Dial.*

"Regarding Mr. Saintsbury's work we know not where else to find so compact, yet comprehensive, so judicious, weighty, and well written a review and critique of Elizabethan literature. But the analysis generally is eminently distinguished by insight, delicacy, and sound judgment, and that applies quite as much to the estimates of prose writers as to those of the poets and dramatists. . . . A work which deserves to be styled admirable." — *New York Tribune.*

THE MACMILLAN COMPANY,

66 FIFTH AVENUE, NEW YORK.

A HISTORY

OF

EIGHTEENTH CENTURY LITERATURE.

(1660-1780.)

BY

EDMUND GOSSE, M.A.,

Clark Lecturer in English Literature at Trinity College, Cambridge.

Price, $1.00, net.

NOTICES.

"Mr. Gosse's book is one for the student because of its fulness, its trustworthiness, and its thorough soundness of criticisms; and one for the general reader because of its pleasantness and interest. It is a book, indeed, not easy to put down or to part with." — OSWALD CRAWFURD, in *London Academy.*

"Mr. Gosse has in a sense pre-empted the eighteenth century. He is the most obvious person to write the history of its literature, and this attractive volume ought to be the final and standard work on his chosen theme."
— *The Literary World.*

"We have never had a more useful record of this period."
— *Boston Evening Traveler.*

"A brilliant addition to critical exposition. Written in a finished and elegant style, which gives enchantment even to the parts of the narrative of a biographical and statistical character, the work illumines obscure writings and literature and brings new interest to famous ones. One of its great excellences is the easy transition made from one style of writing to another. The plan is distinct and well-preserved, but the continuity between parts is so close that unity and coherence mark the work in a material degree." — *Boston Journal.*

THE MACMILLAN COMPANY,

66 FIFTH AVENUE, NEW YORK.

A HISTORY

OF

NINETEENTH CENTURY LITERATURE.

(1780-1895.)

BY

GEORGE SAINTSBURY,

Professor of Rhetoric and English Literature in the University of Edinburgh.

12mo. Cloth. $1.50.

NOTICES.

" We should far exceed the limits of our space if we attempted to illustrate a quarter of the good things to be found in this ' History.' We will not venture even to touch what will be to many the most interesting portion of it, the chapter on the novel since 1850. The biographical details are judiciously selected, skilfully worked in, and pleasantly told. While it is possible that another hundred years may shake some of Mr. Saintsbury's conclusions, for the present a student who follows him with deference will have the company of an unusually well-furnished and an eminently sane guide, and will be likely to reach a much more satisfactory state of knowledge than by attempting to find his own way through the wide fields of this great century's literature." — *The Critic*.

" No student or reader of that great body of literature which because of its modernness comes nearest to our hearts and brains, but would find Mr. Saintsbury's opinions interesting and suggestive. He forms these opinions at first hand." -- *Public Opinion*.

THE MACMILLAN COMPANY,

66 FIFTH AVENUE, NEW YORK.

4